Craig Carter

Space Explorer

(Book 1)

Ilona Hawkins

TSL Publications

First published in Great Britain in 2018
By TSL Publications, Rickmansworth

ISBN / 978-1-912416-45-5

Cover image by James Sands

AUTHOR'S NOTE

I have used the known planets as a backdrop to my story. Please bear in mind that this is a work of fiction and therefore not really an indication of the atmosphere, etc of each planet.

PROLOGUE

Craig Carter was playing in his parents' back yard. His mother watched indulgently, as her ten-year old son ran energetically around their small townhouse garden. He had his favourite toy with him, and was waving it about, making rocket-like noises. It was a scaled down model of the latest spacecraft. She smiled at her tousle-haired son, and was filled with pride.

Craig was an intelligent young boy who did well at school, and was very popular with his peers. He was always out visiting his friends, or else they would come and play with him at his home. Today though he was alone, but he didn't seem to mind, as he was lost in a world of make believe.

"Come along honey, lunch is getting cold!" his mother called.

He smiled at his mother.

"I'm coming, Mom! First, I must save the galaxy from the evil conjurer! He's changed the weather patterns of the world, and now it's going to snow every single day, unless I stop him."

Craig stared out into the distance, and took aim with his toy laser gun. He shot at an imaginary being, somewhere in the distance.

"Come along right now, young man," his mother insisted. "You can play outside later."

Craig grumbled. "Awww Mom, I missed the evil Mercurius, and he got away!"

His mother smiled at him, and took him by the hand.

"Now dear, I'm sure you'll be able to deal with Mercurius later. He only got a temporary reprieve! The great and brave Craig Carter will catch him soon enough. After all, no one can escape from your clutches for very long. Now though, you need all your strength so that you can live to fight another day. If you don't eat, you won't be a match for the evil villains, now will you?"

Her son thought about it, and then he smiled. "I guess he can wait for a while. I'm feeling hungry anyway."

The young boy sat down at the table, and placed his toy spaceship next to him. When he had finished eating, he went outside again, and his mother smiled as she watched him fighting the imaginary criminals.

That evening Craig's father worked late, and his son was already in bed when he arrived home.

"Craig must have been tired tonight," remarked his father. "He never even stirred when I kissed him hello."

"I'm not surprised!" replied his wife. "It takes a lot of energy to save the world, you know."

His father grinned. "I saw him holding his spaceship! I'm glad that he likes his birthday present so much."

"Our son loves anything to do with space, sweetheart," his wife laughed.

"He certainly does. He's determined to become a space explorer when he grows up."

Alice Carter placed a mug of steaming hot tea on the table in front of her husband, and sat down nearby. "Well he's still very young honey. He has his life ahead of him, and maybe he'll change his mind when he grows up."

"It's possible of course, but Craig is very stubborn. Technology is advancing in leaps and bounds. New planets and stars are being discovered all the time," Brian Carter replied.

"I know that," Alice sighed, "but all the same, I have to admit, that I would be very concerned if Craig wanted to make a career out of it. I know space exploration sounds so glamorous, but it must be very dangerous up there. Many of the planets are still unexplored as yet. Who knows what he could encounter out there?"

Brian put his arm comfortingly around his wife's shoulders and smiled at her. "Darling, Craig is only ten years old, and he has his whole life ahead of him! He may change his mind when he gets older. If he doesn't, then we'll deal with it when the time comes. He has an adventurous mind and there's nothing wrong with that! Would you rather he sat in front of the television screen like the rest of his friends, and just watched cartoons, or played on his cellphone like the rest of the world?"

"Well no, of course not Brian! He knows what he wants in life, and that's a good thing."

"Yes it is," her husband agreed.

The next day, Craig was in the garden. It was the weekend, and Brian watched his son while he played. As usual he was fighting the evil foes that wanted to rule the galaxy. It was a beautiful day, and after a while Craig sat down on the ground, and wiped his sweaty forehead. His father handed him some juice, and he drank it in a few mouthfuls, licking his lips in appreciation.

"Mmmm that was great Dad."

"Being a hero is thirsty work isn't it?" his father laughed.

"It sure is!" Craig agreed. Then he became serious. "Dad I really want to explore space when I grow up. I know that you and mom will miss me, because it's not as though I'll be in another country. It could mean that I'm away for months, maybe years at a time. I know how you both worry about me."

Brian tousled his son's ash blond hair teasingly, and looked into his blue eyes. "We both worry about you, but only because we love you, Son. That's what parents do – they worry about their children. One day maybe you'll understand what I mean, when you have children of your own."

His father tilted Craig's face upwards, and pointed at the clouds. "Whatever you want to do when you grow up, will be your decision Son. You must do what you'll enjoy. If you want to explore space, then do what you can to make that dream a reality. You should also consider other options, just in case. We can talk about this again at a later stage, okay?"

"Sure Dad and thanks!"

"It's my pleasure Son," beamed his father.

Craig smiled, and held his toy rocket high in the air. Once again he rushed round the garden and began fighting his imaginary enemies.

CHAPTER ONE

SEVEN YEARS LATER

Craig Carter sat on his autocycle, and looked up at the impressive NASA building. Nervously he adjusted his tie, and made sure that his hair was combed perfectly. He cleared his throat, climbed off his motorbike and headed towards the entrance to the building.

The young man walked into the reception area, and smiled at the lady behind the desk.

"My name is Craig Carter, miss. I have an appointment with Commander Simms."

The receptionist consulted her computer, and smiled at the nervous man.

"Yes you do. Please wait a few moments. The Commander is busy with another applicant at present."

Craig walked to a row of chairs and sat down to wait his turn.

Half an hour later he was called into the commander's office. Simms invited him to sit down, while he read through the young man's résumé. After a few minutes, he put the data disk down, and smiled at the young applicant.

"So Mr Carter, you would like to become a space explorer."

"Yes sir," he replied shyly.

Commander Simms got up and, clasping his hands behind his back, he paced behind his desk.

"Why?"

The question took Craig by surprise. "Excuse me?" he asked stupidly.

"Why do you want to become a space explorer?"

Craig sighed. "It's all I've ever thought about. I have wanted this for most of my life."

Commander Simms looked at his hopeful candidate.

"It must be glamorous to go out in space. You get to explore new worlds, and fly in spacecrafts."

"Yes sir," he grinned.

"I bet you imagine that women love a man, who has such incredible adventures. Women will fall for you like ninepins."

Craig's smile got wider. "Oh yes indeed sir."

Commander Simms turned to his applicant, and banged his fist on the table, making Craig jump in surprise.

"Mr Carter, exploring space may sound very exciting to you but it isn't! It's hard work and it means a lot of self-sacrifice. You'll be away from your family for months, maybe even years. Any semblance of a normal life will just fade away. Being an explorer is a very lonely job. Apart from the loneliness, there is great danger up there, amongst the stars that you gaze at every night. Many explorers have gone insane with all the solitude. You are seventeen, and therefore still very young. I don't think that you can handle it. Even if you can, you'll have to attend the astronaut's course, and it is very demanding. It will take a year before you even qualify, assuming you make it. Why last year alone, twenty trainee astronauts attended the course. Out of those twenty, only four were successful. If you want to explore space because you think it's glamorous and exciting, then think again! No one will pin medals on your chest, and put your name up in lights. Ours is a very lonely profession, I assure you."

"But Sir, I can do it!" Craig protested.

Commander Simms looked at the handsome young man, and shook his head. "No Son, I don't think you can! You want to do this for the wrong reasons. I suggest that you go home, and think about what I have just said. You are just seventeen, and far too young for this. If you still want to do this in two years' time, then maybe I'll reconsider your application. You are welcome to apply then. Goodbye Mr Carter."

Craig was angry, and glared at the Commander, but Simms was busy arranging his data files neatly, and it was obvious that the interview was over. He left the building and his mind was in a whirl.

That evening Craig's father returned from work, and found his son moodily throwing a basketball into the net. One look at his son's angry face told the story.

"It didn't go well I take it?"

Craig threw the ball viciously against a wall. "No it didn't! All I got was a lecture about the demands of space exploration, and then I was told that I'm not mature enough to do the course. I was told that I can reapply in two years' time, when I'm older."

"I'm truly sorry Son," replied his father compassionately.

Craig spread his hands out in a gesture of helplessness. "Dad, what must I do now? All I have ever wanted, was to be a space explorer. I have been dreaming about this all my life, and now my hopes have been dashed! I was so confident that I would be accepted. I never imagined that Commander Simms would refuse my application outright!"

"What did he say Craig?" asked his father kindly.

"He said that I want to explore space for all the wrong reasons. He also said that I was too immature to go out into space now, and he told me to wait a year or two. If I was still interested, then I could apply again." Craig complained. "Two years is a lifetime! I want to explore space now!"

Craig shook his head miserably, and walked away. His father wisely left him alone.

The young man sat under a tree, and thought long and hard about his future. Despite Commander Simms's words, he was determined to explore space, but he had to find another way to do this.

The next day Craig went back to the space Control Centre. This time however, he didn't ask for Commander Simms. Instead he wandered over to the technical part of NASA. He stood for a while, and watched as various mechanics bustled around the huge area, looking into the depths of various spacecrafts. Wires and lights were trailing everywhere.

Craig saw that there were different types of spacecrafts. Some were obviously fighter crafts, while others were made to carry passengers. There were large shuttle crafts the size of airplanes, and small ones that only had room for two or three people. There were also many spaceships, that looked as though only one person was needed to pilot them. He walked around, and several of the workers glanced at him. Although the area was a restricted one, no one asked him to leave.

After a while one of the mechanics approached Craig. "Hello Son, my name is Don Appleby, and who might you be?"

Craig grinned shyly, and shook the hand that was offered. "I'm Craig Carter."

"It's good to meet you. Are you enjoying the tour?"

"Oh yes I am, but I should be leaving now," he replied nervously. "I shouldn't be here. I actually sneaked in, and if the security guards decide to come and investigate, I might get into trouble."

The man smiled. "No harm done! You don't look like a terrorist. You aren't one, – are you?" he teased.

Craig coloured in embarrassment. "Oh no sir, of course not! I was just curious about these machines. They are so awe inspiring!"

Don went up to the nearest machine, and stroked it tenderly. "They sure are, and fast too. They can reach light speed faster than you can say your alphabet backwards. Come on I'll give you the full tour!"

Craig couldn't believe his good fortune, and he followed the man obediently. He listened intently to what the mechanic had to say. When the man offered him something to drink, he accepted it gladly. He liked the man immediately, and soon he was telling Don of his hopes and dreams. He told him all about his interview with Commander Simms as well.

When he had finished, the man placed his hand gently on Craig's shoulder. "You know Craig, this may not be what you want to hear, but Commander Simms is quite right. You are far too young to be exploring space right now. You should be older before you apply. It is a dangerous business!"

Craig stayed and chatted for a while, and then he left the assembly area. His face was set and determined as he made his way to the reception area once more. He approached the receptionist and asked if Commander Simms was available. The receptionist checked for him and when her boss answered, she explained that Craig wanted to see him. He was asked to go in, but was told that he could only speak to the commander for fifteen minutes, because had an urgent meeting to attend.

The young man knocked on the door, and when asked to

enter, he did so. Simms looked expectantly at him over the top of his computer and addressed his visitor. "Yes Mr Carter, what can I do for you? Are you going to try and convince me to change my mind about hiring you to explore space?"

"No Sir, not at all. I want that so badly, but I respect your judgment in this matter. What I want is to offer a counter proposal."

Simms raised his eyebrows in enquiry. "What would that be young man?"

"Well Sir, I want to explore space, more than anything else right now, but if you feel that I'm too young and immature for the job, could I at least train as a mechanic? I want to be around spaceships all the time, and I'm good at fixing things."

Simms rubbed his jaw thoughtfully, and then he smiled at the man sitting in front of him. "You are a tenacious young man aren't you? I can see the determination in your eyes, and I must admit, I thought that you would just go home, and forget about exploring space. I'm glad to have been proven wrong. Craig, it will be a pleasure to have you on my staff. Welcome to the team!" he replied as he shook Carter's hand. "Come and see me tomorrow morning and we can make this official."

Craig smiled radiantly. "Oh thank you Sir, thank you so much."

He left the building, and it felt as though he was walking on air. Craig hurried home to tell his parents the good news.

CHAPTER TWO

Craig Carter worked diligently at his job, and soon became known as one of the finest mechanics at NASA. Sometimes the astronauts would take him out on quick trips to the Moon base. He learnt to fly the spacecrafts, just by watching his colleagues, and soon he could pilot any ship, but he never flew alone. There was always someone to go with him on these short journeys.

A year passed in this way. The newest recruits who had gone through their training, and had now qualified, were introduced to the technical people. When they left, the technical staff were agog with curiosity, and discussed the new trainees amongst themselves. There were seven trainees in all, three of whom were women. Craig however did not join in the discussion, for he had seen something that had impressed him immensely. His eyes were soft and dreamy, when he thought about one of the women in particular. She had dark brown hair and blue eyes. Her lips were soft and full, and he thought that she was the most beautiful woman he had ever seen in his life. Her figure was trim and athletic, and she walked with the grace and ease of a model.

Comments about the women were ribald to say the least, and the men began to take bets on which one of them they should chat up first. Their laughter rang throughout the work area. Suddenly one noticed that Craig was sitting apart seeming to be in a world of his own.

"Hey Craig, what gives?" asked one of the mechanics. "Have you even heard a word that we said?"

"Huh? What did you say?" he asked dazedly.

"We were discussing the new recruits. What's your opinion on them?"

Carter shook his head, and smiled apologetically. "Sorry guys, I was far away. I guess they're okay, why?"

Another of his friends laughed at this. "Do you think that they are just okay? I think that blonde woman was stunning!"

"No, the redhead was much prettier!" another disagreed. "Who do you think was the best looking in the group we saw Craig? Surely you must have an opinion."

Craig sighed. "Oh yes I do. I think the brunette with the shoulder length hair, is gorgeous. I'm in love with her already," he sighed wistfully.

His friend laughed. "Surely you don't mean Constance Gregg, do you?"

"Yes, I do. She's very pretty!" he explained.

His friends laughed and nudged one another. "Are you going to ask her out?"

"I just might," Carter replied mischievously.

His colleagues just shook their heads. "Forget it Craig; she won't give you the time of day. Her father is some big shot in the army. I hear she's very brainy, but cold as a fish. You're just a humble technical guy, and she's an astronaut. You don't stand a chance!"

However Craig wasn't listening to their advice. Instead he asked a question of his own. "How old would you say she is, George?"

George shrugged. "Probably seventeen or eighteen, I would imagine."

"That's pretty young to be a qualified space explorer, wouldn't you say?" he asked curiously.

"Sure, but she has connections sonny boy! Her daddy probably whispered a few words into Commander Simms's ears, and she was accepted as an astronaut."

Carter shook his head. "That's not possible! I was seventeen when I tried to become an astronaut, and Simms refused my application. I have brains too you know! She must be very good to have qualified at such a young age."

George looked at the other mechanics, and they all disagreed with their young apprentice. Stubbornly Carter stuck to his opinion.

"I'm going to make friends with her," he promised his fellow technicians.

They laughed at their colleague, and one challenged him. "I'm willing to wager one hundred credits that you won't succeed."

"We'll see about that! You have a deal!"

They shook on it and the man smiled. "Well time will tell I suppose."

A few days later, Craig went into the canteen to have some lunch. Miss Gregg was sitting with some of her friends, at a nearby table. As he walked past, he greeted her. "Hello Miss Gregg. I haven't had time to congratulate you on becoming an astronaut yet."

She fixed her cool blue eyes on him, and looked him up and down.

"I'm sorry, have we met?" she asked curiously.

"Sure we have! I'm one of the techno guys who fix the spaceships. Commander Simms introduced you and your fellow trainees to us."

Constance smiled coolly. "I'm sorry, but I don't remember. What's your name again?"

"Craig Carter," he replied, offering his hand.

She shook it, but her expression remained blank. "Sorry Mr Carter, but we were introduced to lots of people."

"I remember you," he smiled.

One of the men who had qualified at the same time, glared at Craig as though he was a bug that had crawled out from under a nearby rock. "Nice to meet you," he replied insincerely, "now get lost! We're busy here."

Craig stared at the man, who was taller, and better built than him. "I wasn't talking to you! I think Miss Gregg can speak for herself. If she wants me to leave then I will," he challenged the man.

Miss Gregg placed a cautionary hand on the well-built man's wrist. "Stop it Donny. He's just being polite."

"Yeah stop it," Craig repeated. "I was talking to the lady. Who are you anyway?"

The man stood up, and he was a good few centimetres taller than the mechanic. "I'm her boyfriend!" he replied coldly.

For a few moments they glared at one another, and then Constance broke the awkward silence.

'Maybe you should go Mr Carter," she replied. "It was nice to have met you."

"Sure and it was good to meet you too. I'll see you around I guess."

"I'm sure that you will," she agreed.

Carter went to get some lunch, and then sat some distance away from the trainee astronauts, with his back to them. He didn't look up when they left the dining room.

In Craig's spare time, he enjoyed going to the gym at the Space Control Centre. He found that he enjoyed the workout, especially after a trying day. While he worked out the kinks in his spine, from climbing into tiny spaces on the various spacecrafts, he would reminisce on the day that had passed. When he returned home, he was always in a better mood.

On this particular day, he was doing some exercises when Miss Gregg walked into the gym and went to one of the treadmills. She caught his eye and waved at the mechanic. He waved back and watched as she went through her routine. Half an hour later, he was astonished to find her standing beside him.

"Mr Carter, what did you find so fascinating? You never took your eyes off me the whole time."

Craig coloured in embarrassment. "I'm sorry Miss Gregg, really I am. That was rude of me and I apologize."

"No harm done," she replied. "I was just wondering if I had something stuck in my teeth perhaps."

Craig peered earnestly into her mouth, and shook his head. "No miss, you don't," he replied sincerely. "Nothing foreign lurking there, I guarantee it."

Constance giggled. "Stop that at once Mr Carter!" she admonished him. "You're making me quite embarrassed."

Carter raised his hands in mock surrender. "I apologize once again! Now if you don't mind, I'll just take my foot out of my mouth, and slink away. Enjoy the rest of your workout."

She smiled at him, and he began to leave the gym.

"Mr Carter?" she called to him.

"Yes?" he asked a little hoarsely.

"I was wondering if you knew anything about self-defence. I'm looking for a sparring partner."

Craig shook his head. "I would love to help you, but I don't have any experience in that area. Machinery doesn't really fight back, you understand."

He waved goodbye, and left on wobbly legs.

"Oh that girl is wonderful!' he sighed. "I just wish that I had the nerve to ask her out, but I get so tongue tied around her. Besides, Donny will pummel me if I make a move on his girlfriend."

A few days later Craig was in the gym once again, when one of the more experienced astronauts came in to do some exercises. Carter admired the man a great deal, and the astronaut would tell him about his adventures in space whenever he had a moment to spare. Craig looked forward to hearing the stories that the space explorers had to tell. This time though he had another objective in mind.

"Alan, could we talk for a minute?"

The man stopped his routine, and looked at the young mechanic. "Sure, what's on your mind?"

"I was wondering if you could teach me some self-defence moves – you know just some basic stuff, nothing heavy. I was thinking that I might need something to get me out of trouble, just in case someone wanted to rob me. Can you help me?"

"I suppose I could. Everyone has a right to learn how to protect themselves, especially in these troubled times. When would you like to start?"

"As soon as possible," Craig replied.

"Is tomorrow soon enough?" asked his friend.

"Tomorrow will be fine. Thank you," Carter replied excitedly.

The next day, Alan began teaching his young student. Craig made many mistakes but he never made the same mistake twice. His quick mind processed information at an incredible rate, and even Alan was amazed at his progress. He was so impressed by the young man's abilities that he taught him more advanced self-defence than was necessary.

When Alan lay on his back on the mat, for the tenth time in a row that morning, he raised his hands in surrender. "Well Craig, I've taught you everything that I know. You're as good as me now. If you want to pursue this type of training, then I can suggest a few more highly trained people to help you. You've good coordination with both your hands and feet, and I think that you should continue to the next level."

Over the next couple of months, Craig Carter honed his skills. He passed all his self-defence courses, with very high marks. However, while he became skilled in combat, he could never get close to Constance Gregg. She was kind and polite to him when they met, but every time he tried to ask her out on a date, she declined. Craig dated other women, but none of his relationships lasted very long.

One particular day, Craig was busy tightening some bolts in a spaceship, when Commander Simms came to see them. He greeted everyone affably, and they returned his greeting. He made for Carter immediately, and asked him to come into the supervisor's office for a moment.

Once inside, he got down to business. "Craig, I have watched your progress over the last eighteen months, and I must admit that I'm very pleased with your performance. How would you like a change of scenery?"

"That sounds wonderful Sir. What would you like me to do?"

"I need someone to help fly a spaceship to the Moon. It is one of the newest prototypes that you have all been working on, and our Moon base needs it. All the pilots are busy at present, and I know that you can fly almost as well as they can. Anyway, several of the craft on the Moon base need to be repaired, so I want you to stay there for a few weeks. The astronaut I'm sending, has to attend a number of meetings on my behalf. I unfortunately have to attend another meeting elsewhere."

"Who is the pilot, Sir?" he enquired.

"Constance Gregg," replied his boss. "You leave in the morning, so get some things ready for the journey."

Yes Sir, I will, and thank you!"

Simms waved dismissively, and Craig beamed in delight at the thought of spending some time with the beautiful Miss Gregg.

The next morning, he arrived early, and hurried to the canteen to get something to drink before the journey began. He was surprised to see that Constance was already seated at one of the tables, nursing her drink. Craig took his drink over, and sat down at the table with her. "Hello Constance," he greeted her.

"Hello Craig," she acknowledged.

They sat in silence for a time, and Craig broke it. "Are you excited about the journey to the Moon?"

She looked at him over the rim of her mug, and sighed. "It's just the Moon base you know. I've been there many times before."

Carter smiled. "Well I'm excited anyway! I've been to the Moon a few times myself, delivering supplies and so on, but not that many to call it routine. No journey in space will ever be routine for me, I guarantee it. I love every moment."

Miss Gregg fixed her blue eyes on him, and a shiver of delight went up his spine.

"Well I'm just going to finish my drink, and then I need to freshen up," she replied coolly. "I'll see you later!"

He realized that she didn't want to talk to him, and he got up. "I'll see you in a while then."

She didn't look up when he left, and he saw her staring into her mug, as though looking for inspiration. As there was still time to spare, he went to talk to his colleagues.

Before Constance came aboard, Craig had already stowed his gear away. She nodded at him, and sat in the pilot's chair. Craig sat in the co-pilot's. They began their pre-flight check, and soon they were in space. When Constance was satisfied that everything was functioning normally, she put the ship on automatic pilot. Craig had been meaning to talk to the woman he admired so much, but every time he had tried to get close, she had brushed him off. Now she had nowhere to go, and he decided to ask her some questions. He asked her if she wanted anything to drink, and then went to fetch it from the galley. As she sipped at her drink, finally Craig could stand it no more. He looked at her and her eyes met his.

"Is something wrong?" she asked.

"I was just about to ask you the same question Constance. The answer to your question is yes, there is something wrong. I just wondered why you behave the way you do when I'm around."

"How would that be exactly?" she asked curiously.

"Oh, like I seem to crawl out from under a stone, and you're frightened to step on me in case you get something unmentionable on your shoe."

"I do not!" she replied indignantly. "I always speak politely to you."

"Constance it's none of my business I know, and I'm really sorry that your boyfriend Danny, or whatever his name is, can't be here with you. I know that you would rather be with him, than on a spaceship with me. After all I'm just a humble technician, not a space pilot."

Constance turned to her companion in surprise. "Why are you so angry with me? I have never looked down on you, ever! You perform an important function, and if it wasn't for people like you, astronauts would never be able to do their jobs properly."

Craig threw his hands up in despair. "I don't think I'll ever understand you! For months now, I have been trying to get your attention, and you walk past me as though I don't exist. I suppose it's because your boyfriend claims all your spare time."

Miss Gregg glared at the man next to her. "Donny is a creep! Not that it's any of your business, but I broke up with him a couple of days ago. He just won't leave me alone, and it's becoming tiresome. Last night, I told him to get lost!"

Carter smiled. "So then there's hope for me yet?" he asked teasingly.

Constance looked at him, and smiled mischievously. "I could pencil you in sometime this century I guess, but right now though, I'm trying to get over that jerk. He's been seeing other women behind my back for ages now. He just thinks that I'm stupid, but I knew all about them. Well now he can have them. I certainly don't want him."

His companion interrupted him.

"I don't know very much about you Craig. How long have you been working at Mission Control?"

"I started eighteen months ago. Originally I had planned to train as an astronaut, just like you did, but Commander Simms felt I wasn't mature enough to handle it. He said that

I was doing it for all the wrong reasons. I was seventeen at the time, but I turned eighteen the following month."

"I'm eighteen," she confessed. "How come I got into the program and you didn't?"

"I guess you had the right reasons, plus I heard your father is a very influential man in the army."

Constance flushed angrily. "How dare you insinuate that I had help," she snarled. "Yes, my father is a General in the army, and yes, he taught me how to fight. I learnt a great deal from him, but I never used his name to gain anything. Everything that I have achieved, I did by myself."

Craig backed away, and spread his hands out in a gesture of surrender. "I'm sorry, that was stupid of me! I meant no disrespect! I see what Commander Simms was getting at. I guess I was very immature when I applied for the job. Next time I apply though, it will be for the right reasons."

"You're going to try again?" she asked incredulously.

"Yes, I am! I've always wanted to be a space explorer. The good commander said that I was welcome to try again at a later stage, and I will. What's more I'll succeed this time."

CHAPTER THREE

A transmission coming through interrupted them, and Constance took the call. As the journey to the Moon was only an hour's flight from Earth, they soon saw the landing bay, and touched down without a hitch. There was only time for hurried goodbyes as someone picked Constance up in an official car. Craig was left to secure the ship and organize a ride to his hotel. Even though they were booked into the same hotel, they hardly saw one another.

One week later, both of them had finally managed to get some time off, and they went to a restaurant a few blocks away. They enjoyed a quiet dinner in a pleasant atmosphere. It was very late when they began walking back to their hotel. A shadow detached itself from a dark shopfront, and began to follow them at a leisurely pace. From the opposite side another two merged together. Craig turned around, thinking he heard something, but the shadows had melted back into the darkness.

"Did you hear that?" he whispered.

"Yes, but the street is deserted," she replied softly.

"I still don't like it. Let's walk faster!" Carter replied tensely.

They lengthened their stride, when suddenly two figures materialized in front of them while a third appeared behind them. All were carrying deadly laser guns. Carter turned around in a slow circle and studied them, but it was too dark to make out any distinguishing features.

"What do you want?" Constance challenged them. "We have neither money, nor anything else of value on us."

A man spoke to her, and his voice was muffled. "We don't want money," he sneered. "We want you."

Carter's hands bunched into fists, and his voice was dripping with menace. "Get lost now, while you can still walk. The lady isn't interested in having anything to do with you."

The circle closed tighter, and Constance pushed Craig behind her. She saw that there was no way out of the situation except to fight.

"Like my friend said, I'm not interested. Go away, or I'll have to hurt you."

The criminals studied her intently, and began to laugh. "You couldn't fight your way out of a paper bag miss."

Craig took a step forward, and his companion stopped him. "I'll take care of these creeps in a jiffy. You just keep out of the way, and try not to get hurt."

He wanted to pass a sarcastic remark, but changed his mind. Instead he moved aside, and all three assailants closed in on the woman. He watched in fascination, as she moved with the grace and agility of a cat. The fight was over in a very short time, and all three robbers were writhing on the ground.

"Wow you certainly know how to protect yourself!" he replied admiringly. "Remind me never to make you angry."

"Thanks for your help!" she replied sarcastically.

"You were doing just fine," he grinned. "Besides, you told

me to keep out of the way, so I did."

Constance began walking away, but Craig stopped her. "Aren't you going to call the police?"

"No, why should I? They were just little punks who met their match. I don't have time to get involved with the law. My talks here are too sensitive to make waves!"

Alarm bells began ringing in the young man's head, and he offered her his mobile device. "You need to contact the police. This was no accident! They were sent after you on purpose."

"That's utter nonsense! It was a simple mugging, and they hoped for a bonus," she replied, handing his device back to him.

Carter was reaching for it, when he caught a movement out of the corner of his eye. One of their attackers had struggled to his knees, and he was holding a knife. Craig sprinted over to him, and kicked the knife away. Then in one fluid movement, he kicked the man in his head, bringing him down again. They heard his head crack painfully against the paving, and the crook became unconscious. The other two made no threatening moves, but watched the young couple warily. The mechanic picked up one of the guns, and pointed it very firmly in their direction. With his free hand, he reclaimed his device and called the police.

They arrived quickly and arrested their would-be attackers. The policemen asked Craig and Constance to come down to their headquarters and give a statement. They climbed into the back of the police cruiser, and Miss Gregg stifled a yawn.

"Now see what you've done!" she admonished her companion. "I have to get up early tomorrow morning and now I'm going to have a very late night. That was just a random mugging I'm sure. We should just have left them alone, and gone back to the hotel."

"No, I have a bad feeling about the situation. We're doing the right thing, I'm positive," her companion replied.

At police headquarters, they gave their statements. It was late when they were returned to their hotel. In the morning, Craig saw Constance grab a piece of toast before heading out the door. She waved to him and he waved back. Later he went back to the Control Centre on the Moon, and continued repairing the broken ships. When they stopped for their lunch break, Craig decided to phone Constance. Her phone rang for quite a while before she picked it up.

"Are you all right?" he wanted to know.

"Sure I am. Why wouldn't I be?" the woman replied.

"I'm glad to hear it, but I want you to be careful today. Have you heard anything from the police yet?"

"No they haven't contacted me as yet – and you?"

"Me neither," Craig replied. "I hope that they find out who those creeps were working for."

"I still think that you're making a mountain out of a molehill," she replied.

"Maybe, but somehow I don't think so. You are probably dealing with sensitive issues at your clandestine meetings. I know that you're simply telling the delegation what Commander Simms had suggested, but my feeling is that you are probably bound to upset some of the factions who are against change in any form. You're the youngest representative so maybe they thought you were the best person to make an example of."

Constance gasped. "Oh no, do you really think so? Now you're scaring me!"

"It's just a guess," he replied hastily. "However, don't relax your guard. I think you should be offered some police protection, just in case."

"What can I base that assumption on, Craig? If I ask for protection, the police will just think that I'm an hysterical female. I have to give them some concrete proof that my life is in danger, and I'm not even sure that it is."

"I still don't like it!" Carter growled. "I'm worried about your safety. At least for tonight let me sleep in your room with you. I'll sleep on the couch," he replied kindly. "You can rest assured that your honour will remain intact."

Constance grinned at her friend. "It's not necessary, really. As far as my honour is concerned, I think that it will remain untarnished anyway. If you made a move, I would just have to flatten you," she giggled playfully.

"You certainly are good at taking care of little problems, so I won't hassle you, promise!" he teased.

Miss Gregg then became serious. "Thank you for your offer Craig. I'll accept gratefully. Maybe there's nothing to worry about, but I would rather not take the chance."

"It's settled then. I'll come over after supper. Meanwhile, when you go to your meetings today, don't travel alone. Always make sure you've people around you at all times. Hopefully the police'll have some answers for us later today."

"Maybe they will. I'll see you tonight then. Bye Craig, I have to go now. The delegates are returning from their lunch break."

"Bye Constance," her friend replied.

Later that afternoon, a policeman arrived at the Space Control Centre and asked to speak to Craig. They were shown into one of the manager's offices, where the young man was invited to sit down.

"Is everything all right Sergeant?" the mechanic replied apprehensively.

The officer shook his head regretfully. "No; we have a problem. Your attackers are dead."

"Dead? How?" he asked incredulously.

"We think that they took poison, because they didn't want to be questioned. My superior is very unhappy about the situation. Why would simple would-be thieves take their lives over something so insignificant? I beg your pardon Mr Carter; I know it was harrowing for you and your friend, but usually these thugs hire clever lawyers, and get out on bail. This behaviour is very unusual."

Craig shook his head. "No, I think there's more to it than that. Someone very important must have hired the crooks to kill Miss Gregg. They would most probably have done the same to me, seeing as I was with her at the time. Whoever gave them their instructions didn't want them to get caught, because the trail would have led straight back to them. I think those three thieves were terrified of their boss, and they committed suicide rather than face him."

The policeman looked at the young man curiously. "What are you basing your assumption on?"

"Well it just seemed like too much of a co-incidence, that's all. Miss Gregg is here as Commander Simms's representative, and she's having many secret meetings with important delegates. I don't know why, but I think someone doesn't want these talks to take place. Perhaps by killing Miss Gregg, they're hoping to stall the talks."

"Assuming you are correct, why would they choose Miss Gregg specifically? Surely there are others who would be more suitable?"

"I know it sounds crazy, but they probably thought that Miss Gregg would be a pushover, seeing as she is so young. Anyway, the senior delegates have their own bodyguards, so it would be more difficult to get at them. They were surprised when my friend attacked them, because they expected everything to go as planned. Miss Gregg may be young, but she is a highly skilled space pilot and the training that she underwent is very strenuous."

The policeman looked at him with renewed interest. "Mr Carter, are you really just a mechanic? You aren't working undercover perhaps?"

Craig laughed. "Good heavens no, I'm really just a technical guy. I only hitched a ride with Miss Gregg, so that I could work on our spaceships here on the Moon base."

The Sergeant shook his head in disbelief. "Well Mr Carter, you are uncannily accurate! We came to a similar conclusion, and what you said certainly does make sense! We have no proof of course, but we'll be watching the delegation very closely from now on. They may have been scared off, but we aren't going to take any chances."

"What about Miss Gregg? Shouldn't you offer her police protection?"

The law enforcement officer shrugged his shoulders. "We haven't the manpower to do that, unfortunately. I don't like it at all, but if another attempt is made to disrupt the talks, we don't want to frighten them off. Miss Gregg is going to have to take her chances I'm afraid."

The space mechanic's jaw was set and determined. "I'll see

that nothing happens to that young woman! I'm going to look after her myself. As long as I am around, I'll see that she isn't harmed."

The Sergeant shook Craig's hand. "Miss Gregg is very lucky to have a friend like you on her side. I wish you both luck, and I hope that things will settle down now."

"I hope so too," Craig replied fervently. "I'll have to tell Constance about this conversation. I don't want her to get careless. Is that all right?"

"By all means Mr Carter. I would have told her myself, but as you know she's in meetings all the time, and I cannot get to her anyway. You take care now!"

"Thank you officer; I will."

The man left the building, and Craig returned to work.

That evening, he was waiting for Constance, when she came out of the building.

"This is a pleasant surprise Craig. I was going to take a cab back to the hotel, and you have saved me the trouble," she smiled.

"Well I'm glad to help. I just wanted you to know that as long as you remain here on our Moon base, I will take you to your destination and fetch you in the evenings once again. During the day if you go anywhere, just promise me that you won't travel alone."

"That is very kind Craig, but you really don't have to do this. You also have your work to do."

"I have cleared it with my immediate superior here, and he said that it was okay for me to do this."

Constance looked intently at her friend. "You're still worried about my safety, aren't you?"

"Yes I am. I think that I should spend every night on the couch in your room, until you return to Earth. I don't want to take any chances, not now."

Constance put her hand on his knee. "Craig, is something wrong? Have you heard from the police at all?"

"Yes, I have, but I'll explain everything after supper, if that's okay."

After their dinner, Craig kept his word, and explained what had happened during the day. Constance bit her lip nervously, and paced the floor. "So you were right!" she exclaimed miserably.

"Yes and I truly wish that I had been wrong. At least now, you know what the situation is. When do you think you'll be leaving here?"

"I think that I'll be here only one more day, perhaps two at the most."

Constance stayed for three more days. Over dinner, she told her friend that she would be returning to Earth the next morning.

"That's wonderful Constance. What time do you want me to pick you up?"

"I'm going home on a passenger craft Craig. Commander Simms has been in touch with me, and he said I should tell you that you still have to stay here a few more days. He told me that he would let you know when you can return to Earth."

The next morning Craig drove Constance to the departure lounge, and he stayed until he saw her board the passenger shuttle. Only then did he leave the terminal. He returned to work, grateful that Constance was now headed back to Earth, and safety. However even though his friend was now safe, Craig was concerned. He knew that whoever had tried to stall the talks, had been responsible for the death of the three crooks. The fact that they had committed suicide, worried him more than he cared to admit. What had been so important that they were prepared to kill Constance?

When Craig had a tea break, he went into the canteen of the Control Centre and singled out one of the officials. He learnt that although Constance's part was now completed, the talks were still continuing. The Minister was obviously lonely, and he told Craig more about the talks that he was attending. The mechanic listened intently, and remembered every detail of their conversation. Constance had never told him what the talks were about, and he had respected that. The Minister of Transport, John Taft was much more forthcoming.

Carter learnt that the talks concerned national safety of

travellers throughout the galaxy, and also that security for the Moon base and other planets, was high on the agenda. Apparently, the Moon base had been threatened by some unknown faction, who was determined to blow up the communications network. Several space police were looking into the matter, but they were working undercover and no one knew who they were. When the minister got up from the table, he patted Craig on the shoulder, thanked him for his sympathetic ear and swore him to secrecy.

Craig watched the man go, and was filled with a sense of foreboding. His first instinct was to hurry to the police, and tell them what he had heard, but reason prevailed. All he had was the word of an obviously lonely man, and to make matters worse, he had smelt liquor on the man's breath. Although it seemed too fantastic for words, it had an element of truth to it. During the discussion, John Taft had mentioned several members of the delegation by name, some of whom were in favour of the talks while others strongly opposed them. Carter committed those names to memory and returned to work on the spaceships.

The next day Craig was working on the engine of a ship when some policemen arrived and were shown into the space commander's office. He closed the door firmly, and the mechanics noticed that the discussion was very animated. About an hour later, the police left. Everyone was curious, but nothing was said.

That evening Craig received an unexpected visit from the Sergeant, who had taken his and Constance's statements a few days earlier. Bemused, he showed the man into his room and invited him to sit down. The policeman got down to business immediately. "Mr Carter I decided that I had to come and see you tonight, because I have some disturbing news!"

"Does this have anything to do with the visit by the police to the Commander's office today?" Craig asked curiously.

"It does indeed! This actually has nothing to do with you, but I have good instincts, and mine are telling me that you need to know why the police were at your workplace earlier today."

Craig sat up straighter and the man continued. "Last night Senator Taft was the victim of a hit and run accident. He was walking down the road, just two blocks away from his hotel, when a car slammed into him, killing him instantly. I'm sure you're aware that he was one of the members of the peace delegation."

Craig was horrified. "I know who he was! Am I to understand that the reason you have come here, is to tell me that you don't believe it was an accident?"

"Yes, I believe this was a deliberate attempt to stall the talks, as you surmised earlier. They didn't succeed in killing your friend, so they tried again."

"What happened to the hit and run driver?" Carter enquired.

"He's in jail, but the man is high on some designer drug, and we can't get any information out of him. He doesn't even remember hitting the senator."

Craig was worried and said so. "Sergeant, I would suggest that you place a guard on that man immediately. If what you say is true, he'll die as well, I'm convinced of it. Whoever is pulling the strings, is very high up in the chain of command, and won't leave any witnesses."

The Sergeant peered closely at Craig. "Mr Carter, you never cease to amaze me! Are you *sure* that you aren't an undercover agent?"

Carter denied it. "I'm just a humble mechanic, I swear."

"Well you have excellent instincts Son. I think that you are in the wrong profession. Anyway, I've already placed the perpetrator under twenty-four-hour surveillance. When that drug passes out of his system we'll question him extensively, and try to find out who sent him."

"Sergeant I hate to sound pessimistic, but what if it really was an accident?"

"Do you believe that?" asked the policeman.

"Not really," he sighed.

"Well neither do I. Anyway when the driver has recovered we'll know the truth. Now I have taken up enough of your time. I just wanted to ask you a favour."

"What's that?"

"Just keep your eyes open okay. If you see anything suspicious, or hear something unusual, will you let me know?"

"I'll do my best," Craig promised.

"As long as you don't take any unnecessary risks, understand. These people are playing for keeps, and I don't want you becoming a casualty as well."

"I'll be careful," he promised. Even as he spoke the words, he knew instinctively, that the drug addict in custody, only had a short time to live.

After the policeman left, Craig suddenly remembered that he had forgotten to tell him about the conversation he had with the deceased Senator. He was about to call him back, when abruptly he changed his mind.

Craig left his hotel room and went straight back to the Control Centre. He told the security staff he had a lot of work to do on the spaceships and wanted to put in some overtime. They scanned his access card and allowed him to enter. Instead of going to the workshop however, he made his way to the offices instead. He switched on a computer and typed in a secret code. For the next few hours, he studied the dossiers of the delegates who had shown up for the peace talks, concentrating especially on those who were opposed to the talks. His eyes widened in surprise, when he opened one of the dossiers in particular. Carter read the information on the screen for a while, and then he switched off the computer, and left the building. That night, sleep eluded him.

He returned to the workshop as usual in the morning, but he couldn't concentrate on his job. During the night he had thought of a daring, but foolhardy plan to expose the mastermind behind the murders of Senator Taft, and the three criminals who had tried unsuccessfully to kill Constance. He knew, without being told, that the hit and run driver was dead as well. A phone call from the Sergeant later that morning, confirmed his suspicions. The cause of death had been an overdose of the drug that he had been on when he was placed in police custody.

CHAPTER FOUR

After supper that same evening, Craig went to the hotel, where most of the delegates were staying. He went up to the receptionist, and gave her his best smile.

"Miss, may I have a word with Senator Petersen please?"

"Do you know what his room number is?"

"No, I don't, but I have something that he wants."

The woman looked suspiciously at him, and he held up a spectacle case.

"I work as a mechanic at the Control Centre," he explained. "Senator Petersen left his glasses behind, and my boss asked me to return them to him."

The receptionist smiled kindly at the young man. "I'm not supposed to give his room number out to just anyone. Security reasons you understand," she explained unnecessarily.

"Of course, but I'll only be a minute. He's as blind as a bat without them! Why don't you just give him a call, and tell him to expect me – or else you can take them upstairs for me if you like."

The woman looked around. "I can't do that! There's no one to look after the reception desk for me." She shrugged her shoulders in resignation. "His room number is 305, and it's on the third floor. Just hurry back, okay."

Craig favoured her with his most winning smile. "Thank you Miss."

The mechanic climbed the stairs to the third floor, and made for the suite. As expected his way was barred by some security men. He explained about the glasses and they searched him expertly for weapons. When none was found they allowed him to go in. They closed the door behind him, and he looked around the luxurious suite. Senator Petersen was seated on a couch but he wasn't alone. Another senator was with him.

Craig's expression hardened, and he no longer looked like the innocent mechanic everyone knew. He greeted the men by name.

"Good evening Senator Petersen, Senator Miles."

They nodded a greeting.

"Who are you young man? Do we know one another? You seem vaguely familiar," Senator Petersen remarked.

"Yes Sir, we've met. My name is Craig Carter. I'm a techno mechanic at the Space Control Centre, where you have been holding talks with the rest of the peace delegation, along with your colleague here."

The Senators exchanged looks and Senator Miles nodded.

"He is a mechanic there. I've seen him around," Miles confirmed.

Senator Petersen folded his hands across his chest and looked at the mechanic. "What can I do for you young man?"

Craig smiled coldly. "I think you and me need to have a chat. We can discuss this in front of your friend here, but I would advise against it."

"What is so important that you cannot discuss it in front of my colleague, Mr Carter?" Petersen asked.

The mechanic shrugged his shoulders. "I don't really care either way. I just thought that you would want this to remain private, but if you want to ruin your reputation…"

"What do you want?" Petersen asked curiously.

Craig looked at Senator Miles, who made no attempt to leave.

"Oh fine, have it your own way then!" he replied. "The fact is, I need some money – lots of it in fact. As I'm sure you know, mechanics don't exactly earn a fortune."

"What's your point young man?" Petersen asked crossly.

"My point Senator, is that you are going to give me some credits. In return you'll get something from me."

"What would that be exactly?" Petersen sneered.

"You get my silence about your little conspiracy."

Craig didn't miss the look that passed between the two men. He glared angrily at them. "Oh come on, don't act so stupid! You know exactly what I'm talking about."

"Do I?" asked Senator Petersen carefully. "Maybe you would

care to enlighten me about the so-called conspiracy theory of yours."

Carter sighed in exasperation. "Oh very well, seeing as we are now fellow conspirators, so to speak. I'm talking about the attempted murder of Constance Gregg, and the murder of Senator Taft by your hirelings. Only problem was, you used cheap labour and your scheme backfired, so you had the hirelings eliminated. That way they couldn't tell the police about your little plot."

Senator Miles licked his lips nervously, but Craig pretended not to notice.

"That is an imaginative scenario young man," Petersen replied evenly. "So tell me, have you shared your knowledge with anyone else perhaps?"

"No of course I haven't! I want to keep all the money for myself! I'm going to come into a small fortune, aren't I?" he remarked slyly.

"That depends," Senator Petersen replied warily. "Would you mind telling us just how you came to this conclusion?"

Carter smiled secretively. "Not just yet Senator! Firstly, do we have a deal? I want one million credits transferred to a bank account, which I'll name later. If you agree to this, we can have a cozy chat if you like."

There was an uneasy silence in the room, and Craig stood up.

"Fine, I'll just go and test my theory on the police then. Maybe I should've gone there first. I'm sure that they'll listen to what I have to say."

Craig made for the door, and reached out to turn the doorknob, when a cold voice stopped him in his tracks.

"That won't be necessary Mr Carter. You have made your point abundantly clear. Maybe we should discuss this."

Carter turned around, a smile on his face. His smile disappeared quickly, when he saw the gun aimed at his midsection.

"Hey, you don't need to point that thing at me!"

"I believe I do, Mr Carter. Join us here if you please."

The mechanic reluctantly went to join the two men. He sat down in the chair he had just vacated, and Petersen pressed his hands down firmly on Craig's shoulders. He whispered to his friend. "Go and lock the door, quickly!"

Senator Miles complied, and then joined his friend. Petersen rummaged in his desk drawer, and pulled out a necktie, which he handed to his colleague.

"Here, use this to tie him up securely."

Craig opened his mouth to protest, and Petersen glared at him. "If you try and warn anyone you will die right now. Behave, and you might just live a little while longer. Do you understand?"

The mechanic's bottom lip trembled, and he nodded. Mutely he allowed Senator Miles to secure his wrists behind his back. When that was done, Miles joined his friend on the other side of the desk.

"What are we going to do now?" Senator Miles hissed.

"Take it easy Sam! I'll take care of the situation."

"But Ian, you assured me that everything was watertight! You killed everyone who could link us with the murder. How did this kid make the connection?"

"It doesn't matter! This young man is going to tell us everything before he dies," Senator Petersen promised.

Both turned to their captive and Petersen smiled coldly.

"So Mr Carter let's hear your story. How did you find out about my little scheme?"

Craig was silent, and Petersen thoughtfully lit a cigar. He puffed on the cigar, and glared at the bound man.

"Mr Carter you were more than willing to tell us about your cleverness, now you have clammed up. Please – enlighten us."

Stubbornly Craig remained silent. The man rummaged around in his desk drawer once more, and pulled out a clean handkerchief, which he handed to his friend. "Gag him!" he snapped.

Senator Miles tied the piece of cloth around Craig's mouth. Then, anticipating what his colleague was about to do, he wrapped his arms around Craig's neck, and held him tightly. Craig knew that if he struggled, they would more than likely break his neck. Even so he stiffened involuntarily.

"Mr Carter, this is getting very tiresome indeed!" Ian Petersen sighed. He unbuttoned two of the buttons on Craig's shirt, then he took two large pulls on the cigar. The end glowed bright red. Realizing their intentions, a muffled scream emanated from their victim's throat. Craig continued screaming soundlessly, when Petersen cruelly jammed the lighted end of the cigar onto his chest until the glow was extinguished. He smelt his flesh burning.

Senator Petersen looked in disgust at the ruined cigar, and threw it into the wastepaper basket.

"See what you made me do! I ruined a perfectly good cigar, and they are very expensive."

He ripped the gag from Craig's mouth, and the mechanic took a deep breath.

"Now will you tell us what you know?" he snapped irritably.

"*Yes, please don't hurt me again!*" he cried desperately. "*I'll tell you everything.*"

Craig cleared his throat, and began the story.

"I got involved in this situation when you tried to kill Constance Gregg. It looked like a random act, but your goons made the mistake of underestimating that young lady. Space explorers are given rigorous training, and she beat your thugs to a pulp. She's a friend of mine, and the way your goons acted, seemed somehow out of context. I got suspicious and told the police what I thought. They believed me. Senator Taft and I had a little chat the night before he died. He named those who were against the talks and both of your names came up, amongst others. You had no way of knowing that of course, nor did anyone else. That night I went back to the Control Centre, and did some snooping. I checked on your dossiers and my search led straight to you Senator Petersen. For a man of your experience, you were very careless. You should have deleted anything that could incriminate you."

"Who are you really Mr Carter?" Petersen snapped. "Are you working undercover? You must be a cop!"

"No sir I'm really a mechanic, I swear! I just keep my eyes and ears open. You would be amazed just how many people drop their guard around mechanics. I have learnt many useful things over the years, just by being invisible."

"Continue with your story Mr Carter. We're dying to hear what you found in the dossier," Petersen ordered.

"What I found out blew me away. Your real name is Igor Petrovsky. You were born and raised in Russia. Your father was a Russian general, while your mother was an American. You learnt how to speak English from your mother, and you worked at it, until all trace of your Russian accent was gone. You rose quickly in the ranks of the Russian army, and soon made some influential people sit up and take note of you. You were recruited as a Russian spy when you were thirty years old. Because of your knowledge of the American way of life you were given a new identity by your KGB masters, and sent to America. Your charismatic nature made you a born leader, and soon you had entered politics. Now you are part of the peace delegation, but all you want is war! Russia has never gotten over the fact that although Russia was the first to enter space, America has fared better over the years, and is now more advanced as far as space travel goes. All these years you've enjoyed the American way of life, but your loyalty has always been to Mother Russia. You are in fact a double agent!"

Petrovsky smiled and nodded his head. "Young man, I must commend you! What a pity you have to be terminated, because of this knowledge! Russia could really have used someone like you! Maybe you are a mechanic, but it's such a waste of good talent!"

"I haven't finished the story yet!" Craig replied. "You're in good company here with your friend and colleague. He's Russian too. In fact, he's your cousin. His name is Sambrovitch Milissivitch. I hope that I have pronounced it correctly. Personally I don't blame him for calling himself Sam Miles. It's quite a mouthful isn't it?"

Craig looked over at the Senator, and smiled mirthlessly. The man's jaw was slack with astonishment, and the mechanic continued with the story.

"Sam here thinks the world of you. Of course his career has not been quite as illustrious as yours, but he did make it to Senatorial level, though just as a junior minister, not a senior one like you. You are the mastermind behind this whole operation, while your buddy here just does your dirty work for you."

Petrovsky smiled at his captive, and he was genuinely impressed. "Mr Carter, truly you are an amazing person. It seems that you have many hidden talents. Pity you got cocky, because it is going to cost you your life. What a waste!" said Petrovsky, as he took out his gun, and pointed it at his prisoner's head. Hastily his cousin stepped in front of the bound man.

"Are you out of your mind? You can't kill him here, not without arousing suspicion! Do you want to blow our cover, after all that we have strived to do to keep it intact? How will you explain it to the security police standing outside?"

Calmly, Petrovsky screwed a silencer onto his gun. "You leave those little details up to me comrade," he replied soothingly. "Don't I take care of all the loose ends? Move aside now cousin and let me do what I must."

Milissivitch hesitated, and his cousin shot him through the heart. His body jerked spasmodically, and his leg kicked violently out at the chair on which Craig was sitting, sending it skidding across the polished floor. It slammed into the wet bar sending some of the contents spilling onto the ground. Petrovsky chuckled evilly. "Sorry my friend but you were becoming a liability."

While Craig had been telling the Russians his story, he had been working on the material around his wrists, and it had loosened considerably. He pulled his hands free, but as he jumped up from the chair, Petrovsky had him in his sights. An insistent knocking came at the door.

"Senator, what's going on in there? We heard a commotion. Open the door!"

Igor Petrovsky smiled victoriously. "You lose American! You killed Senator Miles, and I killed you in an effort to save my friend. I'll be a hero!"

"I don't think so!" Craig exclaimed, as the door burst open. The Senator was momentarily distracted, and Carter kicked the gun out of his hand. It ended up under the dressing table, out of reach of both men. Petrovsky grabbed for his throat, and Craig punched him hard in the face. "It's not so easy when your victim isn't tied up is it Petrovsky."

The Russian dabbed at his bleeding face. Petrovsky pointed accusingly at Craig. "He shot my friend! I demand that you arrest him immediately."

The policeman ignored the angry man, and turned to Craig. "Well done Mr Carter. We'll take it from here."

The Senator put his hands behind his head, and sank to his knees. Craig walked to the desk and picked up the spectacle case. He waved it in front of Petrovsky. "I filmed this whole conversation." He then took out his mobile device, and showed it to the Russian spy. "Just in case the video didn't work, I recorded the whole conversation as well. Your career is finished!" he replied, as he handed the case to one of the detectives, then walked out of the door and never looked back.

The next day Craig was again in the Sergeant's office. His burn had been treated, and he had a dressing on it.

"Mr Carter, we are in your debt! You took a chance going into the lion's den like that. You nearly lost your life yesterday."

"I knew that it was dangerous Sergeant; that's why I told you what I planned to do, so that you could organize this sting operation. I would never have managed to do it alone. I had some doubts in the end though!"

"I'm sorry, but I couldn't send my men in earlier. I had to make sure that you got his confession first."

"Did the video recording come out clearly?"

"It was perfect! Every gory detail is there for the world to see! You're an incredible man Mr Carter. Your government will be very proud of you. So in fact will that young lady of yours. Constance Gregg is a lucky woman!"

"She's just a friend!" Craig laughed.

"Well young man, if you are prepared to do something like this for a friend, imagine what you would do for family. I would want you on my side anytime! It's been a pleasure knowing you. When are you returning to Earth?"

"I've nearly finished my work here. I should be around for another day or two, and then I'll go home."

The policeman shook his hand vigorously. "Well good luck then. I wish you every success with your career, whatever you decide to do."

"Thank you very much sir."

Craig left the building, and a figure blended into the shadows and watched him intently.

"So this is Craig Carter! I'll be watching him very closely over the next few years. He brought my father to his knees, and I'll avenge him. We'll meet sometime I guarantee it."

Ivan Petrovsky stared at the young man until he turned the corner. Without being aware of it, the young mechanic had made a powerful enemy. Ivan Petrovsky was destined to play a large part in his life in the not too distant future.

Another two days had passed, when Craig's mobile device rang and the face of his boss stared back at him.

"What can I do for you Sir?" he asked politely.

"Craig, your work there on the Moon, has been completed. I want you to leave for Earth this afternoon."

"Yes Sir, I'll be on the next passenger ship."

"There's no need for that, young man. I've asked for a fighter craft to be made available, and you are going to fly it home."

"But Sir," Craig gasped, "I have never flown solo."

"It doesn't matter! You know how to fly the spaceships, even better than some of the pilots. See you this afternoon! Besides, from what I heard, you have earned it. Constance owes you her life."

"It was nothing," he replied modestly. "Thank you for this opportunity, Sir!" he grinned.

"It's my pleasure Son."

Craig walked out of the Control Centre, feeling very excited.

*****

Not long afterwards, Craig again approached Commander Simms to apply for the job as a space explorer. This time his application was successful, and he began his training as an astronaut. By the time he turned twenty he had completed the difficult course, and passed, coming first in his class. He was given his first mission, and he completed it with another more experienced astronaut. Many missions were just routine flights to the various planets that had been discovered over the years. He usually took supplies to them in the beginning, just to gain experience, but he never complained.

Thus, began the illustrious career of the great Craig Carter, who was soon to become a legend in space.

CHAPTER FIVE

A few years later, Craig was sitting in his superior's office, waiting patiently for him to begin.

"I've sent for you, Craig as it's a matter of some urgency. As you may recall, we sent Roland Stone to Venus to see how things were going over there. You remember, we discovered life there way back in 2090, and made friends with the inhabitants of the planet."

"I remember, Sir," replied Craig politely.

"Well as I was saying, we sent him there, and we haven't heard from him since he landed."

"It's possible that he had some trouble with his craft and he could be repairing it, Sir."

"That possibility did occur to me Craig, but I need him to come home urgently, because his two children are desperately ill. We did many tests on them, but even with our advanced medical technology, we can't cure them. I want you to take a ship and go to Venus. If he's still there and having trouble with his craft, then you must give him yours. If you can, try to repair his ship and return to Earth with it. If it's something more serious, you'll have to stay with the Venusians until a crew can come and repair it."

"I understand Sir. When would you like me to leave?"

"It shouldn't take longer than two hours to prepare a ship for you. I'll call you then."

Craig nodded and went into the waiting room where some of his friends greeted him.

"Hey Craig, I hear that the Commander is sending you on a mercy mission to fetch Roland. Pity about his kids huh?"

Craig nodded sympathetically. "Yes it is. I wonder why the doctors can't trace this disease? What sort of symptoms do they have, Ray?"

"Well, it appears as though they are an unnatural green colour. They also seem to be listless and have no energy."

"*Green*!" exclaimed Craig, horrified. "Is it contagious ?"

Ray shrugged his shoulders. "It's hard to tell, but we're keeping them under strict quarantine at the moment. The only logical conclusion we can think of, is that Roland brought it back with him from another planet."

"What if he has it too?" asked Craig curiously.

"I don't know if he has it of course, but you don't need to worry. I'm going to give you an injection just before you leave. At least you won't catch anything out there in space."

Craig was relieved. "Well thank goodness for that!"

They spoke for a while, and finally Carter was summoned to the launch bay.

He climbed the ladder into his ship, which was shaped like a motor car without wheels. It was large enough to move about in. Carter settled down at the controls, and flipped a few switches, making the engine hum noisily. It throbbed powerfully and the computer came on line with all the relevant data. Craig spent five minutes checking that all the gauges were in working order, and then the all clear was sounded. He pressed a switch, and the rockets responded, lifting him vertically upwards. The roof opened like a flower in bloom and he cleared the bay. Once he was safely out, the roof closed behind him again, and soon he was in the blackness of space.

The journey to Venus took one full day, and finally he put down on the surface of the planet. The planet itself was very soft and marshy. All of the inhabitants looked like walking plants and there were many different species. Their speech was part hissing and part squeaking. Craig and the other space explorers were able to understand the inhabitants by using a translating device, which was worn on their wrists. It looked like a wristwatch, however when it was switched on, it became a verbal translator. All the beings on every planet spoke in their own language, and the machine automatically translated the words for the benefit of all concerned. The leader of the plantlike creatures looked like a large tree. They all had the ability to blend into the vegetation on their planet, and anyone scanning the planet would only see flowers and trees, not beings who walked around. However, they knew Craig, so they showed themselves.

He raised his hand in greeting and they responded.

"Welcome Craig! It's good to see you again." greeted the leader.

Craig smiled at the being. "It's good to be here among friends once again, but alas I'm not here to socialize, for one of our spacemen is missing. Roland Stone was here a few days ago, and I wondered if he was still on Venus."

The Venusian smiled at his friend. "Ah yes, he was here, but he left some time ago – he said he was returning to Earth."

"Oh I see, but he still has not arrived," replied Craig in confusion.

"Perhaps he went to another planet," the being suggested. "I'm sorry that we have no further information for you."

Craig smiled at the beings. "Don't worry, I'll just have to speak to my superior, and see what he wants me to do."

Carter returned to his ship and contacted Earth.

"This is Craig Carter calling Commander Simms. Come in Sir."

Commander Simms appeared on the vid screen. "Do you have any news for me?" he enquired hopefully.

"Sir, the Venusians claim that Roland left Venus a while ago. He should have returned by now."

"That's strange," remarked Simms pensively. "We haven't heard from him at all. Where are you at present?"

"I'm still on Venus. Have you any further instructions for me, Sir?"

"I'm not sure what to say. Maybe you should return to Earth and I'll send out a rescue team to search for him. Something must have happened, because he hasn't contacted us."

"With respect, Sir, I'm already in space and I'd like to search for him myself. He's a friend of mine and I'm sure that I'll find some trace of him. I request permission to continue the search."

"Very well Craig, I have no other missions for you to undertake at present, so you're welcome to look for him. If you need help, just ask for it, okay."

"Thank you Sir."

Craig frowned, and the Commander stared quizzically at him. "Craig, what is it?"

"I don't know if this is relevant at all, Sir, but could he perhaps be in the hands of the Russians? They would jump at an opportunity of capturing one of our astronauts."

Commander Simms was thoughtful. "It's possible of course. They could've intercepted him somewhere, and taken him prisoner. If that's the case, then you'll be in extreme danger too, because the Russians have been trying to lay their hands on you for years now."

Craig smiled at his superior. "Don't worry about it, Sir. I'll take the utmost care not to fall into their clutches."

He ended the transmission and returned to the Venusians.

"Any luck, Craig?" the leader asked.

"No unfortunately not. Commander Simms says that he hasn't returned to Earth yet, nor has he heard anything further. I'll have to go to each planet and search for him. Please notify Commander Simms if he comes back here, or you hear any news about him."

"We would be glad to of course. I hope you find him soon."

The Venusians waved as the craft took off once again and vanished into space.

Craig typed data into his computer, and plotted the best course to take. Then an idea struck him, and he decided to return to the Moon.

"I should've looked there first of all. Due to overpopulation on Earth, a settlement was built on the Moon some years ago. He could have reached there and maybe I won't have to look all over the galaxy for him."

Carter was tired and decided to sleep for a while, but first he programmed the computer to wake him at an appointed time. He lay down on the bed and strapped himself in, while his craft continued on autopilot.

As he approached the Moon, a tiny shock wave passed through his body, waking him up. He announced his intention to land and a place was cleared for him. His ship touched down gently on the surface of the Moon, and he shook hands with a scientist friend of his.

"It's good to see you again Craig. What brings you to the Moon?"

"It's business unfortunately. Roland Stone has vanished and I'm trying to find him. I suspect that the Russians had a hand in his disappearance."

His friend stared at him and motioned him to a private office, where he closed the door.

"That's a serious accusation, pal. What gives you that idea?"

"It's just a hunch at this stage, but the circumstances of his disappearance are very suspicious. I went to his last known destination, and the Venusians say that he left quite a while ago, but no one has heard from him since. Did he contact the Moon at all?"

"Not to my knowledge. I'll ask around if you like."

"Thanks pal!" said the grateful explorer.

His friend contacted various people on the Moon, but no one had heard from Roland Stone at all. Regretfully he conveyed this to his friend.

"Sorry Craig, no one has heard from him. What are you going to do now?"

"I guess I'll just have to go from planet to planet. I'm hoping that he won't be too far away. Thanks for your help though."

The man nodded and Craig left his friend. He went to replenish his supplies for a long journey and also refueled his craft.

Once everything had been organized, he took off once again and set course for Mars.

"I'll just fly by Mars, as it doesn't support any life."

He trained his sights on the planet, and then let out an exclamation of surprise. Craig zoomed in on a wreckage of a ship on the surface and the name was clearly visible.

"United States; that's Roland's ship all right, but where is he?" Carter flew a little closer and scanned the entire planet, but there was no sign of his friend. He switched to thermal imaging and slowly scanned the wrecked ship both inside and out, but there was no sign of life at all. Relieved and yet puzzled, he prepared to lift off once again. He put his rockets on full thrust and blasted away from Mars.

Then he contacted the Control Centre.

"Craig to Commander Simms; come in please Sir."

"I'm here, go ahead Craig."

"Sir, I've found Roland's ship, but there's no sign of him. I'm hovering over Mars at the moment. I've scanned the whole planet, but it doesn't look very promising. I can't find a trace of him anywhere!"

"Thank you for that information Craig. Let me know if you have anything else for me."

"Yes Sir, will do."

He broke transmission, but a Russian ship was within range, and they heard everything. Colonel Ivan Petrovsky was very pleased. "Ah, so my rival, Craig Carter is searching for his missing friend! I would get a promotion if I could capture him, but that man is shrewd. I wonder where he'll look next."

Craig prepared to visit Neptune, but the journey was long. To save time, he put his ship into time-lapse mode, and streaked off to the planet. A short while later, he emerged above Neptune and prepared to land.

Neptune was a planet where the occupants lived underwater. The planet consisted mainly of water and very little land, but the ground was also very stony and nothing could grow on it. His ship landed gently and Craig climbed out, and walked towards the water. As he did so, an inquisitive head popped up out of the water. Craig's smile was friendly. "Hi Lolita, how are things with you?"

The girl smiled and spoke in a high-pitched voice. She had been taught English and greeted the explorer excitedly.

"Hello Craig, I'm fine thank you! Did you want to speak with my father?"

"Yes I would like to. Is he available perhaps?"

She smiled at him. "Well he's busy at present, but you're welcome to come down to the palace and wait for him. He shouldn't be long."

"I didn't pack any oxygen tanks this time, so I was hoping that he would come up and see me," replied the explorer apologetically.

Lolita smiled excitedly. "We have invented a new device called 'gills', which I'll bring you later on. It allows you to breathe underwater without any oxygen tanks. Meanwhile, could I stay and chat to you awhile?"

"Sure, I'd like that," Carter beamed. "How is your mother these days? The last time we spoke, I heard that she was ill."

"Oh, she's fine now Craig," said Lolita as she climbed out of the water, and came to sit down next to her friend on the ground. The explorer was aware once again of her incredible beauty. Although she was only sixteen, she had a curvaceous figure and lovely long legs. She looked human, but her hands and feet were webbed. All the women had long hair and green eyes. The men were very handsome and also had the piercing green eyes, while the older Neptunians had white hair, and their eyes turned grey as they aged. Lolita's parents were the reigning King and Queen of Neptune. The girl wore only a few scales which covered her voluptuous breasts, and a very brief pair of panties, and they sparkled like silver in the light.

Lolita laughing at him brought Craig back to the present. "Craig, what are you staring at?"

He smiled sheepishly and apologized. "I'm sorry, it's rude of me."

"You always stare at me like that, you know."

"Probably because you are so beautiful," he replied.

She laughed musically. "Do you really think so?" she teased.

"Of course I do and you know it. Are things okay underwater, Lolita?"

"Well now that you mention it, no they aren't going well at all. We are having a problem and my father was considering asking for Earth's help in this matter."

"Perhaps you'd better get those 'gills' for me then, so I can visit with your mother and father."

She nodded and dived gracefully into the water, returning a few minutes later with the gills. By this time, Craig had changed into a swimming costume, and was waiting for her to appear. She opened her hand, revealing the strange gadget.

"Here Craig, put these two up your nostrils as far as they can go, and this one attaches to the roof of your mouth. When you dive underwater, just breathe normally and they'll stay in place. It'll probably feel a little awkward at first, but you'll soon get used to them."

Carter did as she instructed, and they got ready to dive into the water.

Suddenly Lolita looked up, and screamed shrilly. Craig followed her frightened gaze, and saw a Russian spacecraft hovering above them. The hatch opened, and Craig grabbed Lolita's hand and jumped into the water with her, just as a ray hit the ground, right where he had been standing just seconds ago. They swam quickly underwater and Craig felt as though he was going to sneeze, but when he told Lolita, she assured him that it was normal and he would soon get used to it. When they were very deep in the water, Craig stopped for a breather.

"Whew, that was too close for comfort, Lolita. Those Russians nearly had me then."

"I don't understand! Why would they want to kill you?"

"No, they wanted to capture me. That was a stun ray."

"Why would they want to do that?" she asked, confused.

"It's a long story, Lolita, but the Russians have been after me for as long as I can remember. You know that Russia and America don't get on all that well together. What I don't understand though, is how they knew I would be coming here.

Anyway it doesn't matter right now. Let's go and see your parents."

They swam hand in hand down to the palace, and the awesome beauty of the place struck Craig once again. In the distance, he saw the King and Queen waiting on the palace steps to greet him. The plexiglass door opened for them and then closed again. The entire city was enclosed in a strong plastic bubble, and once inside, the doors closed automatically. Craig watched as some exotic fish peered at them through the bubble.

Craig walked towards the entrance to the palace and bowed to the royal pair. He kissed the Queen's hand, as was the custom.

"The king is exactly as I remember him. His hair is white and still hangs down to his shoulders I see. That robe of scales he's wearing is quite magnificent – he really does look like a monarch. The Queen is just as beautiful as ever, and I can see where Lolita gets her beauty from," Craig thought.

The king put his arm around Craig's shoulders, and the women discreetly took their leave.

Once they were seated comfortably, the king handed his guest a goblet of wine, which he accepted gratefully.

"Your Majesty," Craig began. "Lolita told me that you are experiencing some trouble here and wanted to ask Earth for help. What seems to be the problem?"

"Yes, we are in quite a state at the moment. Some plant has begun growing wild in our waters, and anyone who passes too close by is caught in the tentacles. I don't know where it originated, but it definitely wasn't here a few days ago. It's quite uncanny Craig, every time we blast one of the tentacles off these things, they simply grow back again. We are living in fear of our lives, and the waters are infested with them. We only discovered these when one of the children went out to play, and never returned. We searched for him and found him in the grip of one of these plants. When we tried to rescue him, we found ourselves surrounded by more of them, but somehow we managed to get the little boy away. If they keep growing at this rate, we'll all face extinction."

"That's terrible, Your Majesty. Did you perhaps ask Saturn to help? They are the most advanced race in our universe."

"They were the first I thought of, Craig, but they are busy with some problem of their own. In fact they suggested I ask Earth for assistance. Commander Simms told me that you were coming to see us, so I deferred it until you got here. Do you think you could help us, please?"

"I'll certainly try, but I'll need someone to guide me to the place. Also, could you let me have some kind of weapon?"

"Of course I can! Lolita knows where this place is, so I'll send her with you. Do you want some of my followers to accompany you?"

"No, not yet Your Majesty. I first want to see what I'm up against and then I'll ask for assistance."

He nodded and clapped his hands twice. Soon Lolita appeared. "You sent for me, Father?"

"Yes I did; Craig wants you to take him into the place where the child was grabbed. Be careful though!" he warned.

"I will," she promised. "Come Craig, follow me."

She swam off gracefully and he followed her.

Once out of the palace gates, they made their way to the turbulent waters. Craig was holding onto a spear gun and they swam onwards for a while. Not long afterwards, they came to the border. Lolita pointed in the general direction.

"Craig, they were spotted just beyond that stretch of coral. We need to be careful from here onwards."

"All right then, just stay close to me. Your father will never forgive me if you get hurt."

A little tremor passed through her body and she held onto Carter more tightly.

"Don't worry, I'm going to stick really close by!" she exclaimed nervously.

"Listen carefully though Lolita; if I can't manage to hold them off by myself, I want you to swim back to the palace and get help, okay."

She nodded. "All right, I'll do whatever you say Craig."

They swam about for a while, but there was no sign of any plants and Lolita became concerned.

"I don't like this, Craig. We've been swimming in these dangerous waters for nearly half an hour now, and there aren't any plants in sight."

"Are you sure this is the place?" he enquired as he looked around cautiously.

"Yes, this is definitely the right spot!" she confirmed.

They swam for a while longer, then stopped to sit on a log.

"Lolita, I want you to stay here for the moment. Maybe they disappear after a few days, but if not, then perhaps they conceal themselves in the sand. I'm just going to swim over there by that coral reef and take a look around."

He swam away from her and poked a stick in the sand. Suddenly Lolita screamed a warning. *"Look out, Craig!"*

He turned quickly and saw a monstrous tentacle hovering above him. He swam faster, but the plant seemed to lash out, and he caught a glancing blow on his shoulder.

"*Craig!*" screamed Lolita desperately.

"I'm okay – it just touched me."

Lolita screamed once again.

"*There's more behind you Craig!*"

He spun around once again and saw many tentacles surrounding him.

"*Get away from here Lolita! Warn your father and get help!*"

She obeyed and quickly swam away.

He watched as the tentacles twined together, blocking his only means of escape, but they didn't come closer. He took the initiative and swam straight for them, watching as they uncoiled in order to stop him from escaping. Then suddenly he turned around and swam through the gap that they had made, leaving them behind. One plant however reacted swiftly and pursued him. He stopped and faced the enormous thing, spear gun ready in front of him. For a moment he stared at the menacing thing and then his lips curled in a snarl.

"Right, you asked for it!" He pointed the spear gun at the plant and aimed for the centre of the mass to which all the tentacles were attached, and pulled the trigger. Carter scored a direct hit and the plant fell dead to the seabed and shrivelled up immediately. Instead of fleeing, he watched the other plants, but they didn't approach him at all, so he took the opportunity and swam quickly out of the dangerous waters.

"Whew, at least I've found their weak spot. I'd better get hold of Lolita before she goes to her father. He needs to send some of his best men out to kill those things."

He caught up with her, just as she was about to enter the palace.

"Craig, oh thank goodness you're okay!" Lolita exclaimed as she hugged her friend tightly. "I wasn't sure what would be left to rescue when we went back out there to look for you."

He grinned at his friend. "I was just lucky, but I've found their weak spot. Your people must aim dead centre into the plant, otherwise they won't be able to kill those creatures."

Lolita then turned her attention to Craig's shoulder, which had begun to bruise slightly.

"How is your shoulder, Craig?"

"There's nothing to worry about. It's just a bruise."

They reported to the king and he was grateful. In the days that followed, Craig helped his friends to get rid of the deadly plants, and then he regretfully took his leave of them. Lolita was very unhappy.

"Oh Craig, can't you stay just a little longer?"

"I would love to, but I'm on a mission. Roland has to be found soon, but I'll come back again, I promise."

She swam to the surface with her friend and he handed her the gills.

"Goodbye Lolita. I hope that we'll see one another soon."

"Bye Craig and good luck. I hope that you find your friend!" she called, as she slowly sank from sight.

CHAPTER SIX

As Craig walked to his ship, he gazed up into the sky, but there was no sign of the Russian craft. Craig was puzzled by the fact that the Russians had given up so easily, but he knew they would be planning something, so he took extra precautions.

Once in space, he consulted his computer again.

"Let's see now – I'll set course for Pluto. That planet has tiny life forms, but they are hostile beings. I'll just skim over the planet and see if I can spot anything."

He couldn't relax, as he was constantly on the alert for spacecraft following him. His computer beeped a warning, and he stared down at the console.

<*Warning, fuel is low!*> the computer said.

Craig stared at the monitor and shook his head in disbelief. "No, that's impossible! According to my gauge, my fuel is almost exhausted, but I checked it when I landed on Neptune and there was more than enough. A leak must have developed somehow!"

He punched in various codes, but there was no evidence of any leaks, and then it dawned on him.

"Damn those Russians! I'll bet that they came down and sabotaged my ship, when I went to join the king on Neptune. They left me just enough fuel to get into deep space, so they must be around somewhere! I need to know where the next space station is, so that I can refuel before I run out of gas." He pressed some keys on the keyboard of his computer and a map of the universe was revealed, but his hopes were dashed when he realized that the only space station within reach, was a Russian one.

"*Damn them!*" he exploded, "I daren't ask for fuel there. They'll capture me and I can't let that happen. All I can do right now is contact Commander Simms and tell him of my plight. He'll have to send someone from our space station to help me."

Craig moved to the radio and began his transmission.

"Craig Carter calling Commander Simms – come in Sir."

There was silence and he tried again, but a diagnostic check revealed that the transmitter had also been tampered with. Carter sighed unhappily. "Well, so much for that idea! I have no fuel and I can't contact Earth!"

He took out his mobile device and contacted Commander Simms on his private number, but the phone suddenly went dead. Craig was furious.

"I should have expected this. The Russians are jamming my mobile device and I cannot get through to my boss either!"

He decided to go as far as he could and then take his chances. Craig hoped he would perhaps meet a friendly ship, which could tow him to the American space station. The Russian space station came into view on his monitor and stubbornly he continued past it. He looked at his fuel gauge, and saw that he had fuel to last another fifteen minutes only before he ground to a halt.

The Russians watched his progress keenly. Colonel Ivan Petrovsky smiled as he saw the ship pass by.

"Craig Carter is an idiot! How far does he think he'll get?"

One of his junior officers grinned happily. "What does it matter, Comrade! When he comes to a stop, we can go out and proposition him."

"He won't give himself up – he'd rather die out here than fall into our hands."

"Maybe, but let's give him the benefit of the doubt."

Fifteen minutes later, Craig's ship came to a standstill. He took out his device, and speed dialled Commander Simms's private number, but all he got was a *'no service'* message. It was obvious the Russians were still blocking the signal.

"Oh well, all I can do now is try and repair the transmitter," he sighed.

No sooner had he replaced his mobile device on the console, when it began to ring. Craig snatched it up, but it showed an unknown number. He picked it up anyway and heard a stranger's voice. The person had a Russian accent.

"Good day to you Mr Carter! I see that you are experiencing difficulties with your ship. May we be of assistance?"

"Who is this?" he asked curiously.

"My name is Ivan Petrovsky. We have never met before, but I know who you are."

"How did you get my number?"

Petrovsky laughed. "Ah Mr Carter, I know a great deal about you, and something like that is easy to find – when you know the right people. I'm looking forward to meeting you face to face and would be honoured to have you come aboard my ship."

Something about the man's surname bothered Craig, and he wondered briefly where he had heard that name before. He searched his memory and it came back to him instantly. Igor Petrovsky had been arrested a few years earlier and Craig realized that the man on the phone was obviously a relative looking for revenge.

"I appreciate your invitation Mr Petrovsky, but I'll have to decline your most generous offer. I've been in contact with my boss, and he's going to send a rescue ship to my current location."

Petrovsky practically purred with delight. "I see! Have it your own way then Mr Carter, but we'll stick around, just in case."

The Russian disconnected and smiled at his crew. "Mr Carter is stubborn, but let's give him some time to reconsider our generous offer. If he doesn't come willingly, we'll just have to take him by force. He isn't going anywhere!"

Craig began checking if he could fix his transmitter. While he was busy, Commander Simms was very concerned. For the tenth time that day, he consulted his technicians.

"Have you managed to raise him yet?"

"Not yet, Sir," replied the technician.

Morosely, Commander Simms returned to his office and stared into space. A few minutes later, his intercom beeped and he depressed the switch.

"Have you managed to locate him?" he asked hopefully.

"Not yet, Sir, but your Russian counterpart would like to speak with you."

Simms was concerned. "*Oh no, this can only mean trouble,*" he thought unhappily. Aloud he spoke into his videophone. "All right, put him through."

The Russian commander's face appeared and Simms' tone was curt as he spoke to him.

"All right, I'm listening. What do you want, Commander?"

The man beamed at him. "Commander Simms, good day to you. I have a message for you, which has just recently been handed to me by Colonel Ivan Petrovsky. He knows where your man, Craig Carter is."

Simms sat bolt upright and paid attention. "Really, well where is he?"

The man smiled like a cat that had just helped itself to a large bowl of cream.

"Mr Carter is at this moment floating aimlessly in deep space near Neptune, as he has run out of fuel. Colonel Petrovsky is on his way to...er...assist."

Commander Simms fought for self-control, but his anger surfaced. "Craig had plenty of fuel – more than enough in fact. No doubt your employee had something to do with this!" he exclaimed angrily. "You are jeopardizing a mission!"

The man smiled triumphantly. "I'll keep in touch with you Commander. Oh incidentally, Mr Carter's transmitter has also malfunctioned. He can only pick up short range transmissions, and his mobile device is also not working."

Commander Simms was furious. "How dare you endanger one of my employee's lives in this manner! If you cause him any harm, your government will hear about this!"

The man looked hurt, but Commander Simms wasn't convinced.

"Commander Simms, I am contacting you as a courtesy only. Your man is in trouble and we only wish to help him. I didn't have to contact you, but I felt that it was my duty!"

The screen went dead and Commander Simms hurled his coffee mug across the room, and watched as it shattered against the far wall. Then he got up and went to the technicians. "Patrick, I want you to contact the Moon base and any others in the vicinity of Neptune. Craig is marooned in space and the Russians are closing in on him. According to Craig's flight plan, he's heading for Pluto. Anyway, sound the alert and let's see if we can help him at all."

In the meantime, Craig had dismantled the transmitter and he found a part missing.

"So, that's why my radio isn't working! I can communicate from a short range of about twenty kilometres. I don't have any spares for this transmitter, so I can only hope that Simms is going to send a rescue party out to look for me."

Another fifteen minutes elapsed before Carter looked through his observation window and saw the Russian spaceship approaching. He scanned the skies desperately, but no friendly rescue craft was in sight. Petrovsky contacted him again on his mobile device, and this time he wasn't smiling.

"Come now Mr Carter, let's get down to business! Your fuel has been exhausted and there are no friendly craft around to save you, except for us. We must insist that you accompany us to our space station."

Craig stared at his rival. "You are responsible for my state of affairs. Obviously you sabotaged my craft while I was on Neptune."

The Colonel nodded happily. "Precisely, comrade. It would have saved so much time if the stun ray had hit you, but alas, you were too fast for us."

"I refuse to accompany you. I know how much it would mean to your country if I were captured. If anyone tries to gain entrance to my ship, I'll blast them into a million pieces."

Colonel Petrovsky's tone was polite, but firm. "You misjudge us, Carter. On the contrary, we'll treat you very well."

"You're wasting your time, comrade!" exclaimed Craig stubbornly.

Petrovsky sighed theatrically. "Alas, then I have no choice but to take you by force."

Abruptly the screen went dead and Carter was left to ponder what the Russians next move would be. Anxiously the space explorer scanned his instruments, hoping desperately for just a small window of opportunity in which to somehow get his ship going again, but the empty fuel gauge mocked him. He didn't have long to wait, when a beam shot out from the enemy craft and latched onto his helpless ship, which began to move slowly as the Russians towed it.

All too soon, the Russian space station came into view, and the two ships flew inside the large hatch, which opened to receive them. Carter watched helplessly as many armed men surrounded his ship, but he refused to get out. His radio beeped and stubbornly he refused to answer it, determined to make life difficult for his enemies. A whispered conference then took place and several Russians left, only to return with a large gun mounted on a stand. Carter knew that it was a powerful laser beam, and the Colonel contacted him.

"If you don't come out of there immediately, we'll cut your ship open like a can of beans and fetch you ourselves. You have five seconds to make up your mind; one...two...three..."

Realizing that it was useless to argue, Carter opened the hatch and emerged with his hands behind his head. All eyes were focused on him as he made his way down the steps, and then he was ringed by many of the guards. Petrovsky reached out his hand and removed the explorer's laser gun from its holster. Then, indicating that Craig should follow him, he moved off, with several guards taking up the rear. The explorer was taken to a large room, where he was ordered to sit down on the bed. He did so and the door closed electronically. Carter stared around him and paced moodily around. He was left alone for half an hour, and then Petrovsky entered and sat down in a chair, indicating another one to his captive. Craig faced him.

The Russian smiled coldly and looked at the explorer. "I hope that you're in a reasonable frame of mind, comrade."

"What do you want from me, Petrovsky?" the explorer asked angrily. "Kidnapping was still a felony the last time I checked."

"It still is," confirmed the Russian, "however that doesn't bother me at all."

"So you are Ivan Petrovsky! Are you related to Igor Petrovsky perhaps?" Craig enquired.

The man's eyes became cold and hard. "He was my father!"

"Was?" asked Carter curiously.

"Yes Mr Carter, was! He's dead now! He was returned to Russia in disgrace a few years ago and he never recovered from that. My father was a proud man, and you stole his dignity. He couldn't live with the shame! One day when my mother and I were out, he placed his gun in his mouth and pulled the trigger. He blew his brains out and left us all alone. I have lived with his shame all these years, and I have you to thank for ruining our lives. From the day that you had him arrested, I have watched your career take off. I know all about you! In fact, I have followed your career over the years, and I know that you rose from being a mechanic to a space explorer. You may not have undertaken many missions as yet, but you have still managed to gain a reputation of sorts. You may not know this, but I was with my father on your Moon base when the peace talks were taking place. My father told me how you tricked him into confessing about his part in the attempted sabotage of the peace talks."

"He tried to kill a friend of mine, and succeeded in killing another Senator, who was just doing his job. If my memory serves me correctly, he also had three other criminals murdered, plus let's not forget the fact that he shot his own cousin too! He deserved what he got!" exclaimed Craig savagely.

"The friend that you are referring to is the beautiful Miss Constance Gregg, yes? I believe the two of you have become very close over the years."

"She is my girlfriend," he replied.

"I know," replied his enemy.

Carter paced around his cell. "Is that why you decided to capture me? Is it because you want revenge?"

"Partly, but actually I am acting on my superior's orders. We heard that an American spacecraft was nearby, and my superior asked for volunteers to pursue it, with the sole intent of capturing the occupants. When I found out that it was your ship, I came up with this brilliant plan and I succeeded. Now we have you and I'm satisfied with the result. If I had my way, I would kill you, but my boss needs information which you will provide. Our President wishes to see you. In a few days' time, a transport craft will arrive here and take you to your new destination. When you reach Russia, you'll be required to surrender the plans for the new spacecraft that

America is building at present, as well as other sensitive information."

"By force, no doubt," grumbled Craig. "I won't give that information up willingly."

Petrovsky shrugged his shoulders. "That is not my concern at present. I've captured you and the rest is up to my superiors."

"Once this information exchanges hands, what's going to happen to me?"

"Your skills could be valuable to Russia, so you'll most probably have your memory erased and be given a new name and face. You'll spend the rest of your life serving Mother Russia."

Craig was thoughtful for a few minutes, while he digested this piece of information, then he spoke. "Colonel Petrovsky, your arrival has interfered with my mission to find my friend Roland Stone, and I have reason to believe that he too is your guest. I would like confirmation of this fact."

Petrovsky looked at him curiously. "What makes you think that we have him as well? Doesn't he also possess the same information in his head as you do?"

"I guess so, why?"

Petrovsky smiled indulgently. "Well, if we had him, why would we bother to capture you? We could get the same information from him."

"I guess that makes sense," assented Craig.

For a while, the two men sat in silence and then Petrovsky excused himself. "Perhaps when you have joined forces with us, we'll meet again Mr Carter. Until then, I must bid you farewell, for I have other important matters awaiting me in space."

The door opened and then closed behind Petrovsky, leaving Craig to ponder on his situation. Some food was brought for him. While he was eating, his knife slipped off his plate and he knelt to retrieve it. Something shiny caught his eye and he bent to examine the object more carefully. It was a thin rectangular object, and he smiled as a plan formed in his head. When the supper tray was removed, Craig placed the object in the doorway and the door remained unlocked. He could hardly sit still, but knew that his timing was crucial, so he forced himself to wait until he judged everyone to be asleep.

Craig then pried the door open and stepped cautiously outside, but no one was there to stop him. He moved quickly to the landing area, and stayed in the shadows to avoid being seen by anyone. Then he filled up his tank with fuel from the Russian supply. Carter knew that he couldn't waste time searching for the part from his radio, so he decided to do without it until he reached the safety of the American space station. Only one more obstacle stood in his path. A guard was stationed in a booth that contained the switch to operate the hatch. The explorer crept behind him and knocked him out, taking possession of his laser gun at the same time. Then, satisfied that no one else would oppose him, he threw the lever and watched the hatch open. Within seconds he was airborne and on his way to safety.

The explorer arrived at the American space station and was welcomed warmly.

"*Craig, oh Craig, it's good to see you again!*" shouted a welcome voice.

Craig turned around and his girlfriend Constance threw herself into his arms, and despite all the onlookers, she kissed him passionately. "Oh Craig, we heard that the Russians had caught you. How did you manage to escape? Commander Simms has been in constant contact with us."

"Let me speak to him, Constance."

He hurried to the communications room and contacted his superior. "This is Craig calling Commander Simms. Come in please sir."

"It's wonderful to hear your voice, Craig. The Russians told us of your plight and it's good to have you back!"

"Thank you, Sir. I managed to escape from them and I'm presently at our space station. Sir, the Russians don't have Roland either."

"They don't? Oh my, well you had better continue looking for him then. Has your transmitter been fixed yet?"

"It's being repaired as we speak, Sir. You had better cancel the rescue craft you sent out to look for me, Commander."

"I'll do that Craig. Did you see Constance?"

The man smiled happily. "Yes I did, Sir. Why is she here though?"

"She's on a mission for me," his boss replied.

Craig's face became solemn. "Oh then I guess she can't continue with me for a while."

"I'm afraid not. Get your supplies together and then get moving. You've been up there for a fortnight already."

"Yes Sir," replied Craig obediently.

He signed off and went to talk to Constance until he was called to board his ship. He waved goodbye and was on his way once more.

He set course for Pluto and while he was travelling he was thoughtful.

"If Roland is on Pluto, then he's dead anyway. The Plutonians hate us and wouldn't have any compassion, but I'm still worried, as Roland's ship was lying wrecked on Mars. I don't understand where he could be, because he can't travel without a spacecraft."

Pluto appeared in his sights and he contacted them via the radio.

"This is Craig Carter of Earth."

The leader waved his six arms around angrily.

"What do you wish of us, Earthling?" he snapped.

"I am looking for another Earthling like myself and I was wondering if he was perhaps on your planet."

"There are no Earthlings here. None of you are welcome! Even if he had come here, he would be dead, just as you will be if you land! Leave now or we'll fire on you!"

Craig didn't need a second warning, so he fired his rockets and sped away from the planet. His radio beeped, signalling an incoming transmission and the explorer pressed the transmit button. Commander Simms's face appeared on screen.

"What can I do for you Sir?" asked Carter politely.

"I'm sorry to bother you, but there's an emergency. One of our explorers went off course and he was headed towards

Mercury. I'd like you to go there and see if you can offer him any assistance. I realize that it's out of your way now, but you're still the closest to the area. It'll mean a delay of a further two days, but it can't be helped."

"Very well Sir, I'll alter course immediately. I'll contact you in two days then."

Craig changed course and headed for Mercury.

His alarm woke him and he stood up, conscious that he was perspiring heavily.

"Oh wow, the heat from Mercury's very intense! I'd better put up my heat shield before I get roasted alive."

After this was done, he orbited around Mercury, scanning for signs of the missing explorer. Craig gasped as a trail of smoke caught his attention and he saw something burning fiercely on the surface. He moved in for a close range shot and his stomach lurched. A spacecraft lay on its side and he scanned it. The name of the craft identified it as one of theirs, but there was no sign of the pilot. The instruments on Craig's ship began to glow and he moved further away from the intense heat. When he scanned the surface once again, he found the charred remains of an unfortunate male lying some distance away. Carter sent out a scanner beam and it panned up and down the charred body, sending back details of the DNA in the body. He fed these into the computer and pulled up the man's file. It was a match. With a heavy heart he contacted his superior.

"Commander Simms, Sir, I found him, but he's beyond help."

"Is...is...he?"

Craig nodded sadly. "I'm afraid so, Sir. I couldn't even salvage what's left of him if I tried."

Simms was downcast. "All right, thank you Craig. I'll have to inform his family then. Could I ask you to bring me some uranium from the planet Uranus, on your way back?"

"I'll do so, Sir," he replied.

CHAPTER 7

On Uranus, Craig landed on the planet and filled some containers with Uranium. As he walked, he kept an eye out for signs of his missing friend, but he wasn't there.

"How strange it feels to be here collecting samples of Uranium. It's hard to believe that on the 21st day of July 1969, Neil Armstrong landed on the Moon and collected lunar rock samples. He was doing much the same as me. Time certainly has moved on!"

He collected his Uranium and stored it inside his ship, and then set course for Saturn.

"I don't like going through Saturn's rings, because I'll lose all contact with mission control, but it can't be helped. I remember that time when Brayce Dennings got lost in these rings. It took us days to locate him and guide him out of there, but fortunately he wasn't badly hurt, and his craft suffered only minor damage. These asteroids can cause quite a bit of damage, but fortunately I can go into time lapse and avoid them all."

Craig approached the surface of Saturn in time lapse and when he was clear of the rings, he brought his ship out of the sequence and prepared to land on the planet.

Suddenly he froze as a beam of pure energy coiled about his waist, pinning his arms effectively to his sides.

"What in blazes...?"

He turned and stared into the face of a creature he had never seen before. It was humanoid in shape, but the entire body was silver. Three gleaming red eyes glowed in its head. The arms were as strong as a nylon rope, and its mouth looked like a dark hole. The creature greeted him telepathically and he was confused by the sound inside his head.

"*You need not fear me, Earthman.*"

"But how did you come to be here? Where did you appear from?" he asked verbally.

"I live on Saturn of course, and I was able to materialize inside this ship of yours by mere concentration."

"Release my arms; I want to land my ship!"

"How careless of me," remarked the being as it freed Craig.

As he began the landing procedures, Carter was puzzled and many questions formed in his mind.

"*Who is this strange creature and where does it come from? Where are the real inhabitants of this planet?*"

His instincts told him that this creature wasn't to be trusted.

The ship landed safely on Saturn, but Craig refused to leave it.

"What's going on? I know the beings who live here. What have you done with them?"

"You needn't concern yourself with them." the creature replied.

The explorer put his hands on his hips in a gesture of defiance. "I can't accept that explanation. They are friends of mine and I'd like a straight answer."

"Don't be difficult Mr Carter," replied the being.

The explorer was taken by surprise. "How did you know my name?"

"It doesn't matter right now. Get out of here, or do you want me to help you?"

Craig detected some menace in the creature's voice, as it had switched to verbal speech. As he didn't know what he was up against, he decided to wait and see. When he stepped down from his ship, he was confronted by many of the creatures and he stopped. Angrily, the one who had materialized inside his ship, pushed him roughly forward.

"Hey, watch it!" warned the annoyed explorer.

They stared at him and he disliked them immediately, but he stood his ground.

"I demand to see my friends right now!" he exclaimed angrily.

The one whom he took to be the leader approached once again and grabbed Craig's wrist.

"We give the orders around here, Carter," said the creature, as it allowed some power to flow through the explorer's wrist and he gasped in pain and surprise. The creature then released him and he rubbed his tingling wrist.

"So, you are electrical beings! I still want to know where my friends are."

"You'll be taken to them in due course. Consider yourself lucky that I only generated a little power into you; I could easily have killed you."

"Your strength has to be renewed some time or another," said Craig, thinking aloud.

"Yes it does, but we can go for ages without topping up. Your ship contains many useful items that we can use!"

Craig's hand moved slowly to his left wrist and he pressed a button on his watch. Behind him, his ship rose into the sky and disappeared from sight. Immediately his arms were grabbed roughly, but the creatures were too late.

"Bring your ship back here this instant!" ordered the leader.

"No! That ship is for my exclusive use, and I don't want anyone or anything to compromise it."

The leader glared at him. "Fool, we can transfer ourselves to your ship and bring it back down here."

Carter grinned mischievously. "I guess you could – if you could see it! I put it into time lapse, so good luck finding an invisible ship."

The being realized that Craig had outwitted it and it wound an electrical beam around his neck.

"Let's see if you can stop me strangling you."

Craig remained calm. "This is a waste of time! I want to see my friends now."

The silver creature removed the beam and walked ahead of the Earthling. "Follow me then."

The group moved to one of the buildings. A door opened and the being stood aside to let Craig pass. Once he was inside, it closed and locked the door once more.

The Saturnians huddled together in fear, afraid that the beings had come to harm them. On seeing who it was, one of the Saturnians hurried forward and hugged Carter tightly. She was half his size and her head reached to the explorer's breastbone.

"Oh Craig, is it really you?" she sniffed.

"It is me, little one," he confirmed, as he kissed her gently on the top of her head.

The Saturnians were the most beautiful race in the entire universe, measuring only one metre in height. They had transparent wings, and looked extremely delicate. The Saturnians resembled humans in every other way. The men were a few centimetres taller than their female counterparts. This race was the most intelligent in the entire universe.

The woman held tightly onto her friend, almost as though he would disappear if she let him go, but eventually she released him, and began to cry. "Oh how can I be so happy, when you have also been caught by those...those creatures? Forgive me please Craig."

He stared at her and cupped her chin in his hand. "There's nothing to forgive, Lara. I must admit that I'm pretty confused at the moment. How did these creatures manage to take over your planet? Surely you could have stopped them?"

One of the men spoke to Craig. "They tricked us! A large container crash-landed on our planet a few days ago, and naturally we went to investigate, but it was a decoy. While we were trying to figure out what it was, these beings took us by surprise. We tried to reason with them, but they killed a few of us. We value our people and don't want to see more destruction, so we gave in to them."

Craig shook his head disbelievingly. "You know what your problem is Karnd; you don't believe in violence, and they took advantage of the situation. Why didn't you ask Earth to help you? We would've been privileged to do so, because you have helped us so much in the past."

Karnd shook his head regretfully. "No, I couldn't do that! It was bad enough that our people died, but we didn't wish for the same fate to befall another race."

"I understand your sentiments, Karnd and I'm the last one who should tell you how to run your planet, but sometimes violence has to be used."

"I have no wish to disagree with you, my friend, but take your planet for instance. The Americans are always fighting with the Russians. Why can't you pool your ideas and work together?"

Craig recalled his brush with the Russians and shook his head. "No, that's impossible! The Russians would like to capture me, and then use me against my own country."

Karnd shrugged his shoulders resignedly and gave up trying to convince his friend. Jorrel, another of the Saturnians then came to speak to him.

"You carry a laser gun with you I notice, Craig."

"I always do! Those beings overlooked it fortunately."

"You aren't thinking of using it are you?" he asked nervously.

"If I have no choice, then naturally I will."

Jorrel looked at his friends and also gave up.

The door opened suddenly, and they all scrambled to their feet as the silver creatures came in and shepherded them outside. Craig didn't miss the look of terror on the Saturnians' faces. Once outside, he took hold of Lara's arm and demanded to know what was happening.

"Oh Craig, they force us to work for them! We have to pick up heavy rocks and deposit them at another site. They want us to build them some sort of structure to live in."

"Lara, something must be done soon. You don't need me to tell you that they plan on living here permanently. Your lives won't be worth anything if they remain here."

Their conversation was cut short by one of the creatures, who hit Lara across her back, sending her sprawling. "Get moving! There's work to be done!"

Craig hurried to her and helped her up. "Lara, are you okay?" her friend asked gently.

She nodded dumbly and hurried to join the rest of her friends.

The creature shoved Craig, who glared angrily at him. An electrical beam lashed out and he sidestepped nimbly, avoiding the blow.

As the creature moved in for the second time, the explorer picked up a large rock and took careful aim. He flung the rock with all his might, and it slammed into the head of the being, damaging the middle eye, and with a loud gurgle, the creature crashed heavily and lay still. The shocked onlookers could only stare in horror and for a moment, even Craig was surprised. The creatures stared disbelievingly at their dead companion, and then they turned their attention to the man who had done the damage. Craig's instincts took over and he began to inch cautiously away, knowing that he had overstepped the boundaries. The explorer didn't get far before some of them had teleported themselves in front of him, so he tried to change direction, but the leader materialized right in his path and grabbed him by the hair. He struggled for his freedom, but a bolt of electricity flowed through him and stopped him in his tracks. His head felt as though it would explode and he fell to the ground, temporarily stunned. Dazed by the onslaught against him, he didn't resist as some of the beings pulled him to his feet. The leader was angry and the Saturnians looked on fearfully.

"So, you killed one of us! You'll pay for your crime, Earthling. I'm tempted to kill you right here and now, but our custom dictates that there must be a trial. You'll be confined to a cell until morning, when your case will be heard."

The space explorer stared at the being that he had killed, and he gasped as the dead creature began to pulsate rapidly. There was a flash of light, and the being disappeared, leaving only a small scorch mark on the ground to show where it had lain.

Craig was silent as they marched him off to a cell and pushed him inside.

While Craig was languishing in a cell, Commander Simms was becoming apprehensive.

"I wish Craig would contact me. I hate these long silences! He must have landed on Saturn by now, so why hasn't he reported to me?"

The Commander went to speak to the radio operators, but no one had heard from Craig at all.

Carter in the meantime had begun pacing in the cell, trying to think of a way out of his predicament. He stared at the laser gun still nestling in his holster.

"I could escape from here now by burning my way out of this cell, but I can't leave the Saturnians in this mess. I have to try and help them get rid of these creatures."

Startled by a hissing noise at the window of his cell, he found Lara standing outside.

"Lara...what...?"

"Oh Craig, I'm sorry about the mess you're in – it's our fault!"

"Don't worry about it Lara; I understand, really. I know you would've warned me if you had been able to, but I most probably would still have tried to help you – I just would have come more prepared for trouble."

"Your trial will take place tomorrow morning and they'll find you guilty – you know that. I know you never back down from a fight, but this is one battle you're sure to lose. Please, just beg for mercy. Maybe then your punishment won't be death."

Carter smiled and reached for her hand. "I know you mean well, but I don't want to live here forever as a slave. I've never seen these creatures before, and I don't know what I'm up against. I could try and get help from Earth I suppose, but I don't want to involve others in what could mean a fight to the death. It's obvious these creatures are very powerful, but I need to learn more about them before I endanger others."

Lara stared miserably at him. "I don't understand, but your motives are honourable. All right, I just hope things work out well in the morning. I'd better get back before they notice I'm missing."

The next morning, Craig was led into the courtroom. All the seats were arranged in a circle and the explorer was escorted to the middle. His trial began with one of the silver creatures coming forward.

"Speak, Zark!" the leader commanded.

"Excellency, this Earthling is dangerous and should be eliminated. I saw him throw a rock at my friend, and it was done deliberately. He meant to eliminate your loyal subject!"

There was a general uproar and all the remaining silver creatures nodded in unison.

"Kill the Earthling!" they chanted.

The leader stared pensively at the explorer.

"Mr Carter, you killed my colleague in full view of everyone. Is there any reason why the sentence of death should not be carried out?"

Craig looked at these strange creatures, then turned back to the leader. "I did kill your subject, but it was an accident. I was unaware that my course of action would result in his death. I met your race for the first time yesterday, so I don't know you. I apologize for my error in judgment, but what's done is done."

"So, you admit killing my colleague then! Earthling, we were minding our own business when you happened to land on Saturn, and your course of action has led me to believe you aren't trustworthy. It seems to me that your entire planet is filled with people like you who disregard the law."

Carter's mouth dropped open in surprise and he glared at the creature.

"Really! What gave you the right to come here and terrorize the peace-loving Saturnians? You have invaded their privacy and you're making them work as your slaves. I understand from my friends here that you killed some of them, so what's the difference? At least I'm honest enough to admit I made a mistake, but you killed some Saturnians deliberately to make a point..."

The other creatures were working themselves into a frenzy, and drowned Carter's voice out. "*Kill him! Kill the Earthling!*" they shouted.

The leader banged on the table and called for silence, but the room was filled with the angry murmuring of the others.

"Well it seems as though the decision is unanimous, Earthling. I pronounce you *guilty as charged!*"

A loud cheer went up as the beings formed a ring around Carter. Those who had been assigned to guard him, came forward and formed a protective barrier around the condemned man.

"Get back all of you!" commanded the leader. "He's going to die by my hand as custom demands. I am your leader!"

They moved aside unwillingly, and the guards led the explorer out, escorting him to a wall.

Carter was angry. "That wasn't a trial! On Earth everyone is innocent until proven guilty."

"This isn't your precious planet!" snapped the leader curtly.

He looked at the Earthling and then took aim. For a moment, Craig wondered idly why none of the Saturnians were present, but he was secretly glad, because he didn't want them to see him die.

As the young space explorer awaited his fate, there was a general uproar, and he watched in morbid fascination as the Saturnians suddenly appeared, firing at their tormentors. Several shots connected with the evil creatures and many fell down, never to rise again. With an exclamation of shock, the leader and all the remaining creatures teleported themselves away from Saturn. A loud cheer started up and Lara threw herself into Craig's arms and he hugged her tightly. "I can't believe what just happened! You Saturnians are so peaceful, yet you used violence – very effectively though I must admit."

Jorrel smiled respectfully at his guest. "Sometimes we must use violence to defeat our tormentors. You showed us this by throwing that rock at the silver creature, and that was when we realized the wisdom of your argument. Thank you, Craig."

"And thank you – all of you, for saving my life."

Karnd then came forward. "No doubt you would like to resume your search for your friend, Craig and it would be most impolite of us to keep you here, although you are more than welcome to enjoy our hospitality for a while longer."

"Thank you all, but I must leave," said the explorer regretfully. "I hope I'll see you again soon."

Craig pressed a switch on his watch, and his ship appeared and landed on Saturn. He climbed aboard and waved to his friends. Shutting the door behind him. He lifted off and set course for Jupiter.

CHAPTER EIGHT

Craig wasn't very familiar with the Jupitarians, as they were still an unknown quantity, though they appeared to be friendly. This planet was very primitive and contained the cavemen species, but the explorers from Earth had learnt to use sign language and in this way they communicated with the beings. Carter landed on the planet and they stared at him with suspicion and wonder. It made a strange combination – the past and the future. It was obvious that Jupiter was going to be the "Earth" of the future, should the planet be destroyed.

The inhabitants greeted Craig in a friendly manner and stayed for a short while, but they signalled to him that no one fitting Roland's description had landed on their planet, so he took off once more. In space, he contacted Commander Simms and told him of the events that had taken place. Simms was relieved to hear from him, but he was ordered to return to Earth, because it seemed as though Roland had vanished without a trace. With a heavy heart, Carter agreed and set course for home. He prepared himself for the journey and went into time lapse once again.

Waking up some time later, he moved to the observation window and stared disbelievingly outside. He was approaching a planet, but it wasn't Earth.

"Where am I? According to the computer, Earth is still a long distance away. What planet is this?"

The explorer ran to the computer and tried to alter his course, because it looked as though he was going to crash land on the unidentified planet. He struggled, but his controls wouldn't obey him, and the surface loomed closer and closer. Carter stared in horror as he plummeted down at great speed. He tensed his body and prepared for impact, but suddenly a section opened up, revealing a large cavern, and his ship headed for it. Once inside, his rate of descent slowed considerably, and he floated gently downwards until his ship came to rest on a metallic platform. The hole above him closed, shutting out the light. However it didn't stay dark for very long. Creatures he had never seen before confronted Craig. They were bathed in a luminous blue light and their bodies were round, shaped like the sun itself. They each had two thin legs and two tiny arms. They were soft spoken and appeared to be friendly, but having met the silver human-like creatures, he was understandably wary of these strange beings. They seemed to sense this and one spoke gently. "Peace to you, strange one. From whence do you come?"

"I'm from the planet known as Earth."

"Ah!" exclaimed the creature sagely, "we have heard of that planet, but we didn't know what the inhabitants looked like."

They stared at the laser gun he was clutching tightly in his hand, and smiled. "You can put away that formidable weapon, Earthling; we mean you no harm."

Reluctantly he obeyed, but his hand hovered close to the holster.

"Where am I?" he asked curiously.

"You are on Sonambra," replied the creature.

"Sonambra?" he asked blankly.

"Yes, when translated, it stands for the planet of the sun."

Craig was confused. "But when I landed here, it didn't feel hot at all."

"Of course not! You didn't have time to feel hot, because I opened the portal that separates us from the surface. In actual fact, this planet is situated a little way beyond Mercury. We live underground and not on top, because we could not hope to survive on the surface. Please accompany me to my air-conditioned quarters and I'll answer any questions you would like to ask me."

The explorer followed his host to a little room, and they sat down on curious little chairs.

"Earthling, what do you wish to know about us?"

"Well I'm curious. Since this planet is a little further away than Mercury, surely it must be bathed in radioactivity."

Sonambro nodded. "Yes indeed, but that doesn't bother us."

Craig was alarmed. "But it is dangerous for earthlings! If I remain exposed much longer, I'll die! Radioactivity is deadly to me and others of my species."

The next statement made Craig sit bolt upright in alarm.

"You mean that the other we found can also suffer from radiation?"

"Are you talking about another one who looks like me?"

"Yes, we found him on our planet a few days ago," replied the sun being.

Craig was horrified. "Oh no, my superior sent me to find him! He's a friend of mine who has been missing for some time now. Is there some way I can get immunity from the radiation on this planet?"

"Yes, I'm able to help you counteract the effects, but you'll have to trust me. Will that be a problem?"

Carter shrugged. "I have no choice I suppose."

"Very well then, I must ask you to approach me."

Craig began walking towards the being, who put up his hand when the explorer was only a few centimetres away from him.

"Turn around with your back to me and place your hands at your sides. Once I have completed my task, you'll feel dizzy for a few minutes, but it'll soon pass. Are you prepared to continue?"

"I am," he declared.

"Good, now remain still while I place my hands on your shoulders. I suggest you close your eyes or you may be blinded."

Carter closed his eyes and he felt the hands upon his shoulders. He felt a tingling sensation run through his head and down his spine. The grip relaxed and the being removed its hands. Immediately, Craig felt dizzy and he was helped to a chair, but he recovered quickly.

"How strange, I feel as though something has been added to my body."

"Something has, Earthman; look at your hands."

Craig obeyed, and gasped when he saw the difference. His entire body was bathed in the luminous blue light that shone out of the Sonambrians.

"There, you are now immune to the effects of radiation."

"What of my friend – the other Earthman?"

"I shall take you to see him. Come this way please."

Craig followed the sun creature to another section of the building, and then it pointed to a window. Carter peered inside, afraid of what he might see.

Roland Stone was sitting down on a bed, his head in his hands. From that angle he looked normal, but at that instant, he looked up and Craig noticed that his entire body was glowing in a very strange way. His eyes looked very bright.

"Oh dear, I had no idea that radiation affected your species like that. I have never seen his face before, as he always kept it turned away every time I approached. I thought it was because I blinded him with my radiance. If you want to go in, you may, because you are immune to the radioactivity."

The explorer went inside, but Roland turned his face away.

"Go away! I look terrible!"

In response, Carter put his hand under his friend's chin, and forced him to look into his eyes.

His face, neck, and arms were covered in angry sores. Roland appeared not to recognize his friend at first, and stared blankly as if he was talking to a stranger.

"Roland it's me, Craig Carter. Commander Simms sent me out to look for you. I had abandoned the search, when a lucky break caused me to land here. I'm glad I've found you."

"You're glowing!" accused Roland.

Carter wanted to point out the fact that his friend was also glowing, but in a different way.

"I know. I was given immunity from the radiation. I wonder if you can still be cured. I'll ask the leader."

A whispered conference took place, and then the sun being came inside.

"I can try and help your friend, but it'll take longer as he has been exposed to the effects of radiation for so much longer."

"Just do what you can, please." Carter replied.

"Before I do so, may I be permitted to know your name?"

"Of course – it's Craig Carter, and my friend here is Roland Stone. We are both Americans. Do you have a name?"

"I am called Sonambro," replied the creature. "I find your

name very hard to pronounce; would you mind if I called you Cragus, and your friend Rolus?"

"I don't mind," grinned Craig.

The sun being placed his hands upon Roland's shoulders and began the procedure once again. Carter watched fascinated and he was obliged to shield his eyes as a number of flashes lit up the room. When he opened his eyes once again, Roland was lying unconscious on the floor and the sun creature began to sway on its feet. Craig caught it, just as it was about to fall.

"Here, hold onto me," he replied kindly.

"Thank you, my dizziness will pass soon. Your friend's condition took more energy out of me than I had imagined, but he should be fine. It's best to leave him where he is and allow him to recover by himself. We may damage him if he is moved now. We should know the results in a few hours."

A few hours later, Craig and Sonambro returned to the room and found Roland sitting dazedly on the bed. He turned to look at them when they approached, and Carter saw that his eyes seemed more normal. Roland stared curiously at them, and a flicker of recognition showed in his eyes.

"Hello Roland. I must say you look much better than you did earlier," Craig replied.

The man seemed puzzled, but smiled at his friend. "I feel fine thanks – never better in fact."

Sonambro clapped his hands delightedly. "If you will excuse me, I'll leave you two alone for a while. You must have plenty of catching up to do."

"Thank you Sonambro! I'll come and talk to you later," promised Craig.

He engaged Roland in conversation, but received only one-syllable answers. His friend apologized, saying he had been through so much in the last few months. Craig excused himself and went to find Sonambro.

"Ah Cragus, have you brought your friend up to date on all the news?"

"Yes I did, but he seems...well...distracted. Is it possible that the radiation could have affected his brain maybe?"

Sonambro stared at his new friend. "Oh dear, I hope not. What led you to this strange conclusion?"

"I don't know – it's just a feeling I have. The reason I was sent to find him in the first place, was because I had to give him my ship so that he could return to Earth and be with his family. His two children are sick, yet when I mentioned this to him, he didn't seem interested. I find this strange, because I know him very well, and his family means everything to him. The Roland Stone I know would have got into my ship at the first available opportunity and returned to be with them."

"What are you trying to say, Cragus?"

"It sounds really preposterous, yet...yet, it's almost as though he's a stranger to me. Sonambro, how did you find him?"

"Well we scanned the surface and our monitor picked him up wandering around over there. We opened the entrance, as we did for you, and he just fell inside."

"Was there any sign of a ship that he could have come in?"

"No, he was alone up there. We found no wreckage at all."

Craig was thoughtful for a while. "I don't like it; I know that his ship was destroyed, because I saw it on Mars. I have a bad feeling about this."

He returned to Roland, who had a silly grin on his face.

"Roland, what's going on here? Why are you grinning like an idiot?"

He smiled dreamily. "I don't know. I guess it's because that creature gave me immunity to the radiation. I feel wonderful – invigorated actually."

Craig wasn't fooled.

"How did you land here?" he asked his friend.

"I came in my ship – how else."

Craig stood up and paced the floor.

"You're lying! I saw your ship on the surface of Mars. It was beyond repair. Who are you really? You look like my friend, but you aren't him."

Roland smiled wickedly. "Can't you guess?" he asked as he began to walk slowly towards the explorer.

Craig took a step backwards, as realization dawned on him. "I should have figured it out! In a strange way, it makes sense. I met the silver, humanoid-like creatures on Saturn, and they are the only ones I know of who can teleport from one planet to another. What I can't figure out though is, why have you taken possession of my friend's body?"

"Ah!" exclaimed the silver creature admiringly, "it seems that you are quite clever for your species. No doubt you have gathered that your friend is a prisoner on my planet, and this is an experiment. His consciousness is at present imprisoned in my body. We live on a planet far away, but I was thinking of taking over this planet. Saturn was my first choice, but this planet is far more useful to me. All this energy will make my people very powerful."

"Why you..." spluttered Craig, as he turned to run from the room, "I'm going to warn the sun creatures!"

"You aren't going anywhere Carter!" said the creature as it lunged for him, and grabbed him firmly around one of his wrists. "You spoilt my plans on Saturn, but I won't allow you to do so again. As you can see, I've acquired great powers and I challenge you to free yourself – if you can! This planet has a tremendous power source and I've absorbed a lot of energy. I could crush you with one hand tied behind my back, but don't take my word for it!"

His lips curled back in a sneer as power surged through Craig's wrist, and an excruciating pain shot up his arm. He forced the explorer, gasping, to his knees. Then Tyrus stopped, and Craig rubbed his aching wrist.

"See, I told you so! If you aren't convinced, I'll show you again."

"I believe you!" Craig exclaimed.

The evil creature smiled victoriously. "I have another problem. I don't want you warning the Sonambrians of my plans, but I can't kill you either without them getting wise to me. You wanted to see your friend, so I'm going to reunite you with him. I'm taking you with me to my planet."

"I won't go willingly!" said he defiantly. "How do you plan to take me, without the Sonambrians getting suspicious?"

The creature just smiled coldly. "You have no choice, because if you don't come with me, I'll return to my planet and kill your friend. Then his poor sick children will be without their father, and your mission will be doomed to failure."

Craig knew the being would carry out his threat, and he didn't want his friend's blood to be on his hands. The creature read his mind, and knew he had won.

"All right, I'll go with you. Are we going in my spaceship?"

The creature shook his head. "No, too much time has been wasted already. I'll take you in my ship. It's too far for us to teleport to my planet."

"But my ship..." he began.

"Roland" held up his hand in a dismissive gesture. "Make some excuse to the sun creatures and tell them you'll be leaving with me in my spacecraft. Come on, it's time to go!" He prodded Craig in the ribs. "If you try to warn the Sonambrians, I'll unleash some power into your spine and you'll be paralysed for life."

They walked to the lounge and Sonambro stood up.

"Ah there you are! Would you care for some refreshments perhaps?"

Craig smiled stiffly. "No thank you. I have found my friend and he's anxious to return home. I want to thank you for your hospitality. Roland says his ship is parked on the surface and we'll use his craft. Could I ask you to keep mine here for a while? Someone will pick it up another time."

"Of course, think nothing of it. Go well Cragus and you too, Rolus." He leaned forward as though to embrace the explorer. Sonambro lowered his voice and spoke urgently. "*I know you are in trouble, and that he's not your friend – he didn't deceive me for a moment. Go with him Cragus and rest assured, help will be on the way. I know where his kind live. Good luck my noble friend!*"

He opened the door and the two of them climbed back up to the surface. Once the doors had closed, the silver being grabbed Craig around his waist and they both disappeared. They reappeared in a strange spaceship where the creature detained him in a small utility room.

Soon they landed on the creature's planet when again he was taken to a room and locked inside.

"I hope that Sonambro keeps his word! I don't want to be held on this planet for too long."

His thoughts were interrupted by the arrival of one of the silver creatures, and Craig got up quickly.

"It's only me, Craig!" exclaimed his friend. "Oh how I hate this hideous body."

"Roland...Roland Stone! Oh it's good to see you again, my friend. You led me quite a chase, you know. I've been searching all over the universe for you!"

"I believe so and I'm sorry for all the trouble I've caused."

"It wasn't your fault Roland! How long have you been like this?"

"It's only been a few days. How I wish I could return to my own form."

"I'll think of some way to change you back, don't worry. Do you know how to get to their laboratory?"

"Yes of course."

"All right then, let's put our heads together, so that we can think of a way to get off this planet."

Roland left before the others could discover him, and later the leader allowed Craig to come out. The being grinned at him. "Have you seen your friend yet?" he asked

Carter shook his head. "No I haven't, not yet anyway."

"That's strange! I thought he would be anxious to come and talk to you."

"Well he hasn't!" lied Craig. "Now that you have me here, I want to know what you plan to do with me."

"I haven't really decided yet. I was toying with the idea of killing you, but you could prove valuable to me. Twice now you have thwarted my plans to take over two different planets. Maybe I'll keep you here and study you. Once I have found out all I need to know, I'll launch an attack on your precious Earth."

Craig stared at the leader. "Seeing as we'll be seeing lots more of one another, I'd like to know your name."

"You can call me Tyrus."

"Well Tyrus are you going to keep me locked up forever, or am I free to walk about?"

"For the moment, I'll grant you your wish. If you give me cause to distrust you, then I'll confine you again. I have some business to attend to now, but later on I wish to interrogate you."

Carter moved away from the electrical being, but he wasn't happy. It upset him to see Tyrus walking around in his friend's body, so familiar to him, yet still so alien. He walked a short distance away, and when he saw that no one was paying attention to him, he took out his mobile device and searched for a signal. The phone screen lit up and he stared miserably at it, but there was no signal. He cursed softly, and then pressed one of the icons. Immediately a distress signal began to flash silently. Craig switched off the device, but the signal was programmed to continue until someone came in range of it. It would then give details of Craig's whereabouts and the coordinates of the planet. It was a long shot, but not impossible.

"Until the Sonambrians, or another friendly planet intercept my distress signal and come to rescue me, I'm helpless. All I can hope to do right now is snoop around. Maybe something interesting will come to light. I shudder to think what he meant by interrogating me, but I know it won't be pleasant. It disturbs me when I don't know my enemy. Somehow I have to trick that leader into the laboratory so that Roland can regain his human form. That creature's name certainly suits him. Tyrus, the tyrant and he certainly is that!"

Craig moved some distance away from the creatures, but several were always in the background, watching and waiting for him to disobey their leader. One came closer and he looked enquiringly up at it.

"Craig, it's me again," said Roland. "It seems that Tyrus has been very busy lately. I don't know how it happened, but he was in contact with a Colonel Ivan Petrovsky. Apparently this Petrovsky has offered him a deal and he's very pleased. He asked for you in exchange for the information."

Carter picked up a small stone and flung it contemptuously away from him.

"Damn it, this Tyrus is bad news! I met Colonel Petrovsky while I was looking for you. He was going to send me to Russia so that I could be brainwashed. First however, he told me I would be tortured for valuable information. I got away from him, but this will probably mean a promotion for the Colonel if he succeeds. Did they mention what was going to happen to you at all?"

"Yes, I overheard Tyrus talking to some of his followers. Apparently, the good Colonel decided I could be useful as well, but I don't know what that odious alien agreed to."

"Roland, things are getting out of control now. When is Petrovsky due to arrive here?"

"Tomorrow sometime. I think our plan will have to be implemented sooner than expected, don't you?"

Carter nodded vigorously. "Yes, you need to get transferred to your own body soon. If Petrovsky is coming for us, then Tyrus won't kill us, but he warned me to behave. Knowing his reputation, what's to stop him torturing me to teach me a lesson?"

Roland stared miserably at his friend. "Yes, I know him a little better than you, and this looks like it could be just up his alley. Well, what should we do?"

Carter was determined. "No, we implement the plan now. I'll have to take that risk. How do you feel about it, Roland?"

"Let's do it. Anything is better than being imprisoned in this horrible body. Just make it convincing, okay."

Suddenly Craig stood up and flung a rock at Roland, winking as he did so, but it missed as he had intended. He lunged at Roland and they began to fight, while several of the creatures looked on in amusement. They fought convincingly for a while and then Craig "slipped", allowing Roland to seize him. His arms were pinned behind his back with a circle of pure energy; just enough to make it look convincing, while Roland placed a hand on his shoulder, and shoved him in the direction of Tyrus and his friends. An amused gathering began to form and Craig began shouting at the top of his voice.

"Let go of me!" he yelled angrily.

Tyrus approached and spoke to his "follower". "What seems to be the trouble here? Has this Earthling been up to his tricks again?"

"Yes Excellency, I gave him an order and he threw a rock at me, but fortunately it missed. We fought, and I managed to subdue him."

"So, he obviously can't take good advice. Take him back to his cell – I'll deal with him later."

"I shall do so at once, Excellency!" His "follower" replied.

They moved away. When they had gone a short distance, Roland released Craig's arms and the explorer darted off in the direction of the laboratory.

"Don't just stand there, you fool – go after him!"

Roland broke into a run and followed him, with the leader close behind.

Once inside, Roland stepped into the one cubicle and waited. Tyrus stormed in and cornered Craig at the entrance to the other cubicle, but as he reached for the explorer, Craig side-stepped and tripped him and Tyrus fell headlong into the second cubicle. With a shout of triumph, Carter slammed the door shut and locked it securely. Following Roland's instructions, he reversed the process and the machinery whirred into life. There was a series of flashes and strange noises and then the computer relayed a message. <*Transformation complete*>

Triumphantly, Carter opened the doors and both Roland and Tyrus stumbled out. Roland looked down at his body and gave a whoop of joy.

"You did it, Craig, you did it!"

They shook hands vigorously and hugged each other delightedly. Tyrus was furious.

"Curse you meddler! I have reverted back to my own form again."

"It suits you, Tyrus!" exclaimed Craig cheekily.

Until then, his laser gun had remained holstered, but now he drew it out and pointed it at Tyrus.

Outside, the drone of many engines could be heard and Craig smiled gleefully.

"Well it looks as though the cavalry have arrived, Tyrus. Come any closer and I'll dispose of you like I did your friend on Saturn. I'm sick and tired of your hospitality, and so is Roland here."

Several frightened silver beings hurried inside.

"Excellency, we are under attack!"

Ignoring the laser gun and the two Earthlings, Tyrus ran outside and everyone else followed.

Craig waved to Sonambro, who waved back. Both worlds began to fight one another and the two humans were forgotten during the exchange. The two friends watched in fascination as both beings fought one another. Sonambro came up to them.

"Sonambro, meet the real Roland Stone!"

The sun being smiled and shook Roland's hand. "Yes, your eyes do look better now! Cragus, here is your ship; I suggest you leave now while Tyrus is occupied. We'll keep him busy for you."

Craig shook his hand gratefully.

"Thank you for helping us, Sonambro – we couldn't have done it without you."

"Think nothing of it, Cragus. I hope you'll come and visit us sometime when you are in the vicinity."

Both men waved and then Craig's ship lifted off the planet and was soon gone from sight.

As they watched the planet disappear, Roland smiled at his friend. "Thank you for coming to my rescue, Craig. I cannot thank you enough for all the trouble you went through to help me."

"It was a pleasure, chum!" exclaimed the explorer happily. "I'm just glad you're all right."

All went as planned and soon they watched Earth came closer and closer.

"How strange it is to see Earth again!" remarked Roland, "I was missing for almost three months."

"Yes you were. I'd better contact Commander Simms and tell him we're coming in."

Roland looked at his body. "Craig, that glow has disappeared from around our bodies."

Carter looked at his hands and smiled. "So it has – well Sonambro told us that it would disappear in time."

He moved to the console and pressed a button. "This is Craig Carter calling Commander Simms!"

Instantly the screen lit up and a relieved Commander beamed at his employee. "Craig! It's good to hear your voice! You gave us some nasty scares you know!"

"I realize that Sir, but I found Roland and he's unharmed."

Roland moved into focus and the Commander beamed cheerfully at him. "Welcome back, Roland – I'm truly glad you made it. Come on home!"

"Yes Sir!" exclaimed both men simultaneously.

A little while later, the craft settled noiselessly onto the landing pad and both men climbed out, leaving the technicians to secure the ship. Together they went into Commander Simms's office to brief him on the events of the last few months.

A medical examination convinced the doctors that Roland didn't have the same disease as his children. Suddenly he remembered he had bought them a toy on a previous mission and he hurried to fetch it. Tests on the toy proved that it was filled with a strange substance, which could be found in the stuffing. A seam had worked loose, releasing some sort of gas, which when the children had inhaled, poisoned their systems. Once the toy had been destroyed, the children began to get better and before long, they had fully recovered, thus everything was fine again in the Stone household.

In Russia, Colonel Ivan Petrovsky was staring thoughtfully at a computer screen, but his thoughts were elsewhere.

"So, you have eluded me once again, Craig Carter, but you cannot escape me forever. One day we shall meet again, and I look forward to that. Next time, I *will* get the information my country desperately wants."

CHAPTER NINE

At the space station, Craig was again seated in Commander Simms office. He had spent a few days recovering from his last strenuous mission. Now he waited patiently to hear what his boss had to say. Commander Simms poured some coffee for himself and his employee and pushed it over to him.

"Craig, I know you have only been home a few days, and you are still tired from your trip around the galaxy. I just want to reiterate how grateful I am to you for what you have done, and I know that Roland has thanked you as well. You returned him to his family, who were beginning to give up any hope of seeing their loved one ever again."

"It was my pleasure Sir, really. He's a good friend of mine and I was glad to help."

"All the same, you met up with some unsavoury characters along the way. Tyrus and the planet Tyrome will hate you for the rest of their lives, and their life-span could be a long one. Also, Colonel Petrovsky is furious at having lost you."

Craig shrugged dismissively. "It's part and parcel of the job Sir. I wasn't expecting to become humanitarian of the year or anything like that. Space exploration is a challenge and one that I accepted a few years ago, when I was trained for this job. I signed an oath and I intend to stand by it!"

"Yes you will because you work hard at it!" his employer confirmed. "However today I have asked you to come here for an entirely different reason. Craig, you have excelled at what you've done and I'm very proud of you – just don't tell the rest of my astronauts, or they might think that they have serious competition." he winked.

"No Sir, I'll never do that, I swear!" Craig grinned as he placed his hand over his heart.

Simms smiled. "Well young man, I think that you deserve a vacation. You've been working very hard and you need to relax. As of this moment you are on leave for one month. Take this opportunity to go out and enjoy yourself."

"I would Sir, but no holiday is any fun if you have to go alone. I appreciate the offer but maybe another time?"

Simms drummed his fingers on the table. "So, you want to go with someone? Who did you have in mind?"

Craig grinned sheepishly. "Well Sir, I haven't seen much of Constance lately. I seem to go out on a mission, just as she returns from one."

"What am I, your fairy godmother?" he replied with mock severity.

Carter began to speak, and Simms put up his hand. "Just a moment young man. Let me see what I can organize," he replied as he spoke into his intercom. "Miss Steele, send the other astronaut into my office."

The door opened and Constance walked in. "You wanted to see me Sir?"

As she turned around, she saw Craig sitting down opposite their boss, and she smiled at him. He indicated to the chair next to Craig. "Sit down my dear."

She complied, and Craig reached for her hand.

"My dear I'm sending Craig away on holiday for a month. He needs a break – and so do you. I'm ordering both of you to go away immediately – today in fact."

Both young people smiled at one another, and then they grinned at their boss.

"Thank you, Sir!" Craig replied gratefully. "I'll never forget this."

"Go on, scram!" he laughed. "See you both in a month's time. Enjoy yourselves!"

The young couple left, and Commander Simms's secretary came in with a data tablet containing some documents for him to sign. He sighed and looked at their departing backs. "I know what it's like to be young, Sarah. I hope that they have a good time."

Commander Simms had kindly loaned the couple one of the smaller spacecrafts, so that they would not have to depend on public transport, and they were free to go wherever they chose to spend their time, as every planet had spaceports that could accommodate travellers. They decided to go to a nearby planet that specialized in taking care of small parties of tourists. All types of beings frequented this place called Eclipse which had been discovered only a few years before. An enterprising billionaire had decided to invest and had built a luxurious hotel on the planet.

The couple stood arm in arm and looked out of the observation window. The ship was operating on auto pilot. Constance put her head on her boyfriend's shoulder and sighed dreamily. "I can't believe we're finally going away together for a whole month! Mostly we're lucky if we can snatch a quick weekend together."

"Believe it my sweet! I'm looking forward to this holiday, and I am going to enjoy every moment. No criminals or evil beings to look out for!"

Constance agreed. "We can concentrate on us the whole time!"

Carter leered at his girlfriend. "Now you're talking! We still have an hour before we reach Eclipse. I vote we start early," he suggested, as he bent to kiss his girlfriend. She put her hand on his lips. "Hey, hold that thought Romeo! We have to land soon! Curb your impatience mister!"

Craig groaned. "Ohh you sure know how to hurt a guy's feelings. Aww come on, just one itty bitty kiss and then I'll leave you alone."

"Promise?"

"Uh huh, scout's honour," he promised.,

Constance sighed and turned to her boyfriend. Their lips met gently and Craig's tongue probed her mouth. She sighed and surrendered to him.

The vidscreen came alive, and the controller cleared his throat noisily. "Ehrmm, excuse me ship E221, you are cleared to land in bay 2, anytime, when you have finished your examination of one another."

Craig and Constance jumped guiltily apart, and Carter grinned sheepishly. "Got you, tower. See you in a while."

The controller smiled, and the screen went dead. Constance combed her dishevelled hair, while her boyfriend began the landing sequence.

They touched down without even a bump and a courtesy car pulled up and waited for them to disembark. When the steps were in the downward position, a valet took possession of their baggage and headed towards the car. At the same time, one of the pilots taxied their ship to the hangar where it would be stored during their stay.

The couple was dropped off at the reception area where they approached the woman on duty. They mentioned their names and she handed them a card. "Good day Mr Carter, Miss Gregg, your room is number 700 on the seventh floor. Welcome to the Hotel Caprice. I hope you enjoy your stay with us."

The porter took their baggage up to the seventh floor and opened the door for them. He opened the windows to allow the air in and placed their suitcases on the double bed. Craig gave him a generous tip.

"Thank you, Sir. My name is Frank and if you require anything that is not listed in our brochure, please don't hesitate to call me and I'll see what I can arrange. The activities we provide have been downloaded into your mobile devices. This key card is your access to everything that is available. The number is embossed on the card. Enjoy your stay!"

"We plan to," Craig replied.

When the door had closed, Carter lay down on the bed and sighed. "Oh boy, come and feel this mattress! It's awfully comfortable!"

Constance however was looking out of the window. "Oh Craig, what a breathtaking view we have. You can see the hotel pool from here, and their gardens are exquisite!"

Reluctantly he climbed off the bed and went to join his girlfriend at the window. He opened the balcony door and they stepped out onto a paved terrace containing a table and some chairs.

"It is beautiful I have to agree. I can't wait to try out that pool! It looks so inviting." Craig replied.

Constance looked up at the sky and smiled at her boyfriend. "The sky is clear and blue and it looks as though today is going to be a scorcher. Hurry, let's unpack and get down there. I want to make the most of this holiday, starting now!"

The young couple changed into their swimming costumes and went to the pool area where they put their towels on some recliners.

"Last one in the water has to buy lunch!" Craig challenged.

Constance got a head start and laughingly Craig followed behind her. She giggled as he grabbed for her, and she dodged his outstretched arms. Craig tripped over her feet and fell headlong into the water, making a huge splash. He went under and surfaced, shaking the water from his hair.

"Why you little hussy, you cheated! Anyway I went in first, rather ungracefully I have to admit, but lunch is on you."

Laughingly she stretched out her hand to help him up, and he took the opportunity to pull her into the water. When she had surfaced, and wiped the water out of her eyes she put her arms around him and kissed him teasingly. "I don't mind one bit! Your swan dive was worth every moment."

The couple laughed and frolicked in the cool water. They spent the better part of the morning in the pool. When they weren't swimming, they stopped to drink something cool. Constance paid for the lunch, but vowed she would make her boyfriend pay for the next meal.

That afternoon they explored the little planet and took note of all the amenities on offer.

"Wow Craig, we need more than a month if we are going to sample all the delights this place has to offer! Look they even have a massage parlour! I'm definitely going to book a session there sometime. The shopping mall also looks interesting. I could use some new clothes."

"Yes, and look at the movie brochure. All the latest movies are here and I can think of quite a few that take my fancy," Craig continued. "There is also a hiking trail, and since we don't have much available space on Earth to go for long walks, I think that is a definite must!"

Constance ran her finger down the list on her mobile device. "Look, we can even go for diving lessons, or learn how to play tennis."

"Or squash, play virtual reality games, learn another language," Craig continued. "This place is amazing!"

"So much to do and so little time," Miss Gregg sighed.

"Well we'll just have to come back here another time and finish what we don't do this time around," Carter decided.

"Now there's a plan!" she agreed. "What should we do tonight?"

"I think a movie sounds like a good idea," Craig replied.

"Sounds good to me," she agreed.

The next few days passed in a whirlwind of activity, with the young couple finding plenty to occupy themselves.

A week had passed, and the young couple were making their way to the hotel's dining room for supper. As they turned towards the dining room however, Craig stopped suddenly, causing Constance to bump into him.

"Hey, why did you stop so suddenly?" she asked curiously.

"I thought this holiday was just too good to be true! Another guest has arrived and it's someone I certainly don't want to meet up with!"

Constance craned her head and looked over her boyfriend's shoulder. "Who is it?"

"My arch enemy Ivan Petrovsky, that's who," he replied, pointing to a figure walking in the direction of the dining room.

"Oh no, what's he doing here?" she asked dismayed.

"Probably on holiday as well! This place is a tourist attraction, so I suppose he has every right to be here."

"Do you think he knew you were coming to Eclipse?" she asked nervously.

"I doubt it, but the timing is awful! He's the last person I want to see. I escaped from him twice before, and it must have made him feel pretty stupid. He would love to have another chance." Craig replied crossly.

"But Craig, this is a very public place. If he tries to kidnap you here, he will be taking quite a risk. Eclipse is full of holiday makers."

"Maybe so, but I don't like it. I have a bad feeling about this!" Carter replied sourly.

Craig took his girlfriend by the hand and led her out of the hotel. "I think we should eat somewhere else tonight."

They went to another restaurant and while they were waiting for their food, Constance voiced her concerns. "Craig, does this mean that we will have cut our holiday short, and return to Earth? Eclipse isn't a very big planet, and we are sure to bump into him sooner or later. Do you think when he sees us, he'll try something?"

"I don't know what to think! On the one hand, I think we should leave right now, but another part of me says we have paid for a month's stay on Eclipse and we should enjoy it. It's very crowded at present and that could work for or against us, depending on the situation."

His girlfriend placed her hand on his wrist. "Craig, we should just stay here and enjoy the facilities. Obviously, we will have to be constantly on our guard, but Petrovsky isn't stupid. He wouldn't try anything that could spark an international incident."

"Yes, but if we stay he'll see us sooner or later, you can be sure of that," Craig grumbled.

"Let him see us then! I'm confident he won't do anything idiotic. We came here to enjoy ourselves and we should do that. Obviously, we just have to be a little more cautious. When we go on the hiking trail for example, we should stay close together. Even if we lose one another in the crowd, there would be too many people around for him to attempt anything. It will work out fine, I'm sure of it."

"I still don't like it!" Craig complained. "However, if we are extra careful, everything should go well."

"It will," his girlfriend replied confidently.

"I guess we are staying here then."

"Yes, I think we definitely should remain here and enjoy the rest of our holiday!" Constance agreed.

The next day, Craig and Constance were once again at the swimming pool. Craig handed his girlfriend a drink and bent close to her ear. "Don't look now but we are about to receive company," he whispered warningly.

Constance glanced surreptitiously upwards and saw Petrovsky heading purposefully in their direction. He smiled a greeting, and without waiting for an invitation, pulled up a chair and sat down next to them.

"Well hello Comrade Carter, what a pleasant surprise! I wasn't expecting to see you here on Eclipse."

"I didn't expect to see you either," Craig replied.

Ivan Petrovsky turned an appraising eye in Constance's direction. "Mr Carter, would you mind introducing me to your beautiful companion?"

"This is Constance Gregg," he replied stiffly.

Petrovsky gave her a dazzling smile and kissed her hand. "I'm delighted to meet you my dear! I think the sun has some competition here. You are a ray of sunshine on this glorious planet."

"Thank you."

He signalled a waiter and ordered a drink. Once it had arrived he sipped it and engaged the couple in conversation.

"So Mr Carter, how is space travel these days?"

"It's just fine," he replied warily.

Petrovsky turned his attention to Constance. "What do you do for a living my dear? I'll bet you are a high-powered secretary for a very big company!"

Constance smiled sweetly at him. "Well appearances can be deceiving Mr Petrovsky. Actually, I'm also a space explorer."

Ivan's eyebrows rose slightly.

"You are? That is most interesting!" he replied.

"Many women are now travelling in space for their countries. I'm sure that Russia has its complement of lady explorers as well."

Ivan favored her with another dazzling smile. "Touché my dear; you are clever, as well as beautiful."

Craig however wasn't smiling. "What are you doing here, Petrovsky?"

"I'm on holiday, same as you."

"There are several holiday resorts on any number of planets. How come you chose Eclipse?"

Petrovsky looked hurt. "Come now comrade, it was a coincidence, nothing more than that. Besides, I love the atmosphere here and Eclipse was highly recommended. It looks just the place I need to unwind. You know as well as I do that space exploration can be very stressful, and we all need to rest and recuperate."

Craig thought back to his recent mission and decided his rival was probably right.

The Russian took Craig's silence to mean assent and he began talking about his plans for his stay at the pleasure resort. He mentioned that he only had two weeks leave but when Craig asked him what he planned to do on his vacation, he shrugged his shoulders, explaining that he hadn't really had time to think about it, as he had only arrived the previous day. Craig and Constance were wary, and didn't share their plans with him either. Ivan spoke to them for a while longer, but when he had finished his drink, he excused himself.

"I am sure that we will see one another again," he replied affably.

"We probably will." Craig agreed.

Constance watched him as he left and she cocked her head to one side. "Charming devil isn't he."

"He most certainly is, but the devil analogy is quite correct. He would smile at his victim before he killed him, so watch your step. That man is very dangerous! I have read his dossier and it makes for some impressive reading."

Miss Gregg stretched out on the recliner and made space for him to sit. "Well my sweet, you had better enlighten me as to what we are dealing with here. I know nothing about him, other than the fact that he is devious."

By this time Petrovsky had gone inside and Craig began the story.

"Ivan Petrovsky is an excellent space explorer. The dossier said nothing about his childhood, except that it was a military based one. His father was General Igor Petrovsky, General Ivanovitch Petrovsky was his father's father, therefore Ivan's grandfather and namesake. Ivanovitch married an American woman, and that was how Igor learnt how Americans behaved and thought. Igor was just as cunning as his father and soon rose to the rank of General as well. At the age of thirty he was recruited as a spy. He was sent to America under an assumed name, and he entered the world of politics. You met him at the peace delegation, remember."

Constance shuddered. "The man was known as Senator Ian Petersen."

"That's correct. When I exposed him for what he really was, he was arrested and later sent back to Russia. He killed himself because of the shame of failure, and his son has never forgiven me since. He blames me for his father's suicide. Ivan is his only son, and he was determined to do the best he could, with the sole intent of avenging his father's death. Ivan's mother was a sickly woman and she died soon after her husband had committed suicide.'

'Petrovsky was already an astronaut and his determination wouldn't allow him to accept second best. He came first in all his classes and is an expert in everything from weapons to flying any spaceship ever built. The KGB recruited him a few years ago and he often goes on missions for them, but only those that involve space exploration. He is the same age as me and as far as we know, he doesn't have a girlfriend. If he has, she isn't mentioned in the dossier. Ivan prefers to work alone, but has gone on missions with other cosmonauts. He already holds the rank of Colonel. He is a perfectionist, constantly striving to better his already impressive record, and he doesn't care who gets in the way."

Constance thoughtfully sipped her drink. She put it down carefully and turned troubled eyes to her boyfriend. "I like this even less now than I did before! Judging by what you have just told me, you are a reminder of his failure, because you escaped from him when you were on that mission to find Roland Stone. Now I have no doubt that his visit is not a co-incidence. His KGB masters must have found out that you were on vacation here on Eclipse and I think he is determined to finish the job. Remember he has a personal stake in this vendetta against you. He would dearly love to capture you, with or without the KGB's permission."

"You could be right my dearest, but at the same time it seems like such a waste of energy."

"Maybe from your point of view Craig, but Ivan Petrovsky sees it differently I'm sure. You are proof of his failure and he hates that. I don't like the odds."

"What are you saying Constance? Should we change our minds and run like scared rabbits?" Craig demanded crossly.

"It sounds like a good option," she offered.

Craig's eyes blazed in fury. "I won't run away, not now! Even if we do cut our holiday short, he will always be there, hovering in the background, waiting for a suitable opportunity to capture me. If he is here for that sole purpose, then let him do the best he can. I'm a Carter and we never run away from a fight."

His girlfriend knew better than to argue with him when he was in this frame of mind, so she said nothing.

Colonel Ivan Petrovsky had walked slowly back into the hotel, but once he was out of sight of the young couple sun bathing at the pool, he took the stairs two at a time in his haste to get back to his room. Despite Craig and Constance's fears, his visit had been a co-incidence, but he too saw the opportunity that had suddenly presented itself to him.

He took out his mobile device and contacted his superiors in Russia, and an animated conversation in Russian then followed. The conversation lasted fifteen minutes and when Petrovsky disconnected the call, he was smiling broadly.

"This is a truly lucky day for me! I know Mr Carter has a weakness now! He and that pretty young lady look like they are very close. I won't underestimate him again though. That man is cagey and I have asked for reinforcements to be sent here on the next shuttle. When they arrive, I'll put my plan into operation."

Several more days passed and during that time Craig was constantly on the alert for trouble. Now and again he would see Petrovsky taking part in some of the same activities as him. However the Russian never made any threatening moves. Sometimes he would wave at the couple, but he never really spoke more than a few words to them at any time. Constance began to relax slightly.

"He must really be here for a holiday Craig. If he wanted you that badly he would have attempted something by now," she reasoned.

"Maybe, but I still have my doubts," he replied.

The next day Craig prepared to go on a hike up one of the mountains, but Constance declined.

"As much as I would like to accompany you my sweet, I've booked a day at the spa. I'm going to spend the entire day being pampered and beautified."

Carter kissed his girlfriend. "Well if they can improve on your beauty, then the age of miracles hasn't passed. I think you're just wonderful the way you are."

Constance kissed her boyfriend. "Thank you, that's the most charming compliment anyone could ever pay me," she sighed. "I'll see you later then!"

"See you tonight Constance. I've booked a venue in the hotel's ballroom. We can wine, dine and dance the night away."

"That sounds absolutely divine. I can't wait!"

The couple went their separate ways.

CHAPTER TEN

Constance headed for the spa to begin her day of pampering. She spent the morning enjoying the therapeutic effects of the hot springs. Afterwards she was due to have a full body massage and while she was eating the healthy lunch that had been laid out for the participants, she was counting the moments when she would be in the capable hands of the trained masseuse. She moved her neck from side to side and felt the tension there.

Constance went into the massage parlour, along with several other guests where they were handed towels and told where to lie down. Several women then arrived and introduced themselves to their waiting guests.

Miss Gregg's masseuse began massaging her head and neck and in this way, she planned to work her way down to her customer's feet. The space explorer sighed blissfully as she felt the knots begin to disappear and soon she was hardly aware of anyone else in the room. She closed her eyes and dozed briefly.

The explorer was unaware of several figures who silently entered the room and shepherded the customers out quickly and efficiently. Someone moved over to where Constance lay, and indicated to the masseuse to move out of the room. She scuttled away hurriedly, unnerved by the menacing figures.

Ivan Petrovsky took a handful of cream and began massaging Constance's back. Her eyes opened dreamily. "Oh Michelle, you have the most amazing hands! I can feel the tension just oozing out of every pore."

"I'm glad to hear it Miss Gregg," Petrovsky replied. "Many of my girlfriends have said the same thing to me over the years."

Constance was immediately on full alert. She grabbed at the sheet and covered her naked body before jumping off the bed and whirling to face Petrovsky. He watched her expression with some amusement.

"How did you get in here?" she demanded.

"I did so very quietly actually. You didn't even hear me."

She pulled the sheet tighter around her body and tensed to meet this threat. However her eyes roved around the room and she found to her dismay that Petrovsky was not alone. Several men and women blocked her escape, and the way they were standing, left her in no doubt as to what their intentions were. She was very aware of her nakedness and tucked the stray end between her breasts.

"What are you going to do now Miss Gregg?" he challenged.

"By the looks of that flimsy sheet you'll need both hands to hold it in place." He moved his hand in a wide arc that took in all of the people in the room with him. "Every one of these people is highly trained and you will have quite a fight on your hands. I know that the American space explorers are well trained, as are we. If you wish to protect both your health and your dignity, give up now."

The woman weighed up her options carefully but the situation didn't look good. She glanced out of the corner of her eye, and saw her robe lying on a chair not far away. Constance looked around the room but everyone was still quite a distance away. Miss Gregg hesitated only a brief second before she flung a chair at Petrovsky, who was closest to her. He swore as the chair caught him a glancing blow on the side of his hip, and he overbalanced. In that split second, the explorer grabbed for her robe and had put it on and tied it securely before anyone else had made a single move. She ripped the sheet from her body and threw it over the head of a woman who was fast approaching, causing her to trip and fall. Her jaw was set in a grim and determined line as she launched herself at the next assailant, kicking him hard in his genitals. He folded like a limp rag doll.

The others moved in steadfastly and attacked her from all sides. Constance's hands and feet were a blur as she kicked and punched her assailants. She gave a good account of herself, and inflicted some damage on each one of her assailants. Someone landed a lucky punch, and she reeled from the blow. Constance saw double images, and before her vision cleared, someone tripped her, and she fell flat on her face. Petrovsky dragged her unceremoniously to her feet, and her arms were forced roughly behind her back, where handcuffs snapped into place. A woman grabbed a handful of her hair and slapped her viciously through the face.

"Bitch!" she exclaimed vehemently. "You broke my nose!"

Constance was unrepentant. "I think it improves your looks actually."

The woman raised her hand again and Petrovsky grabbed her and twisted her wrist, making her yelp in pain.

"Save your anger for later Anna! As much as I agree with you, I need Miss Gregg alive, so that I can implement phase two of my plan."

"Craig won't give in to you Petrovsky," Constance snapped. "That's why you're doing this isn't it?"

"If Craig Carter loves you my dear, he'll see reason. If not – well I don't fancy your chances. It would be a terrible shame though," he sighed as he ran his hand down one side of her face and looked thoughtfully at the blood on his finger. He sucked the red liquid off and pushed her firmly ahead of him. The others crowded around her so that no one would notice anything amiss. Behind her one of the women went to a cubicle nearby and picked up Constance's clothing.

Constance thought briefly about shouting for help, but she changed her mind when she realized that Petrovsky would have no qualms about killing anyone who tried to interfere, and the last thing she wanted was to have innocent blood on her hands. Grimly she decided to go along with them for the moment. While she lived, she could plot her escape, and she planned to live for a long time to come.

They bundled her into a van with tinted windows and drove away from the hotel without anyone being aware that she had just been kidnapped. Behind her, two other vans followed their leader. Petrovsky, who was sitting beside her, placed a blindfold over her eyes and the journey was completed in silence.

When they arrived at their destination, she was helped out of the car and led into a building. Someone came up behind her and undid the handcuffs, but left the blindfold on.

She remained where she was until she heard the door clang shut, and then she removed the blindfold.

Constance blinked in the light and saw that she was inside a cell. Her clothes were thrown at her feet and the outer door was slammed shut. A key turned in the lock.

Miss Gregg took off the robe and put her clothes back on. She checked if they had left her mobile device in her pocket but was not surprised to see that it had been removed. Afterwards she explored every section of the cell, but was surrounded by solid concrete. A barred window faced her and she looked outside, but she didn't recognize her surroundings. She knocked on the door, but it was constructed of solid steel. A wash basin stood in one corner, and a cracked mirror was stuck on the wall just above it. The woman examined her face and touched a few tender spots gingerly. She washed her face and was pleased to discover that all the cuts were superficial in nature and would heal without scarring. Her assailants had certainly known what they were doing. Morosely she sat down on the bed and stared unseeingly at the floor. Petrovsky may have worked alone in the past she reasoned, but he had certainly wasted no time in getting reinforcements today.

Meanwhile out on the mountain, Craig was hiking with another group of people completely unaware of the drama that had taken place in his absence. He enjoyed communing with nature and was fascinated by all the different flora and fauna that their guide pointed out to them. He was unaware of the person who had joined the party with one sole purpose in mind, and that was to observe his every movement. The man was told not to approach Craig or arouse his suspicions in any way. If Craig left the group sooner, he was to report to Petrovsky, and the man would then implement a way to delay his return to the hotel, until Constance was safely out of reach. It seemed however that Carter had no intentions of leaving before the tour had been completed.

The sun had begun to set when the hikers returned to their hotel. Craig hurried upstairs to shower and change. He was surprised to find that his girlfriend wasn't there, but he assumed that she was either still tied up at the spa, or else she had taken the opportunity to go shopping. He dressed in smart clothes and headed for the ballroom to wait for his girlfriend. He felt a vague sense of unease but admonished himself for it.

When an hour had passed and Craig had begun on his second drink, he became worried. He was just about to go and look for his girlfriend when a waitress came up to him with a note on a silver platter. Thinking that Constance had been delayed, he smiled and accepted the note. However his face creased in a frown of anxiety as he read the letter.

"Hello again Carter! Your girlfriend asked me to give you this note. She has been unavoidably delayed. She's fine however, but whether she stays that way is entirely up to you. The lovely Miss Gregg is at present enjoying my hospitality. You are welcome to join her anytime that is convenient. The waitress will give you a mobile phone, and you are to keep this with you at all times. I'll contact you later."

Ivan Petrovsky.

Craig crumpled the note viciously in his hand. He spoke to the waitress. "I believe you have something else for me miss."

She nodded and handed him the phone. He stared unhappily at it and waved the waitress away. Knowing that it was useless to stay where he was, he returned to their room. He put the phone down on the coffee table and stared at it.

"Damn Petrovsky to hell! I thought it was just too much of a coincidence, and now he has my girlfriend in his clutches. Obviously, he wants me, but why would he take Constance instead? Probably to get my attention, and he has definitely done that. Well I have no option but to wait for his call."

The space explorer paced up and down the room, but the phone stayed stubbornly silent. Several hours passed and it was nearly midnight when the phone rang. He snatched it up anxiously.

"Petrovsky, where is my girlfriend?" he demanded without preamble.

"Craig it's me," said a familiar voice, and he sank down on the chair. "Constance, are you all right? Has that maniac hurt you in any way?"

"No I'm fine really," she assured him. "Petrovsky has me locked up in a cell, and he is standing right here beside me. He wants to talk to you."

Miss Gregg handed the phone to her captor.

"Good evening Mr Carter. See your girlfriend is just fine. I thought it would be a nice gesture to have her speak to you first. In that way you know that she is still alive."

"She had better stay that way Petrovsky, or else you'll have me to deal with. Why have you kidnapped her when you so obviously want me? You could have saved yourself the trouble. She isn't a part of this vendetta."

"That's certainly true comrade, so let's make a deal shall we. You come to me and then I'll release her, it's that simple! If I had tried to capture you first, you would have resisted and I didn't want that to happen. This way you'll come to me willingly, otherwise your girlfriend's body will wash up on the beach in the next few days. I like the idea of my most hated enemy having to belittle himself by giving up without a fight."

Craig's hands bunched into fists, and he had to bite back a sharp retort. He took a deep breath and spoke to his enemy. "All right Petrovsky, you win! I'll do whatever you want me to, but leave Constance alone. Tell me where to go and I'll meet you there."

"Not so fast comrade! Do you honestly think that I am so naïve as to give away my location? You could have the police beating down my door in no time. I'll contact you later. Meanwhile keep the mobile phone that I gave you switched on at all times. If I phone and you don't return my call within thirty minutes, your girlfriend will die. There will be no further discussion on this matter, do you understand?"

"Yes, I understand."

"If I see any police, Miss Gregg will die. When I call you, come alone and tell no one about this conversation. I'll be in touch."

The call was disconnected and Craig stared unhappily at the phone for a time. He shook his head, and sat down to think about the situation. It was late when he finally went to bed, but he tossed and turned during the night, and was glad when morning came.

The explorer spent an anxious morning waiting for the promised call but it was midday and still he had not heard from the kidnappers. Despite Petrovsky's orders not to tell anyone else about the situation, he decided to contact Commander Simms.

"Hello Craig! How are you enjoying your holiday so far? Why have you contacted me anyway?"

Simms took one look at his crestfallen face and unshaven chin.

"Oh dear me, something's wrong isn't it? What's happened?"

"Sir I'm so sorry but the news isn't good. Constance has been kidnapped!"

"*What? Why? How did this happen?*" he demanded.

"I have no idea Sir. Yesterday I went for a hike up a mountain and Constance booked a day at the spa here. The next thing I knew, she had been kidnapped."

"Who did this; have you any idea?"

Craig rubbed the stubble on his chin and sighed. "I'm sorry Sir I guess I'm not making any sense. It's just that I didn't sleep well last night and my brain is foggy. Colonel Ivan Petrovsky is here! He admitted to kidnapping her."

Commander Simms scowled. "Say no more my boy. No doubt he wants you in exchange for her, am I correct?"

"Yes Sir, I don't know what to do! He has threatened to kill her if I don't surrender. I'm waiting to hear from him, but it has been more than twelve hours since he communicated with me."

Someone else walked into Commander Simms's office, and Craig recognized the newcomer as the chief of police. He was a good friend of the Commander's and Simms waved him to a chair, so that he could listen to the conversation. Craig made no objection.

Simms whispered in his friend's ear and the chief of police nodded attentively. Commander Simms then turned his attention back to his employee.

"Craig I want you to listen carefully to what I am about to say. Under no circumstances are you to accede to Colonel Petrovsky's demands. The man is dangerous, and I'm pretty sure that Constance is probably dead by now. You are understandably distraught by what has happened but don't let the situation cloud your judgment. If you were in Petrovsky's shoes, what would you do?"

Carter's face crumpled, and he ran his hand through his dishevelled hair. He said nothing but he knew that his boss was probably right.

"Craig, Petrovsky will extract whatever information he can from you and then you will die. If he decides not to kill you, he could have you brainwashed and used against us. Remember he has threatened to do this before. I know that you love Constance, but the alternative is unthinkable."

"Do you mean I must just leave Constance to whatever fate awaits her?" he replied angrily.

"Yes Craig that is what you must do," Simms replied sympathetically.

Carter shook his head. "I can't do that! I would never be able to live with myself if I didn't at least try to help her. She is a valuable member of your staff, Sir so how can you just condemn her like this? Don't you care about her?" he snapped.

Commander Simms leaned forward in his chair and looked unhappily at his employee. "Craig, you have no idea how bad I feel about this whole situation. General Gregg is a personal friend of mine, and I would sooner hang myself than tell him that his daughter is dead. If there was any way I could remedy the situation I would do so in a heartbeat. Craig you have studied Petrovsky's dossier at length and he has no mercy. Constance is already dead, so don't sacrifice your life for nothing! I want you to walk away from this, do you hear me?"

Craig's voice was steady, but he was having trouble keeping his anger in check.

"Is that an order Sir?" he asked stiffly.

"Yes I'm afraid it is Son," he replied.

"I see," he replied quietly. "Then I guess there's nothing else to be said. I still have two weeks' vacation left, Sir. Must I return home now?"

"No stay and finish your holiday, Craig. Just make sure that it is only a vacation. I don't want you running around half-cocked and putting your life in jeopardy."

"I understand Sir," he replied woodenly.

Craig disconnected and the Chief of Police looked sympathetically at his friend.

"I would hate to be in your shoes, when you have to contact General Gregg. He might just hang you himself."

Simms smiled tiredly. "He probably would, but I won't tell him until I have concrete proof to that effect."

"But you told Craig..."

"I know what I said," he interrupted his friend. "I just don't want to jump the gun yet."

"Preston, do I detect a note of fear in your voice?" the Chief of Police asked in amazement.

"Yes, you most certainly do, and I'm not afraid to admit it. Petrovsky is a trained killer, but maybe he has some use for Constance. If that's the case, she could still be alive. General Gregg is not on my list of priorities right now. That man's temper tantrums are legendary and he would most probably go to Eclipse himself and try to extricate his daughter. Then there will most definitely be an international incident."

"I don't understand your reasoning then. Why did you give Craig the order to stand down if you thought there was even the remotest chance of recovering Constance?"

Commander Simms smiled faintly. "You see I had to cover myself, but Craig is also not one to crumble in an emergency. He goes to great lengths to help his friends, and my orders to have him do nothing will probably fall on deaf ears."

"Do you mean that he will look for her, despite your orders?"

"I sincerely hope so my friend! Right now he is all she's got – if she still lives that is."

The Chief of Police left, muttering about the insanity of certain people.

Back on Eclipse, Craig made a vow to find Constance, either dead or alive, before he left Eclipse. He hoped sincerely that Petrovsky would become overconfident, and then he would kill his enemy if the opportunity arose.

Later that afternoon the mobile phone finally rang.

"Carter here," he remarked.

"Hello comrade, I'm pleased to see you obeying my orders! If anyone else had taken this call, your precious woman would be dead in no time."

"Let me talk to her," he begged.

"Not this time. I assure you that she is in excellent health. She sends her love and asked me to tell you that she is missing you terribly. If you do exactly as you are told, you will both be reunited very soon."

"I'll do whatever you ask! Just tell me what to do."

"I don't want you to do anything before this evening. Have your supper at the normal time and tell no one of your plans. When night falls, I want you to go to the taxi rank around the corner from your hotel. It's in the alley where the kitchen staff go in and out. Take the fourth taxicab, and tell him that Ivan wants to see you. He'll know what to do. Until then stay out of mischief. I have people watching your every move."

"I understand. You will have my complete cooperation. Just don't harm Constance."

"As long as you obey my instructions completely, she won't be harmed, you have my word on that."

Petrovsky disconnected and Craig put the phone away in his pocket.

The young man did some shopping, albeit reluctantly because his mind was on other things. He could easily spot the watchers that Petrovsky had assigned to him, but he made no attempt to lose them, nor did he acknowledge their presence. The only time that he was out of sight of his babysitters, was when he went into the Gents' toilet. No one followed him inside, because they already knew there was no way for him to give them the slip. He came out of the toilets about ten minutes later. A woman, who had been pretending to admire some jewellery in a nearby shop, stuck her hands in her pockets and followed him at a leisurely pace.

That evening he dressed in casual clothing, and went into the dining room to have his supper as he had been told. Afterwards he went to the back of the hotel and looked down the darkened alley. It looked threatening and he knew this was a good place for muggers to hide where they could pounce on unsuspecting people.

Carter went to the fourth taxi and knocked on the window. He informed the driver that Ivan wanted to see him. The man threw his data reader onto the back seat, and came around to open the door for his client. Craig felt the unmistakable prod of a gun in his ribs.

"Place your hands on the car and spread your legs!"

The explorer did as the man commanded, and he was checked thoroughly for weapons. Nothing was found, and the man put the gun away in his jacket pocket. His passenger got inside and closed the door. It locked automatically. They drove for a while and soon were out in a deserted area. It was pitch black and Craig realized the sense of this for, in the darkness he had no idea where they were going.

Suddenly the car screeched to a halt and the driver unlocked the door.

"*Get out!*" the man ordered.

"But this is in the middle of nowhere!" he exclaimed.

"*Now!*" the man shouted and pointed his gun at the hesitant man.

Craig scrambled out and the taxicab turned around the way he had come, raising a cloud of dust in his wake. Carter scratched his head in bewilderment and turned full circle, not sure where to go.

The bushes near him parted suddenly and another vehicle screamed out, making him jump out of the way. The driver opened his passenger door and indicated for Craig to get in. He did so and they continued further down the road, making several twists and turns along the way. The explorer was unsure whether they had doubled back or not, and he doubted if he would ever find his way back to town on his own. He was made to change cars twice more.

Finally, he was taken to a warehouse, where he saw another car had been parked. This one was a luxury vehicle with tinted windows. The door opened and Petrovsky appeared.

"Ah here you are at last my friend! Your journey is nearly over."

"Where's Constance?" he demanded.

His enemy smiled and indicated to the limousine. "She is inside waiting for you. Come over and say hello! You do realize of course that once you have seen one another, you are to trade places with her. My friend over there will return her to the hotel, and you will accompany me."

"If you say so," Craig replied as he came closer.

Petrovsky nodded and stepped aside, so that the explorer could look into the car. Craig placed his hands on the seat, and peered into the gloomy interior. "Constance?" he called.

Dimly he saw what appeared to be a figure wrapped up in a blanket, and he stretched out his hand. "Constance, it's me! You can get out now."

Even as his hand touched the blanket, Craig realized, in that split second, that he had been tricked. He just had time to register that the overhead light had been purposely disconnected, before Petrovsky's knee slammed into the small of his back, pinning him effectively to the seat. Carter felt the prick of a needle going into his neck and he tried to say something, but darkness descended almost immediately. Ivan pushed him further inside and sat down next to him. As the limousine drove away, he covered Craig completely with the blanket that lay on the seat.

CHAPTER ELEVEN

Craig was dreaming. He was fighting with an unseen enemy that was very strong. The more he fought and kicked out at the stranger, the weaker he seemed to feel. His assailant laughed and taunted him, telling him that he would lose in the end. Carter was told to give up before he got hurt, but he refused to listen. He was screaming for Constance and he could hear her somewhere in the background, calling to him, but he couldn't find her.

The strong man de-materialized in front of him and Petrovsky's face came at him out of the mists. He was laughing victoriously. "You are a foolish man Craig Carter! Your love for your woman has made you vulnerable and now you are mine. This is the end of your life as you know it. From now on you will belong to Russia!"

The explorer tried to cry out, but he seemed to have lost his voice. Again Constance called to him. "Craig can you hear me? Wake up please!"

The young man opened his eyes and gulped in some air. For a moment he was disorientated and everything was blurred. He rubbed his eyes and sat up. Anxious arms gripped his shoulders. "Craig, are you all right?"

He shook his head to clear the mists and saw his girlfriend sitting beside him. Thankfully he took her in his arms, and kissed her tenderly on her head. "Oh Constance, thank the stars you're still alive! Where are we?"

"In a prison cell unfortunately. I was so worried about you! I have been trying to wake you for close on an hour now, with no luck."

Her boyfriend rubbed his aching head, which was throbbing mercilessly. "I was drugged! Petrovsky tricked me."

"I know," she replied, "he took extreme pleasure in telling me what happened."

"I'll bet!" Craig grumbled.

He got gingerly off the bed and steadied himself before getting up slowly. He went to the washbasin and washed his gritty eyes with water. Then he rinsed his mouth to get the stale taste out. After that he walked to the barred window and looked outside, but he didn't recognize his surroundings at all.

"Have you any idea where we are Constance?" he asked curiously.

"No I'm afraid not! I was blindfolded when they brought me here. I'm not sure how long the journey was because they may have travelled in circles to confuse me."

"Did they drug you at all?"

"No they didn't," Constance replied.

Craig paced the floor of their cell restlessly. "Honey, did they change vehicles at any time, or take you in a spaceship anywhere?"

"No I was in the same car the whole way. Why? Did you think that they could have taken us to another planet perhaps?"

"The thought did cross my mind, but seeing as I was unconscious the whole time, I just wondered. It doesn't make any difference anyhow I suppose."

"No, I guess it doesn't," she sighed.

Her boyfriend sat down on the bed again. "Constance I'm sorry that I got you into this predicament. The whole thing is my fault! Petrovsky wanted me and he used you as bait. I was foolish enough to believe that he would let you go when I gave myself up to him, but I was wrong. I know how his fiendish mind operates, yet I still fell for his lies. Now he has both of us in his clutches!"

"What do you think he will do with us?" asked his girlfriend.

Carter shrugged his shoulders helplessly. "I wish I knew, but you can bet that he'll tell us in due course. I wish I could reassure you and tell you that he'll release you, but we both know that he won't do that now. If he had been serious about letting you go, you would have been returned to the hotel by now."

Constance agreed. "Put yourself in his shoes Craig. Would you have released one hostage just to gain another, knowing that the first thing the freed person would do would be to contact the police?"

"No, I would do the same thing he has just done," Carter agreed. "All the same I'm sorry about this situation. I put you in jeopardy."

Miss Gregg came and sat down next to her boyfriend and gently squeezed his hand. "Craig, I'm a big girl now and I can take care of myself. I tried to avoid being captured and if it makes you feel any better, none of Petrovsky's goons got off lightly. I gave a good account of myself."

For the first time since he had woken up, Craig smiled. "Good for you my angel!"

"Well what happens now?" she asked.

"I guess we just have to wait for our esteemed host to pay us a visit. He's holding all the aces right now."

They spoke quietly for a while and a few hours later, some men came to their cell and ordered Craig out. He went with them to another room, where his enemy was waiting. Petrovsky indicated to a chair and Carter sat down. The men moved a short distance away but their hands stayed close to their weapons.

"Hello Mr Carter, I trust you slept well," he remarked.

"I had no choice, now did I," his prisoner snapped.

Ivan smiled at his prisoner. "I'm surprised at you! You fell for the oldest trick in the book. You weren't thinking clearly and you made it so easy for me!"

Carter kept quiet and his host continued. "I see that you are still working alone. I fully expected a whole contingent of police to be following you – in fact I was prepared for it. That's why I made you change cars so many times."

"It was tempting, but I had no right to endanger anyone else. This is my problem, not theirs. You on the other hand seem to have acquired some helpers. I thought you also worked alone."

Petrovky smiled. "I do, for the most part, but you my friend are another matter entirely. I learnt long ago not to underestimate you. I must admit though that the lovely Miss Gregg is a welcome distraction. Your involvement with her led to your capture. I believe that I have discovered your weakness."

"Constance can take care of herself, but I felt obligated to help her. It wasn't her fault that she landed up in the middle of this situation. Your fight is with me, not her and I want you to let her go like you promised."

"Sorry I can't do that now. If it makes you feel any better, I had every intention of letting her go, but then I got curious. She gave a good account of herself when we kidnapped her, and that got me thinking. So when she was safely in that cell, I did some investigating. It seems that your girlfriend has developed quite a reputation for herself as well. At the time I had no idea that she had begun exploring space even before you did. I read her file and it made for interesting reading. She has an army background and her father is General Gregg, quite a formidable man himself I understand. She never traded on her name though and did exceptionally well in training, coming first in almost every class. While she doesn't have your finesse in flying all spacecraft ever invented, she does get the job done. She is just more cautious out in space, while you are reckless in the extreme, going to incredible lengths to help those you care about!"

"So, what's your point?" Craig asked curiously.

"My point is that Russia will be able to use a lady with her talents. Since her father is a good friend of Commander Simms, perhaps she can share some secret knowledge with us. We have ways of extracting the information from her."

Craig half rose from his chair and he was pushed down roughly.

"Leave her alone Petrovsky! She doesn't know anything important!"

The Colonel smiled cruelly. "Well we could start with you. I know that you have secrets buried in your brain somewhere. In fact I think that we should begin with you. I've been following your illustrious career over the last few years, and it has made for very interesting reading. Even when you were a technical mechanic, you showed extreme promise. You know the schematics of every spaceship ever built, because you worked on them all before you qualified as a space explorer. Therefore you know all the strengths and weaknesses of all the machines. I could use that knowledge to help my country strengthen our ships. If you refuse to co-operate, I'll torture your lady friend and you know me well enough to believe that I *will* do it."

Carter stared levelly at Petrovsky. "I'm sorry but I won't betray my country. I love Constance but she knows the rules as well as I do. Whatever you want to know I won't divulge willingly. Nor in fact will Constance. We aren't traitors!"

The Russian smiled a slow, lazy smile. "I admire your loyalty towards your country comrade, but you don't stand a chance against the new hypnotic drugs that have been invented. I don't care how we get the information we require, just as long as we get it, and I can assure you that we *will* obtain it. If you fight, so much the better! I'll enjoy watching as the drugs weaken your resistance. However, it would be a great pity if my comrades destroyed your mind, because I admire your courage, I really do. Why don't you just give up gracefully and admit that I've won? Then if you give us the information without any force having to be applied, I promise you that Russia will welcome you with open arms. You can continue exploring space if you want to, but under Russia's flag. We can easily arrange a new face and identity for you."

Craig stared at his enemy. "No I won't betray my country! I love America and I don't want to shift my allegiance to Russia. You can do whatever you think is necessary, but I will not cooperate with you, not ever. I would sooner die first!"

"That too can be arranged," Petrovsky replied coldly. "However, I'll be speaking to my superiors soon. I have done my part, now your life is in their hands. I'll shortly be having this same conversation with your girlfriend. I'm interested to hear how she feels about the situation. Do you think she loves you enough to go through the agonies that we are going to put her through, or will she turn away from America and from you and join us willingly? It will be most interesting to find out, don't you think?"

Craig kept silent and Petrovsky ordered that they take him back to his cell.

Constance looked up anxiously when he joined her once again. "Are you okay?" she asked nervously, "Did they hurt you in any way?"

"No, they are saving that for later. Petrovsky told me just what to expect in the future and it isn't pleasant!"

Craig went on to tell his girlfriend about his meeting with the Russian colonel. Afterwards she stared at her boyfriend in shocked silence.

"Oh Craig what can we do? We have to escape from here as soon as possible. I don't know where we are, nor do I care! I just want to get away and we can find out afterwards how to get back to our hotel."

"Tell me how to do that Constance and I will! Whenever one of us gets taken out of here, there are heavily armed guards everywhere! What chance do we stand of escaping?"

"I...I don't know but we have to do something!" she replied desperately.

Carter turned his back on his girlfriend and went over to the window, where he shook the bars viciously. They remained firmly in place. There was very little to say and the couple sat in silence, each occupied with their own thoughts.

Two hours later, Petrovsky came for Constance and she went with him to the other room. He indicated to the same chair Craig had been sitting in a few hours earlier and he pulled up a chair opposite her. He smiled kindly at Constance. "Well my dear, no doubt your boyfriend has told you of our conversation."

She nodded in the affirmative and Ivan continued.

"Look I don't want to frighten you in any way, but since Mr Carter and I had our conversation I have spoken to my superiors in Russia. The news isn't good! They want complete cooperation from you and your boyfriend, or you will be tortured when we reach Russia. Miss Gregg, how do you feel about joining us? I gave Mr Carter the same ultimatum but he refused our hospitality. Would you like to work for us?"

Constance's bottom lip trembled and she took it between her teeth to stop the vibrations. "I...I don't know," she replied hesitantly. "I love my country and my family! If I pledge allegiance to Russia I'll never see them again will I?"

Petrovsky shook his head. "No, my dear, that would be impossible. If you were not given a new identity and face, America would kill you the first chance they got. You could of course refuse to cooperate, as your foolish boyfriend has done, and we could force the information from you."

Ivan came over to Constance and stood near her. Gently he tilted her chin up and stroked her face. She pulled away instantly. "My dear you are a beautiful woman, and my superiors are cruel. Have you ever had any cause to complain about your treatment since you have been our guest?"

"Well apart from the fact that I'm your prisoner, no I guess not."

"You see, my superiors are not interested in beauty. All they want is results and they will do anything to get what they want. Our methods are very crude and some would say even inhuman. That pretty face won't remain that way for very long. Once you are in Russia, you will cease to exist as a person in their eyes. Please think carefully about this! You will be well treated in my country if you decide to join forces with us. What does America have to offer that we cannot better? Yes you would lose your family, but there are many wonderful people in Russia to substitute them."

"I...I don't know!" she sighed.

Petrovsky walked around and came back to her. "Miss Gregg, how much do you love Craig Carter?"

The question took her completely by surprise. "What? I love him a lot, of course, why do you ask?"

Petrovsky shook his head. "Sorry sometimes my English isn't very good. What I meant to say is, would you sacrifice your life for him? If I said that I would let him live if you died, could you do that for him? Naturally he would still be brainwashed and made to work for Russia, but at least he would be alive. I should tell you however that I put the same question to him and he refused. He was quite happy to see you die. That man has no respect for your feelings. So, Miss Gregg, are you prepared to go through hell and still lose in the end, or will you join us?"

A myriad of emotions crossed Constance's face and the men were silent, waiting to hear what her answer would be.

Finally Constance drew in a quivering breath. "You have to understand that this is very hard for me!" she began. "I love my country and my family and yes I love Craig too, but all the training in the world doesn't prepare an astronaut for torture. I can't go through that, I just can't! Colonel I won't lie to you I hate the thought of having to join Russia, but if you give me your solemn word that you won't harm Craig, I'll do as you ask. If...when you do whatever it is that you must do, will he remember anything?"

"No my dear, he'll have no memory of his previous life," Petrovsky replied gently. "We will put various suggestions into his mind and he'll believe them implicitly. He can still have a family life, just not the family he has at present. Do you understand?"

"Yes, but will he remember me?"

Petrovsky smiled at his captive. "My dear, we could reprogramme him into believing that you are his girlfriend. Is that the problem? Are you afraid of losing him?"

"Yes," she sighed. "Yes I am. I could live in Russia, but I want to be with him."

"We can make a plan I assure you."

Constance nodded. "Fine, then I'll accept your offer."

Petrovsky shook her hand. "Welcome to our little group Miss Gregg. I look forward to a close association with you in the future. We are leaving for Russia in two days' time."

Constance was returned to the cell, where her boyfriend looked anxiously at her.

"Constance is everything okay?"

"Not really! Hold me please Craig!" she sobbed.

Carter put his arms around her and held her reassuringly. Her tears fell on his shoulder and her body shook with sobs. When she had regained control of herself she wiped her eyes.

"Craig listen to me, we have to talk!"

"I'm listening."

"Honey please you mustn't be angry with me, but I have come to a decision. I want you to know that I have agreed to work for Russia."

Craig's face registered shock and apprehension. "No you can't, you mustn't! Why would you do that?"

"Please Craig, I didn't enter into this decision lightly! I gave it a great deal of thought. I may be a good astronaut, but I cannot face being tortured. If I do as they say, I'll live longer and I happen to like living. What is the difference really who I work for, as long as I can do what I enjoy?"

"What are you saying Constance? Do you know that you will have to give up everything that has ever meant anything to you?"

"I know."

"Your family, what about them?" he exclaimed desperately.

"Please Craig let's not discuss this anymore okay. I just wish that you would change your mind and join me. Petrovsky told me that they won't go easy on you."

"I know that! Constance I expected more from you! I risked my life, even put myself in jeopardy because I loved you so much, and this is what I get for my trouble! If I had known about this earlier, I would never have come to rescue you. How could you betray me like this?"

Miss Gregg reached out to her boyfriend and he slapped her hand away. Morosely he went to his bed and lay on it with his face to the wall. Constance tried to engage him in conversation but he refused to answer her. That night they hardly spoke at all.

Meanwhile the couple was the main topic of conversation at the dinner table that evening. One of Colonel Petrovsky's colleagues was confused. "Comrade, I'm sure you have a reason for doing what you did today, but I fail to see the reasoning behind it. I suppose Miss Gregg would be useful to us in some way or another, but both you and I know it is Craig Carter that we really want. He refuses to cooperate with us however."

Petrovsky looked at his colleague in annoyance. "So what if he refuses to do what we want? It doesn't matter anyway, because our esteemed leader has given me his orders regarding the man. He says that he has no use for Mr Carter and we must kill him tomorrow."

"The man is an idiot!" his colleague exploded. "What about the information that he carries in his head?"

"Svedloff is aware of that but he says the man is too dangerous."

"What is your opinion on this matter Ivan?"

"Personally, I don't really care what happens to Mr Carter, as long as he dies."

"Well then what about his woman, Constance Gregg? Is she to die too?"

"Svedloff says that seeing as she wishes to join us willingly, he might find some use for her. If she thinks she will be exploring space however, she's in for a big surprise. More than likely he'll place her in an expensive brothel; otherwise he may keep her for himself."

Both men laughed uproariously at this.

Boris became serious. "Ivan do you really believe that young lady was telling the truth? Could she be stalling for time? She could turn against us as soon as the opportunity presented itself."

Petrovsky put his arm companionably around Boris's shoulder. "Don't worry my friend. I thought of that possibility, but I have a plan. If she passes the test I'll believe her."

"Test?" he asked stupidly.

"Yes indeed," replied Petrovsky delightedly.

Despite Boris' pleas, he refused to divulge his plan.

The next day several men went to Craig and Constance's cell and ordered them out.

They were taken outside where Petrovsky met them.

"Good day to you my friends," he replied jovially. "I hope you slept well."

In fact neither of them had slept much at all. Craig was still reeling from the fact his girlfriend had decided to work with the enemy. Constance was upset at Craig's attitude but she couldn't really blame him she supposed. At the same time she hoped that he would see her point of view before they left. She had told him that they were leaving for Russia in two days.

"What do you want with us now?" Craig asked crossly.

"Oh come on Mr Carter, don't be such a spoilsport!" the Colonel replied affably. "It's a beautiful day outside and as you know, the weather in Russia isn't that wonderful. I thought you might enjoy the sunshine for a while, because you won't be seeing much of it for quite some time. If you would rather sulk in your cell, I can have you returned immediately."

"No, I'll stay here," Craig replied.

As if reading his mind, Petrovsky spoke. "If you try to

escape, my men have orders to shoot you in the legs. A crippled man can still divulge secrets."

The explorer looked around the walled area, but he saw no opportunity for escape. Petrovsky let them walk around for an hour, before he called Constance over.

She went to him and he whispered in her ear. Miss Gregg looked at him in shock and horror and shook her head.

"*No, you promised!*" she sobbed.

Petrovsky looked witheringly at her. "You gave your allegiance, now prove it!"

Craig heard their upraised voices and stared at the little group.

"What's going on?" he asked curiously.

"I have a surprise for you," Petrovsky chuckled.

Craig's eyes opened wide when he saw Petrovsky give Constance a gun.

"*What are you doing?*" he asked in disbelief.

"Mr Carter, my superior has been in touch, and he says you are too dangerous to live. Miss Gregg is welcome to accompany us, but sadly you are not invited. I tried to persuade him to change his mind, but alas he refused."

The colour drained from Craig's face. *"Constance, no!"* he cried in dismay.

Constance looked at the gun in her hand as though it would bite her, and tried to give it back to Petrovsky.

"Please don't make me do this!" she begged.

"Miss Gregg, if you refuse, you'll be tortured. Remember what I told you."

"But I can't do it!"

Miss Gregg looked into the eyes of the Russian colonel and found no sympathy there. She stared at Craig, and his expression was one of shock and disbelief. Mentally she urged him to run away, but he remained in the same position. He looked helpless and vulnerable, and totally shocked. Her eyes took in the scene and she saw that Petrovsky's men had their hands close to their weapons. There was nowhere to run or hide and she came to a decision.

Constance steadied the weapon and aimed it at Craig. Her hand shook, and she held the gun tightly with both hands, to steady it.

"I'm so sorry Craig, but I have no choice. Please forgive me. I would rather kill you myself than have these pigs do it!"

Carter made no sound, but he looked like a lost puppy. His bewildered expression would haunt her forever! She pulled the trigger.

CHAPTER TWELVE

Miss Gregg closed her eyes, but nothing happened. She stared at the gun, and Petrovsky took it away from her. Craig's legs gave way beneath him and he sank to the ground, thankful to be alive.

Ivan beamed at Constance. "Well my dear it would appear you passed the test."

"Test! what test?" she asked in confusion.

"The gun had no charge in it. It was useless. You really meant what you said, and now I believe you."

Constance's expression hardened. "So you didn't believe me before then? How dare you make me do this? You wanted me to kill my own boyfriend!"

"And you were prepared to do it! Miss Gregg I salute your courage. Russia will certainly welcome you into the fold as it were."

Craig was touching himself wonderingly, convinced somehow he must have been shot, but he was undamaged. He didn't trust himself to stand up yet, and remained on the soft grass. When the soldiers hauled him to his feet, he made no protest and allowed them to take him back to the cell. Constance soon followed and he confronted her.

"*How could you do that to me,*" he stormed. "*After all that we have meant to one another. I thought you loved me!*"

Constance sat down on the bed and stared at her boyfriend. "Oh come on Craig, let it go! You know as well as I do the demonstration was a test. You are far too valuable to Petrovsky for him to kill you. I knew that and I thought you did too. Petrovsky would sooner see me dead than kill you."

"Well then what was that little demonstration all about. "*I can't kill him!*" he mimicked in her voice. "Then you aim anyway and shoot at me!"

"It's called acting my darling! I pretended to go along with Petrovsky in the hope he would trust me more. I wanted to have a bit more freedom, so that I could find a way to rescue you and escape, but he didn't trust me anyway. That man is cunning! Anyway, if I had turned the gun on Petrovsky or any of his soldiers, instead of you, I would have died instantly. Your Russian friend would have had a perfectly logical reason to shoot me."

"Everything was an act?" he asked in disbelief. "You aren't really defecting?"

"Of course not! Why would I do that? Why should I swap the freedom of America for the icy cold of Russia? Admittedly if Ivan Petrovsky was an American, I wouldn't mind giving him the once over. He's not that bad looking – for a Russian."

Craig glared at her and she smiled. "I'm kidding, just kidding! I love you Craig Carter, and don't you ever forget that!"

"I'm still curious. How could you be sure that there was no charge in that gun? Petrovsky is a cunning adversary. He could just as easily have given you a loaded gun."

"I had thought about that too. When I aimed at you, my hands were shaking on purpose. No one noticed, but I lifted the gun up slightly and aimed above your head, just in case. If he had really intended to kill you, and the gun had been charged, my next shot would have ended Petrovsky's life."

Carter grabbed her roughly and forced her down on the bed. "Don't ever do that to me again; my heart nearly stopped beating!" he gasped. "You had me completely fooled."

"The main thing is that Petrovsky believes I want to defect. I'm truly sorry about your feelings, but I've achieved what I set out to do."

Further talk was interrupted by Craig's mouth covering hers. She made no protest and her hands encircled his waist.

She gave in to his demands and the kiss was long and sweet.

When the moment had passed, Constance became serious. "You know we'll be leaving this planet sometime tomorrow, but unless something miraculous happens, we'll be heading to Russia. I don't want to get on that ship. How can we escape from here?"

"I don't know!" Craig replied helplessly. "I looked around earlier when we were outside, but every exit or entrance was covered by Russian guards. If we could escape from this prison cell, we could knock out some of the guards and take their weapons. Maybe then we could steal a Russian ship and get away from here."

Miss Gregg walked to the door and examined the lock. "When they first brought me here I tried to pick the lock, but it was impossible. It has some kind of tamper proof mechanism."

Carter tried to open it but he too had to give up in despair. He scratched his head and was silent for a while.

"Constance, I have a plan but it's risky. It could work, but everything depends on your talents as an actress. You fooled me completely, but do you think you could fool Petrovsky?"

"Well I think he trusts me a lot more now than he did before! What's your plan?"

"Okay, Petrovsky now believes that you wish to defect to Russia. He knows I won't go willingly, but he wants us both anyway. I think we should stage a fight! See, you want to go to Russia and I don't. Now let's pretend you've tried to persuade me to go willingly and I refuse outright. You extol the virtues of Russia, and I disagree with you. I yell at you and tell you I hate you, and I never want to see you again. We exchange harsh words, and I hit you."

Constance backed away. "Hey just hang on a minute! I was beginning to like this plan, now you want to clobber me!"

"Well not very hard," he replied hastily, "but it has to look good otherwise he won't believe us."

"Then what happens?"

"Well I'll leave the details up to you. However I suggest you persuade him to take you out of the cell. Get close to him and try to find out where he hides the key to this cell. Then, using your feminine wiles, steal it and free me. Afterwards we can disable some of the guards and steal their weapons. Then we escape in one of their ships."

"Just like that?" she remarked dryly.

"Yes, exactly like that."

Miss Gregg rubbed her chin thoughtfully. "The man isn't stupid you know. I'll have my work cut out for me."

"Well you could always do nothing! I believe Russia isn't bad this time of year. They are having their summer season now," Craig replied sarcastically.

Constance threw up her arms in exasperation. "Fine, I'll do it. When should we start?"

"Now is as good a time as any. It's nearly suppertime, so there should be more people around than usual. Shall we begin?"

Constance shrugged her shoulders. "Sure, why not!"

Carter hurried to the front of the cell and peered through the bars. No one was around but he could hear voices nearby. He walked up to his girlfriend and glared at her, winking at the same time.

"*How could you do this to me? I love you so much, yet you are feeding me to the wolves!*"

"Craig will you listen to me," she urged. "What difference does it make where we live as long as we are together? Ivan will help you get settled, I know he will."

"*No he won't! He hates me and the moment I set foot in Russia he'll kill me. He just wants you for himself, can't you see that?*"

"Don't be stupid! He needs both of us!"

"No, he doesn't! You followed his orders like a puppet! *How could you do that to me?*" he shouted. "*I hate you! Why don't you just go and be with your precious Russian swine and leave me alone.*"

"*Craig please calm down! It's not like that at all, I swear,*" Constance sobbed and her voice had an edge of hysteria to it. "*I love you!*"

She reached out to hold Craig, but he stepped away from her. By now they had drawn an interested audience.

"*Lies, all lies!*" he ranted. "*I never want to see you again!*"

His girlfriend's eyes brimmed over with tears and she wiped them away angrily.

"*Please believe me! I only want what's best for you!*" she pleaded as she went to embrace him once again.

Craig's hand lashed out and his face was suffused with anger. He hit Constance with the open palm of his hand, and she fell backwards, landing on one of the beds. He moved purposefully forward to inflict more damage, and Miss Gregg shrunk against the nearest wall and pleaded with the onlookers. "*Help me please! He's gone mad!*"

Just as her boyfriend had pinned her to the bed, and raised his fist for another onslaught, his arm was caught in a vice-like grip and forced back painfully. Two men pulled him roughly off Constance, and pinned his arms behind his back. He struggled against their combined strength but they held him tightly. He glared at everyone around him. Alerted by the cries, Petrovsky entered the cell and Constance ran to him and put her arms around him. She fingered the bright red welt on her cheek and began to cry.

"*He hit me! Please don't make me stay with him. I'm afraid he is going to kill me!*"

"*Get her out of my sight Petrovsky!*" Craig shouted menacingly. "*She's made it quite clear whose side she's on. I never want to see her again!*"

Petrovsky put his arm gently around Constance's shoulders and led her away. Craig was flung onto one of the beds, and the cell door slammed with a mighty clang. He rushed to the bars and shook them angrily. "*Bitch!*" he swore.

When everyone was out of sight, he allowed himself a small smile of satisfaction. "*That was very realistic! It's up to Constance now.*"

Petrovsky led Constance to a room, and pointed to a chair. She sat down and wiped her eyes with a tissue. Several guards hovered around and he waved them impatiently away. Then he went to a bar in a corner and poured her a drink.

"What's this?" she asked curiously.

"It's Vodka. Try it. It will settle your nerves."

She sniffed the clear liquid tentatively and took a sip. Constance grimaced. "Ugh, this tastes awful!"

Petrovsky smiled. "It does take some getting used to, but it will calm you down. Sip it slowly."

Miss Gregg did so and by the time she had drunk a quarter of the glass, she began to relax.

"Are you feeling better now my dear?" he asked solicitously.

"A little, thank you," she smiled.

Petrovsky sat down opposite her and looked questioningly in her direction. "What happened earlier?"

Miss Gregg shrugged her shoulders and a tear ran down her face. "I...I don't really know! Craig and I were talking and I was trying to persuade him to defect willingly. He just seemed to lose his mind and started screaming at me. The next thing I knew, he attacked me. He's never done that before. Usually he is such an easy going man."

Ivan smiled at his companion. "You can't really blame him you know. Craig Carter is a man of action and he's used to getting what he wants. This time however, he has bitten off more than he could chew. It has taken me a long time to capture him, and finally I have succeeded – with your help of course. When we reach Russia, he'll be interrogated at length and then when we have what we need from him, we'll wipe the incident from his mind."

"But where does that leave me?" Constance sniffed. "He hates me now and I love him so much. He's never going to forgive me for what I did!"

"He won't remember your fight my dear. When we have finished with him, we'll reinforce the fact that he loves you and you can both live happily ever after, just like in the fairy tales that children still read today."

The woman smiled gratefully at Petrovsky, but she knew instinctively that once they had obtained whatever information they required, Craig would simply disappear. She didn't hold out much hope for her own life either. However she smiled at Petrovsky as though she believed every word.

They spoke for a while and then Petrovsky yawned. "I'm afraid I need my beauty sleep Miss Gregg. It's time to settle down for the night."

The woman turned huge frightened eyes to him and she reached out for his hands, and held them tightly. "Please don't take me back to that cell! I'm frightened Craig will try to hurt me again," she replied, fingering her still stinging cheek.

"What am I to do with you?" he asked. "There's nowhere else for you to stay."

She looked beseechingly up at him. "Please, there must to be somewhere else I could sleep. I don't care if you put another bed in the same room as yours. I cannot escape from this place, even if I wanted to."

Colonel Petrovsky smiled amusingly. "Miss Gregg, I have no problem sharing a room with someone as beautiful as you, but morally that would be wrong. Think what a bad example that would set for my troops."

Miss Gregg blushed in embarrassment. "Oh no, forgive me, I never meant to imply anything of a sexual nature. I love Craig and couldn't look at another man in the same way right now – although you aren't bad looking – for a Russian," she smiled wanly. "I just don't want to be in the same room with Craig until he calms down."

Petrovsky thought about it for a while. "I suppose I could give you temporary accommodation with one of my female soldiers. After all it's only for one night! I'm sure tomorrow I could organize somewhere safe on my ship for you to stay."

"I would be very grateful," she replied.

Miss Gregg stood up and hugged herself tightly. "Oh, I don't know if I'll get to sleep tonight! Thank you for the Vodka, but I still can't believe Craig could hate me so much."

She began to cry again and Petrovsky held her hand. "Come along with me and I'll take you to Hannah's quarters. She has no roommate and you can bunk with her tonight. On the way I'll get you a sedative to calm your nerves. You'll sleep like a baby, I guarantee it."

The Colonel held her hand, and she didn't pull away from

him. He introduced her to the female soldier, and whispered quietly in Hannah's ear. The woman nodded and Petrovsky left them alone. Hannah smiled way too brightly and shook Constance's hand, but she wasn't fooled by the demonstration. Even now she knew that Colonel Ivan Petrovsky was expecting trouble.

Hannah handed her a tablet and some water and Constance smiled wanly at her. "I'm so sorry to be a nuisance but I sleep better when I drink a glass of warm milk. Could I perhaps have some with this tablet? Maybe you could join me and have some milk too?"

The woman sighed. "I suppose I could get you something, but my orders are not to leave you alone even for a second. Everyone else is sleeping."

Constance gave a shaky sigh. "Oh, all right then I'll have it with water, but even with the sedative, I doubt I would sleep. I just hope that my crying won't disturb you too much."

She dabbed at her eyes once again. "I'm sorry," she sighed.

Hannah relented. "All right I have a plan, but I must handcuff you to the bed. I'll be back soon," she replied, as she reached for the steel bands. The woman made Constance sit on the bed and handcuffed her left wrist to the bedpost. Miss Gregg didn't argue.

The soldier returned a few minutes later, bringing two glasses of milk with her. She put them down on the side table near Constance's bed. "All right now drink your milk so I can get some sleep," she grumbled.

Miss Gregg smiled apologetically. "I'm sorry but I just need to use the ladies' room first. I don't want to worry you later, when you handcuff me again."

The woman sighed, and undid the handcuffs. She watched as Constance went to the toilet. Hannah came to handcuff her again and she asked if she could just finish her milk first. Under the watchful eyes of the Russian soldier, she put the tablet into her mouth, but at the last minute she let it slide down her sleeve. Hannah turned away for an instant and Constance dropped the tablet into the guard's milk instead.

The space explorer climbed back onto the bed, and allowed the woman to handcuff her wrist again. She snuggled down under the duvet and closed her eyes. Constance watched as her guard drank her own milk. She waited for half an hour and heard the guard snoring softly. Stealthily Miss Gregg reached under the collar of her blouse where the seam was slightly undone, and withdrew a small hair clip. The handcuff came apart in her hands and she left it dangling on the bedpost. She crept over to the sleeping figure and felt the pulse in her neck. It was slow and regular. Hannah would not hear anything tonight.

Miss Gregg climbed out of a nearby window and kept in the shadows. While she had been in Petrovsky's quarters, she had seen the key to the cell in which Craig still languished and was determined to get it, but there were many guards to avoid first. The path to Ivan Petrovsky's quarters was nearby, but it was also too well-lit. Instead she went behind the building where the shadows were darkest. She avoided the guards on duty, but knew she would have to get rid of some of them before she could enter the building in which Craig was imprisoned. First, she had to get the key!

The woman saw no guards around Petrovsky's suite. Blessing her good fortune, she turned the handle of the front door, but it was locked. She took out the hairpin once again and picked the lock, closing the door softly behind her once more. She knew the key was in his jacket pocket and the garment was lying carelessly over one of the chairs. Since she had been there earlier, she knew the way to his bedroom.

The door was ajar and she peered into the gloom and could dimly make out Petrovsky's form in the bed. She tiptoed over to the dressing table and reached for the jacket, and then she froze.

She noticed Petrovsky yawn and stretch and begin to sit up in bed. She panicked for an instant, then dived onto a mat and slid under the bed just as the Russian headed for the bathroom. He closed the door slightly and, taking a deep breath, she crawled out from under the bed and ran to the jacket. Hastily she searched through the pockets and finally her hand closed on the key. She grabbed it and in her haste, the jacket fell to the floor. The door to the bathroom opened again and the light switched off. In that instant she dived under the bed once again. The springs creaked as Petrovsky settled down to sleep. Constance lay under the bed, hardly daring to breathe. Much later she eased her cramped body out and after making sure the Russian was really asleep, she left the room and started heading for the cell block. Miss Gregg swore softly to herself, when she realized she only had an hour left before daylight came. The whole plan had taken longer than she had expected and now time was becoming a critical factor.

Miss Gregg made her way to the cell block and touched the key hidden in her pocket for reassurance. She hid behind a bush and saw one guard stood near the entrance to the cell block and she crept stealthily towards him. He had a dazed expression on his face and she knew he was half asleep. A well placed blow sent him into dreamland. The young woman dragged his body into some thick bushes and, taking his gun went inside the cell block.

Further down the passage, some guards were talking quietly amongst themselves and Constance sneaked past them. A few others were watching a movie. Suddenly one of them turned around and opened his mouth to shout a warning. Constance set the gun to rapid fire and stunned every one of them. They crashed to the ground and she winced, hoping desperately that the others hadn't heard anything. She hid behind the door for a few minutes but luckily no one came. Just to be on the safe side she closed the door so that anyone walking past would not be immediately aware that they were unconscious. No one was waiting at Craig's cell door.

Constance looked inside and immediately her boyfriend stood up and hurried to the bars.

"You took your time! I've been awake for hours!"

"It looked easier than it actually was," she hissed. "Petrovsky isn't a fool you know."

Constance opened the cell door and Craig came out. She handed him a gun she'd stopped to pick up in the room down the passage. They both peered into the room, just to make sure, but everyone still lay as they had fallen earlier. Constance began to pass the room where the other guards had been talking, but Carter put his hand to his lips, and pointed to another door. Miss Gregg raised her eyebrows questioningly, and he took her hand and led her inside, closing this door about halfway as well. Then he moved to a window and opened it. Constance smiled when she realized they would have cover in the form of a large tree.

Once they were outside, Craig whispered to his companion. "Do you know where they keep the spaceships?"

"No but this place isn't all that big. The courtyard where Petrovsky took us earlier is to the right of us, so I imagine the spaceships would be to the left."

Carter strode purposefully off in that direction and Constance put a cautionary hand on his shoulder.

"That place must be well guarded. How are we going to get past them without raising the alarm?"

"I don't know," he confessed, "but we have to try. It's getting lighter every minute now. Once dawn breaks, our chances of escape will be minimized."

He began to move off and Constance stopped him again.

"What now?" he asked irritably.

"I've just thought of something! Even if we manage to steal a Russian spacecraft, we'll struggle to fly it."

"Why?"

"Because all the instructions will be in Russian," she exclaimed miserably.

"We'll just have to improvise! It can't be all that difficult. "Would you rather stay here and face Petrovsky?"

Constance quickened her step. "Let's hurry!" she pleaded.

Even as they started to run towards the hangars, the sun peered through the clouds and bathed them in its golden rays. Carter swore angrily and they began to run faster.

Suddenly a siren blared and he groaned. "Oh no, someone has raised the alarm!"

Both fugitives ran towards the hangars, and threw caution to the wind. Guards poured from every building.

"*There they are; stop them!*" someone shouted. Beams of

deadly light danced around them, and they lengthened their stride.

Petrovsky came running out of the building, still buttoning his jacket.

"*Shoot to wound only!*" he cautioned. "*I want them both alive!*"

Craig and Constance returned fire and several guards fell down. Miraculously nothing hit them and they continued running towards the spaceships. Ivan Petrovsky realized their intention and shouted in Russian. Some of the troops split up and headed for the hangars. Neither fugitive spoke much, but focused on reaching the ships instead.

Craig saw a ship not very far away, and ran for the door. As his hand closed on the recessed handle, a beam from one of the guns just missed his fingers. The next one disturbed the ground at his feet, kicking up dust. Constance gasped, when a beam narrowly missed her ear.

"*Step away from there both of you. It's over and you have lost this round!*" The Russian replied commandingly. "*My next shot cannot miss at this range.*"

Craig Carter slammed his hand against the bulkhead in a fit of helpless rage.

"No; so close and yet so far!" he mumbled miserably.

He looked at Petrovsky, whose mouth was set in a determined line. His eyes were black with fury, and the gun was pointed at Craig's kneecap.

"Just give me one good reason to shoot you," he growled.

Carter looked at his girlfriend and sighed. "I'm so sorry honey, but at least we tried."

Constance glared at their captors. "All we needed was another few minutes, that's all and we would have escaped."

The Russian was not amused. "Now that you have finished playing games with me, step away from that ship!"

Both of them did as he had commanded, and raised their hands in the air.

Petrovsky took a few steps forward, and pointed his gun at Constance. "Now, both of you place your hands behind your neck, and kneel in front of me. I still don't trust you."

They obeyed and their captor glared witheringly at Constance. "You should have gone into acting my dear. In fact, both of you showed amazing talent in that department. I was almost fooled – almost, but not completely," he remarked triumphantly. He looked at both of them. "You have given a good account of yourselves, both of you. I hate to admit it, but your Commander Simms had good instincts, when he placed you in the space program. Now you belong to Russia, and he'll never see either of you ever again. I hope you enjoyed your brief taste of freedom, because it's over, forever."

Craig Carter looked up at his captor and smiled. "No Petrovsky, I have to disagree with you on that! I certainly never underestimated you. I think *your* freedom is coming to an end very soon."

"Have you gone mad comrade?" the Russian asked, indicating to all the heavily armed troops who were pointing their weapons at them. "I don't see any advantage for you!"

"Then perhaps you should look behind you...*comrade!"*

"You should know better than that! It's an old trick, and I'm not about to fall for it!"

One of Petrovsky's men gasped, and spoke to his superior.

"Uh comrade, I suggest that you do as he says."

The Russian colonel turned, and looked behind him. The smile died on his face, when he came face to face with a contingent of soldiers, wearing American military fatigues. Many policemen were with them and every single one was armed. They easily outnumbered the Russians two to one. Petrovsky raised his weapon in a gesture of defiance, and his hand tightened on the trigger.

Craig's movements were a blur, as he jumped to his feet and kicked the weapon out of Petrovsky's hands. The two men fought for a few minutes and no one interfered, sensing that this was between the two enemies only. Finally Ivan Petrovsky fell dazed to the ground. His troops laid down their weapons, and raised their hands in a gesture of surrender. While the Americans were arresting the Russian soldiers, Constance stared disbelievingly at her boyfriend. She was furious!

"You knew that help was on the way, didn't you?"

"Yes I did," he confessed. "I was the one who alerted them."

"Then why did I have to go through this ridiculous charade?" she challenged.

Craig could see an argument coming, and put his hand on his girlfriend's shoulder. "I'll tell you later. Now isn't the time!"

"You bet you will mister," she remarked angrily, turning to leave.

Suddenly everything went haywire. As Constance began walking away from her boyfriend, Petrovsky jumped up and kicked Craig's legs out from under him. Caught by surprise, he sprawled helplessly in the dirt, and he watched in dismay as the Russian made a grab for Constance once again. She saw him coming for her, but was too late to get out of his way. A knife appeared in his hand as if by magic, and he put the sharp blade against the woman's neck.

"I'll never surrender to any American pigs!" he snarled menacingly. "Anyone who tries to stop me will be responsible for the death of this woman!"

He dragged Miss Gregg towards the spaceship Craig had tried to steal, and opened the door. As he vanished inside, he gave Constance a rough shove allowing her to jump off the steps just as the spacecraft lifted into the air. The American soldiers loosed off a volley of shots, but they didn't even dent the ship, which rose into the sky and vanished from sight.

Craig shook the police captain's hand vigorously. "Thank you for coming, but you cut it pretty close. I had serious doubts about being rescued."

"My apologies Craig, but I wanted to catch Colonel Petrovsky in the act and I achieved that. It's a pity he managed to escape."

Craig looked up at the sky. Petrovsky's craft was a tiny speck, barely visible.

"Yes, it's unfortunate! Maybe next time we'll be able to apprehend him. Right now, all I want to do is go back to my hotel and take a shower!"

"I'll take you and Miss Gregg there myself. My men can finish off here. Please, follow me."

Carter looked over at his girlfriend, and he saw that she was still angry. He knew that he had a lot of explaining to do, but he was tired and decided to wait until they had cleaned up at the hotel.

"Mr Carter, I think we still need to talk. Can you come down to the police station after you freshen up? We don't need to trouble your young lady just yet, so she can just relax and wait for you We can take your statement later, whenever it's convenient, Miss Gregg."

Constance nodded her head but kept quiet.

Carter looked at his girlfriend's flushed cheeks and nodded. "Yes, I'll see you a bit later then. Thank you for helping us, Captain."

They were driven back to their hotel, but Constance was still angry, so the conversation was very stilted. When they had cleaned up and had a snack, Craig went to the police station.

He was shown into the Captain's office, and sat down in a chair, facing the officer.

"Craig, I know that you're still on holiday, and I hope that the rest of this vacation will be peaceful. I'll have my men keep a discreet eye on you, just in case Petrovsky comes looking for revenge. How much longer will you be staying on Eclipse?"

"I have only another four days unfortunately. When I get back I'll need another holiday to recover from this one."

"I agree with you. I'm really sorry that we never caught Colonel Ivan Petrovsky. As much as he wanted to capture you and pick your brains, I'm sure that America would have loved to reciprocate in his case as well. He too keeps many secrets."

"The man is a professional and very clever. Unfortunately it was not to be," the astronaut replied. "Look I'm very grateful you came through for us, but I need to clarify some things. Why did it take you so long to rescue us? I gave you the signal in good time."

The policeman smiled secretively. "Mr Carter we were already in position hours ago. We were merely waiting for a suitable opportunity to present itself."

"What if we had managed to escape in that ship?" the young man asked curiously.

"Then we would have watched you go, and still sprung the surprise attack on the colonel. After all he was the icing on top of the cake. The main thing is that you and Miss Gregg were rescued. We can get Petrovsky another time!"

"Yes, there will definitely be another time and another confrontation somewhere else, I can guarantee it. Ivan Petrovsky will never forgive me for this, or for any of our previous confrontations."

The policeman stood up and shook Craig's hand. "Go and give your statement to our stenographer in the next office and then you can return to your hotel. While you are still with us you can relax, because I'll see that nothing bad happens to you. Enjoy the rest of your stay. Maybe the next time you come here, it will be peaceful."

"I hope so," Craig replied fervently.

He left the station and returned to the hotel, where he found Constance moodily watching television. Carter put his hands gently on her shoulders and kissed her lightly on top of her head.

"We need to talk honey. I know you're mad at me, but we have several unresolved issues to discuss."

She turned to him and put her hands over her boyfriend's. "Yes we do! I have so many questions and not enough answers."

Her boyfriend poured them a drink, and they went to sit on the balcony, which overlooked the swimming pool.

Miss Gregg drank half her drink and put it down on the table. Her hands shook just slightly but he pretended not to notice.

"I'm sorry I wasn't completely honest with you the other day. I guess I should have told you beforehand, but I was angry too. I believed you were really going to defect and I was devastated," her boyfriend explained. "Then when you aimed that gun at me and pulled the trigger, I wanted to die because I thought you hated me for getting you involved in my mess.

I understand you had thought of a plan to escape, but it would've helped if you'd clued me in on it as well! At least I would've understood and we wouldn't be fighting now."

"Craig, I'd no idea that Petrovsky was going to test me like that! I did the only thing I could, under the circumstances. I explained my reasoning behind it!" she exclaimed. "I knew you were shocked, but I had no choice. Petrovsky would have shot me if I tried to kill him or his soldiers, as I explained before, so I went along with the deception. I knew how valuable you were to him."

"But what if you had been wrong?" he persisted.

"My darling if I had been wrong, we wouldn't be having this conversation. I explained to you already how I planned to kill Petrovsky with the next shot."

"Would you really have killed him in cold blood?"

"I swear it," she replied, putting her hand over her heart. Do you forgive me now?"

"Oh honey I'm so sorry for what you went through!" Craig replied contritely. "We were both so stressed, and things weren't going well with us. I owe you an apology too. I was so angry with you that I sent you out on that errand, knowing already we would be rescued sometime the next day. I guess I just wanted to get back at you for the fright you gave me. I was out of line and I apologize! You were amazing and we nearly made it!"

For the first time in a while, Constance smiled. "Yes we nearly did! We make a great team."

"We certainly do!" he agreed.

Constance wrapped her arms around her boyfriend's neck and kissed him passionately. "I'm sorry for the deception! At the time I thought it was the right thing to do, but I realize now how stupid I was!"

"I forgive you, as long as you share your plans with me the next time we encounter a problem."

His girlfriend frowned. "I've been meaning to ask; how did you keep in contact with the police? They knew exactly where to find us."

"Well, I never kept in contact with them. They knew where we were. You see, when you were kidnapped and Petrovsky delivered that ultimatum, I knew he would never keep his word, so I took precautions. I went to the police captain and told him the whole story. I knew Petrovsky's goons would be following me around to see if I went for help, but I didn't make it obvious. The policeman approached me in a bar, on purpose and it just looked as though I was having a chat to a stranger. He devised the clever plan.'

'While Petrovsky's goons were following me, the police followed them. The only place where the Russians didn't follow me, was the public toilet in the shopping mall. It was there one of the policemen placed a transmitting bug into my belt. It was so small that Petrovsky's people missed it when they searched me. It served a dual purpose as it was a locator as well. The police then tracked me by satellite, to where Petrovsky held us prisoner and they simply followed at their leisure. They waited until the last minute, but they explained the necessity for this. Naturally they wanted to turn the tables on Petrovsky and take him prisoner, but he got away. I knew the police were going to make their move the night we had our 'fight', because the transmitter vibrated. The captain had told me to give him twenty-four hours from the signal, and they would come and rescue us."

Constance sat down next to her boyfriend and put her head on his chest. Gently he stroked her dark hair. "I wish that we could turn the clock back and take away this ugly incident, but we can't. At least we're safe now and still in one piece, thank the stars."

"Some holiday this turned out to be!" she remarked wryly.

"There will be others," he promised.

"I hope so! It would seem that you, Mr Carter, are a very dangerous man to know. You have influential enemies that don't know how to take 'no' for an answer."

"I agree with you, but all I can do is keep my eyes open and be extra careful! I cannot spend my whole life hiding away. The very nature of my work is the reason I have this problem. I've spent most of my life thinking about exploring space and

I knew, right at the beginning that it would be a difficult task. Even though I have these enemies, I still love my job. Does that make any kind of sense to you?"

His girlfriend snuggled into his arms and sighed. "In a strange, twisted way it makes perfect sense! Nothing can beat the rush of going out into space and piloting a powerful craft at incredible speed. I'm addicted as well."

"Then you don't hold your kidnapping against me?" he asked hopefully.

"How can I do something like that? You had no idea what was being planned. It was just the wrong time and place I guess."

"Do you forgive me for what happened a few days ago then?" he asked hopefully.

"Yes I do! We've been through a bad time, and we weren't honest with one other. Let's just put this behind us now and move on."

Constance kissed him gently on the lips. She took him by the hand and led him back inside. They lay down on the bed and she smiled at her boyfriend. "I know just how to ease those tense muscles of yours. Now just relax and put yourself in my hands."

Craig groaned in ecstasy. "Oh yes Doctor Gregg. That sounds like just the right medicine."

The couple found solace in one another and their tension melted away.

The week passed very quickly and soon they were heading back to Earth. They knew an investigation would be held by Mission Control, as the police on Eclipse had liaised with their employer. Commander Simms gave them time to freshen up before they were de briefed. A few hours later they returned to their respective homes.

CHAPTER THIRTEEN

Craig's parents watched their son as he went into the garden and sat under one of the trees. They knew that he had been through a trying time, but they didn't question him. They were just glad to have him back safe and sound. Alice Carter watched her son moodily staring up at the heavens.

"Oh Brian, I had such a bad feeling when Craig decided to explore space. I still wish sometimes he had chosen another profession."

Her husband put his arm around her shoulders and sighed. "You say that every time he comes home from another dangerous mission. We have to respect his decision! He chose this life for better or for worse, and he has to live with the consequences. All we can do is support him when he needs to talk."

"I know, but this time he was on holiday, which makes things even worse. If he can't relax on vacation, what is he supposed to do?"

"He's dealing with it and so should we," her husband replied. "Now let's give him some space and just be available if he needs."

Constance also found it difficult to settle down again. She had been involved in her share of narrow escapes, but somehow this experience seemed to stay with her. Her parents watched her behaviour with some trepidation. Mark and Alexis Gregg noticed their beloved daughter was very fidgety. They knew counselling was available if astronauts asked for it, but they didn't want to broach the subject. Their daughter was watching a movie on her mobile device. She had earphones connected to it and was listening quietly to the soundtrack.

Mark took his wife aside. "Sweetheart, I'm worried about Constance and I know that you are too, yet she is a strong person and this nightmare will soon be a thing of the past.

She knows how to take care of herself in difficult situations, we both know that. We just have to give her time to recover."

"I suppose so but I just wish she would give up space travel. It's a dangerous profession."

Mark Gregg sighed. "Honey this happened on her vacation! Nothing quite so dramatic has ever happened during her missions."

"Except when that damn Russian traitor tried to have her killed!" his wife interjected.

"Igor Petrovsky took his own life and anyway, that happened a number of years ago. You cannot fixate on that scenario you know. Constance has a sensible head on her shoulders! She can handle herself as good as, or better than most men she comes across. I taught her well. Anyway, she loves space exploration and we shouldn't discourage her at all."

"That's easy for you to say," sniffed his wife. "I only have the minimal amount of training and I only learnt how to fire a weapon, because you thought it was a good idea. I hate guns!"

"You were never interested in exploring space nor in fact was I. Our space police unit is the finest in the universe and I had a chance to join it, but it wasn't something I wanted to do. Let's face it Alexis, she loves her work and we should encourage her always. You know our daughter is headstrong and she was the one who approached me about a career in space travel. Personally I would have been just as happy had she decided to take after you and have a 9-5 desk job. I think we have to encourage her no matter what. She's a fine young lady and I'm very proud of her."

"I am too, but I just can't help worrying about her."

"She's going to be just fine," her husband assured her.

Later that day, Constance went to speak to her mother. "Mom I just want to go and see granny Beth at the retirement village. I'll be home later."

Miss Gregg got into her helicar and headed for the old age home. Her parents watched her go, with mixed feelings.

"Have you noticed honey; every time Constance needs cheering up, she goes to see your mother. Why do you suppose she does that?" Mark wondered aloud.

"She loves her grandmother!"

"I know, but Beth's mind isn't what it used to be, and she talks nonsense most of the time."

Alexis Gregg glared at her husband. "Mark, maybe you don't understand my mother most of the time, but I certainly do. She's a comfort to Constance and I don't see anything wrong with that! Our daughter must get help wherever she feels the most comfortable."

Constance arrived at the retirement village and asked to see her grandmother. The nurse pointed to a tree in the distance, where a slight figure could be seen sitting on the park bench.

"How is she today nurse?" the girl asked enquiringly.

"Your gran is just fine my dear. She seems to be talking to her imaginary friend again though. Despite that strange behaviour she is in good health. Go and see her."

"Thanks, I will," Miss Gregg replied.

She went across to her grandmother who had her eyes closed. Even though she didn't seem to be talking to anyone in particular, she had a benevolent smile on her face.

"Gran?" she asked tentatively "It's Constance! I've come to visit you."

Her grandmother's vivid blue eyes opened immediately, and she smiled at her granddaughter. "Constance my dear, it's so good to see you! I've been expecting you."

She hugged her grandmother impulsively.

"You have? I don't remember telling you that I was coming."

Her grandmother smiled secretively. "You didn't have to my angel! I knew you would come. You always come to me when things aren't right in your life. Right now I sense great turmoil in your life. Why is that?"

"I just wanted to visit you," Constance hedged. "I miss you when I'm away in space. We have so little time together."

Beth smiled and gently admonished her granddaughter. "Don't lie to me missy! I know what you are thinking about. You can't hide your thoughts from me. I guess your holiday was a bit of a disaster, if I'm not mistaken!"

"How do you do that Gran? You seem to know my innermost thoughts."

Beth hugged her granddaughter, and stroked her glossy brown hair. "Sweetheart of course I know what you're thinking about. I've known you all your life and I know when you're unhappy, so tell me what happened on Eclipse. I know you don't want to upset your mother with the truth, but you can tell me anything. That's why you've come to see me, isn't it?"

"Yes it is. Oh Gran, I had an awful time!" she sniffed.

"Tell me everything and don't leave out a single thing."

Constance unburdened her heart to her grandmother and the old woman listened intently to every word. Finally, when she had finished, Beth took her granddaughter's face between two gnarled hands. "Listen to me Constance, what happened to you was unfortunate, but it doesn't mean it will happen again. You must put this unfortunate incident behind you, and don't let it ruin your life. You're much too good for that. Use your gifts for good and you won't go wrong – ever. You have an incredible sixth sense that can help you out of difficult situations. Use it well!"

"I have nothing of the kind," Constance replied.

"Yes you do – you just haven't discovered it yet. When you do, it will be awesome. Your future will always be uncertain as long as you want to explore space, but you know that already. Just take care and you'll be fine. I know you're angry with your boyfriend, but both of you were wrong not to trust one another in the first place. You must forgive each other and move on! Otherwise you'll destroy one another, and that would be a great pity."

"Are you talking about Craig?"

"Yes I am. He is a fine young man. I liked him immediately when you introduced him to me. I certainly am grateful to him for bringing you back to me. Look after him; he's also special in his own way. That man is destined to become a legend in his time."

"Honestly Gran, you say the strangest things," Constance laughed.

"Maybe, but it will come true. I'm good at assessing people

and that young man is very brave and clever, you mark my words. When are you seeing him again?"

"Probably tonight I guess, why do you ask?"

"Well my dear it really isn't any of my business, but I'm feeling uneasy for some reason. Your boyfriend has made a lot more enemies than you will ever do. I sense some conflict in the not too distant future. Just tell him to be careful!"

"What do you mean Gran?" Miss Gregg asked worriedly. "Can you elaborate a bit more for me?"

"I wish I could, but I don't know what's going to happen. I just know he must be cautious always." Beth yawned and stretched. "Well my dear all this brain power is exhausting! I need to lie down, because I'm starting one of my headaches again. Will you walk me back to my room?"

"I'll be glad to," her granddaughter replied.

Beth linked her arm through Constance's and they took a slow walk back to the rooms. Once she had lain down on the bed, she smiled at her granddaughter. "You take care now and listen to your inner voice. I'll see you again soon."

Constance kissed her grandmother on her cheek, and the woman went to sleep immediately.

At home, her mother questioned her. "How was Granny today honey?"

Constance frowned. "She seemed just fine but she was a little distracted. She says the strangest things sometimes. I'm always amazed at the way she seems to know what I'm going to talk about. It's almost as though she can read my mind."

"I know what you mean Constance, and she does seem to have some talent in that area but her mind isn't what it used to be, so don't always believe everything she tells you. You are feeling better though. You've a spring in your step."

"I do feel much better Mom. I'm going to dinner with Craig later, so I just want to have a quick shower. I'll talk to you later."

"Sure honey. You go out and have fun!"

Constance climbed under the shower and while she was drying her hair, she was thoughtful. "*Mom's right of course. I love Granny Beth so much, but she does say strange things. I never know what to believe. I suppose I should just focus on the good things and forget about the rest.*"

That evening she and Craig went out. They had a wonderful time and she felt more content than she had for a long time. Constance mentioned briefly she had gone to see her grandmother, but she never mentioned anything to her boyfriend about her grandmother's prediction.

CHAPTER FOURTEEN

The next few months were a whirlwind of activity. Both young people had missions to complete and hardly saw one another, as they were ordered to visit planets that were far apart.

Craig was instructed to take some space mechanics with him to Neptune, where they were to upgrade the Neptunians' spaceships with the latest technology. Although he would work in an advisory capacity only, the Neptunians had specifically asked that Craig be present. He, together with four of NASA's best technical people left for Neptune the next day.

When they arrived, the king welcomed them warmly and showed them to their quarters. They all wore the gills the Neptunians had invented, for without them they could not breathe underwater. Their hotel was a large cave set against a rock face, and no expense was spared to see that their guests were comfortable. Each mechanic had his own room, but Craig's was a little more sumptuous. All the rooms led to a small splash pool where jets of water spurted out, very much like a spa. In this case however the people could direct the jets to any part of their bodies that they wanted. This was a very popular spot in the evening, when they wanted to relax and unwind.

Once the men had been taken to the spaceships they were required to work on, Craig was summoned into the king's presence. He bowed to the king and responded politely. "How may I help you Your Majesty?"

"It's good to see you again Craig. I'm very grateful to Commander Simms for letting me borrow you for a while. I know you no longer fix spaceships but I would welcome your input anyway."

Craig smiled at the ruler. "Sire, I may not actively fix the spacecraft anymore, but I still keep up to date on all the latest technology. I would never like to be caught unawares in space if my ship broke down. It's not as if I can send for a tow truck you know," he remarked wryly.

"Indeed!" the king guffawed. "I see your point. Anyway we have lagged behind other planets in upgrading our defences and we must fix that as soon as possible."

"Are you expecting any trouble in the near future, Your Majesty?" he asked curiously.

"I sincerely hope not, but we cannot be too careful. I don't think we have anything to worry about but I would rather be prepared, just in case."

"It is a good strategy, Sire," Carter agreed. "You have to move with the times or you get left behind I suppose."

"That's it exactly Craig. Did you bring the blueprints of the weapons I asked you for?"

"I did indeed Your Highness, but we have to find a way to stop the water getting into the weapon system."

"I know, I've been asking my technical people to come up with some ideas. Later today we'll have a meeting with them to discuss this. Obviously, our weapons are waterproof, but we still have to adapt Earth's designs to ours."

"I also have some ideas about that, thanks to our weapon specialists on Earth."

"Excellent, then I look forward to hearing all about it later. We still have a few hours before the meeting, and I know someone who would really like to spend time with you."

An inquisitive head peered around the corner and the king's daughter Lolita came into the room. "Am I interrupting you Father?"

"Not at all my dear!" the king replied kindly. "You go and take Craig on a tour of your newest project."

Carter smiled at the beautiful girl. As usual he gawked at her, because of her incredible beauty. She was used to it by now, and reached out to take her friend's hand.

"Come on then, let me take you away from this place for a while."

"I'll go anywhere with you," he sighed, and Lolita giggled.

Together they swam out of the palace. The princess was very excited and led him to a secluded cove a short distance away.

"This is my sanctuary Craig! Sometimes I just want to be alone and my father has given me permission to do it up and decorate it however I wish. It still needs a lot of work, but it keeps me busy."

They explored the cove, and Lolita explained that she had started her own garden. Several water plants were growing in pots and the colours were exquisite. Lolita explained how she planned to divide the cove up into several sections and he listened to her plans for the future. She had some wonderful ideas and he gave her some advice, when she asked for his opinion.

After a while they sat down side by side on a rock and Lolita sighed. "I love talking to you Craig! You are my best friend in the whole world. Can I ask you a question?" she asked shyly.

"You can ask me anything, you know that," he replied kindly.

Lolita shuffled her feet self-consciously and looked into her friend's eyes. "Craig, if we were compatible, would you marry me?"

Carter chuckled. "Well I don't know how Constance would feel about it, but I would certainly marry you if we were. If that had been the case, Constance would never have stood a chance. Unfortunately, we aren't, so you have to be content with being loved like a sister."

Lolita hugged him and put her head on his shoulder. "I hope we'll be friends forever!"

"We will," he promised. "You can count on it!"

"I'm glad."

Craig watched her sitting beside him, deep in thought. Her

long hair swayed in the water and she moved it away from her face. He marvelled at her profile and decided she was really very special. After a while Lolita took his hand and stood up. "We must be getting back to the palace now. Father will be angry if we're late."

They swam back and Lolita left him to go into the royal conference room where he was to meet with the king's advisors.

The discussions continued for most of the day, and by the following day, the group had begun giving instructions to the space technicians. Various ideas were tried and some worked well while others were discarded. Craig watched the technicians at work and helped where he could. One week later, they were ready for a test run.

Carter went up with one of the Neptunian pilots and they put the weapon system through its paces. The lasers fired perfectly hitting their target. Everyone cheered and plans were implemented to manufacture more weapons for the rest of the fleet.

Two days later, disaster struck! Craig was roused from his sleep by an anxious palace guard.

"Craig, you must come quickly! His Highness wishes to speak with you urgently!"

Craig squinted at his clock by the bed. "It's three o'clock in the morning! Can't it wait until later?" he groaned.

"No you must come now, please!" the Neptunian urged.

The explorer threw on a pair of pants and followed the Neptunian. He found the king anxiously pacing the floor. Despite the early hour, the king was impeccably dressed with every hair in place. Craig smoothed his tousled hair, self-consciously.

"You wanted to see me Sire?"

"Yes Craig I did! Something terrible has happened! There was an explosion in the workshop where the weapons were being assembled. The building is in ruins but fortunately my people managed to salvage some of the machinery. We have set up elsewhere, but this will mean a delay of a few days now, because we have lost some of the weaponry."

"Do you think it was an accident Your Majesty, or was it done on purpose?"

"I don't know what to think! It looks as though there was a short in one of the machines. It blew up and started a chain reaction, but my people are investigating."

"It might have been a genuine accident Sire, but I don't believe in coincidences. You should double the guard on the new premises, and issue instructions that no one goes inside, without being accompanied by one of your security staff. This applies especially to someone doesn't belong there. Do you know anyone who's against manufacturing the new weapons?"

The king shrugged his shoulders helplessly. "You were at the meetings with me Craig. Several people were against this as you know, but I know of no one who would do something like this."

Carter rubbed his chin thoughtfully. "I hope this was an accident Sire, but if it was intentional, it means you have a traitor in your midst."

"How can we find out who did this? No one is going to own up. This is treason!" the king complained.

"I think our best course of action is to do some subtle investigating of those who opposed the manufacturing of the weapons. Will you grant me access to your database and I'll see what I can find?"

The king scratched his head thoughtfully. "You'll be violating the privacy of some very important government officials and they may not like it."

"Then don't tell them Sire. This time all you lost was some machinery and weapons, but if this perpetrator strikes again, you could lose something much more important."

"I agree with you Craig, but I still don't like it. All right I suppose I don't have a choice. When do you want to begin?"

"There's no time like the present Your Majesty. I'm wide awake now, and it would be best if no one knows about this. If word gets back to whoever sabotaged the warehouse, things could get very dangerous. I would like to prevent any further criminal activity, if it does indeed exist. I hope I'm wrong and it was just an accident."

"I hope so too," replied the king fervently.

He took Craig to the computer room and typed in the secret access codes. Then left the man alone to do his investigations. Carter worked steadily until it grew light and by this time he had accumulated plenty of information. He hid the data disk away, went to have breakfast and afterwards returned to his room. Carter wanted to catch up on some sleep before studying the information in depth. He locked the door, climbed into bed and was soon fast asleep.

Some time later he began reading the information he had downloaded. Not much came to light however. Those opposed to modernizing the weaponry were just hard headed beings who didn't like change in any form. Craig investigated their backgrounds thoroughly but found nothing unusual in their dossiers. He hoped the explosion was just an accident. The upgrading of the weapon systems and installation of more modern weapons continued undisturbed in the new warehouse. Guards were in evidence everywhere though, just in case.

The next day when Carter went to the dining room, he was again summoned into the king's presence. His heart skipped a beat. He knew instinctively more trouble was brewing. The king was very agitated. "What's wrong, Your Majesty?"

The king couldn't meet his eyes, and he wrung his hands in grief. "I'm so sorry. I have failed you and Commander Simms!"

"What do you mean?"

"Craig, I don't know how to say this, but one of your technicians is dead. He was found early this morning. There is a cove not far from here where his body was discovered."

"*He's dead, but how? What happened?*"

"I don't know for sure yet. First I wanted to let you know, so you can tell me what course of action to take. Would you like to view the body?"

Craig sighed heavily. "I had better do so I suppose. We should go now."

"Yes of course. Come, we can go in my chariot. The mortuary is some distance away."

The journey was completed in silence and when they arrived, they went straight to the section where the technician was being kept.

The king nodded and the attendant opened a drawer. Craig looked closely at the body but could find no visible marks. The man's face reflected serenity as though he had died in his sleep, but Craig knew instinctively that he had been murdered. All that needed to be established was the cause of death.

When they returned to the palace, the king took his friend into the throne room and closed the door, leaving instructions that they were not to be disturbed. He sat down tiredly on the throne and rubbed his eyes.

"Craig I'm terribly sorry about this. If you wish I will tell Commander Simms. I owe him that, especially since you were all under my protection."

"I appreciate the offer Sire, but as the leader of this group, that responsibility will fall to me. If you don't mind, I would like to delay telling him the bad news just yet. First I would like to know the cause of death."

"Yes, yes of course! You should know that first! I'm so sorry about this lamentable incident."

"I am too, but it's too late for recriminations now. I'm going to tell the rest of my people what happened, and then I'll try to retrace his steps from last night."

"If you need anything, anything at all, you only have to ask me," the king offered. "My security people are yours to command."

"I appreciate that Sire, but I would like to investigate on my own. I'll keep you informed of anything unusual that might have happened."

The explorer excused himself and went to see his staff. They were busy installing some laser cannons into a ship when he arrived. The security police stepped aside to let him in and inclined their heads politely as he came into the room. He clapped his hands to get the Earthlings' attention and the three remaining men climbed out of the ship and smiled at their superior.

"Hello Craig; we have nearly finished installing these cannons. It should take approximately another hour."

"Good work men, but let's just take a break here. I have some bad news."

The smile died on the technician's face. "What is it? What's happened? Is Brent okay?"

"Why would you ask?" Craig queried suspiciously.

"Well after last night, I did wonder about him. He must be nursing quite a hangover because I see he hasn't turned up yet. I saw him going to the bar not far from here."

"Did he seem upset in any way?"

The men exchanged curious glances.

"No, not at all. In fact he seemed quite cheerful," another replied.

"What's happened Craig?" the third technician asked, sounding a little scared.

"Brent is dead! He was found in a secluded cove not far away."

Shock was evident in their eyes.

"*No! How did he die?*" the first man enquired.

"I don't know the answer to that yet, but the king's doctor is busy with the post mortem right now. Once I know the answer, I'll let you know. In the meantime, I'm having a security guard assigned to each one of you individually, just in case it was foul play. Work on the ships is suspended for the moment, until we get to the bottom of this mystery. You can return to your hotel now, and don't leave the building unless the security man assigned to you accompanies you. All your lives could be in danger."

The men left the room in silence, shocked by the recent turn of events. Craig also returned to his room, and despite his protests, a guard accompanied him.

Carter was fidgety as he studied the dossiers he had looked at before, and began re-reading them. Somehow, somewhere there had to be a clue, he decided. It had just eluded him for the present. Later that afternoon, he was collected from the hotel and taken to the palace. The king went into his conference room and again left instructions not to be disturbed.

He sat down, and Craig joined him. His face was solemn. "I assume that the news isn't good, Sire?"

"You are quite correct. Your man was murdered! When the coroner did his post mortem he found nothing! There was no mark on your colleague's body, not even a bruise. He said that the man had drowned."

"Drowned?" asked Craig in confusion. "How could that be? No one in their right mind would remove the gills, when they are down here. We cannot exist without them and everyone knows that!"

"You are correct of course Craig. That's why he became suspicious and did some more investigations. There were no gills in your man's mouth or nose at all. That was when he did the post mortem again, but much more carefully this time. The doctor then discovered a tiny pinprick at the base of his skull, right underneath the hairline. Your man was rendered unconscious with an untraceable sleeping drug, made from a particular type of seaweed. When he fell asleep, his assailant simply removed the gills, and left your technician to drown. He never knew what happened. I'm dreadfully sorry."

Carter turned shocked eyes to his friend. "Sire, you know what this means then, don't you? We have a cold blooded killer on the loose. The fire was set deliberately and made to look like an accident, and now this same perpetrator has killed a member of my team."

"I deeply regret the incident Craig! Perhaps it would be wise if you just took the rest of your team and left. I don't want to see more of your people being murdered."

"Your Majesty, I appreciate your concern, but we still need to finish the installations. Only the team I brought is qualified to do this. If we don't finish the project, you could still be at risk of attack from your enemies," Carter reasoned.

"I know that but it doesn't matter anymore! Your safety is my main concern!"

Craig smiled at the king. "With respect Sire, so is yours. This could just be a smokescreen to frighten us away from here and leave you defenceless. Someone or something obviously has their sights set on Neptune. We have to finish the job we came here to do!"

"I forbid it! You must leave while your team is still more or less intact," the king ordered.

The explorer bowed low and spoke to the king.

"I appreciate your concern Your Majesty, but I cannot comply with your request. I was sent here to do a job and I will finish what I started. I have confidence in your security staff, and I'm sure they will find this murderer soon. The puzzle is falling into place, but I still have to find the few missing pieces, metaphorically speaking of course. Please let me help you! Perhaps one day you can return the favour!"

"I don't like the idea of you risking your life!" the ruler complained.

"Well neither do I, but this murderer must be caught. All remaining technicians will use extreme caution from now on, and we would welcome your security staff looking out for us until we complete what we were sent here to do. Is it a deal Sire?"

The king shook Craig's outstretched hand vigorously. "You drive a hard bargain Craig, but I will gladly accept your help, under the conditions you have described. Hopefully this criminal will be apprehended soon."

"I sincerely hope so," Carter replied. "Right now I have the unpleasant task of telling Commander Simms about Brent's murder."

The explorer contacted his boss at Mission Control and told him what had happened. Commander Simms also wanted them to return immediately but Craig refused. After a heated discussion he finally gave his explorer permission to continue.

Because they were now short one man, Craig pitched in and helped with the work. There was a sense of urgency amongst the men to finish the task and go home as quickly as possible, and Craig couldn't blame them. Yet even as they worked against the clock to finish the installations of the weapons, something kept nagging at the back of his mind. That night he again went to the place where he had hidden the dossiers of all the suspects, intending to take them out and read through them once more. He reached into the cavity and suddenly a cold shiver passed through him. It was empty! The dossiers had disappeared!

Carter's first instinct was to tell the king, but he decided against it. Someone had been nervous enough to remove the evidence, and this made Craig realize that he was on the right track, but who was responsible? He paced up and down recalling the contents of each file in turn. Yet try as he might he could find no one who had anything to gain by the destruction of the new weapon system. The explorer had read the dossiers so many times that he knew exactly what was contained on the data disc. He smiled triumphantly when the beginnings of a plan began to take shape. The perpetrator was too clever to make a mistake, so Craig had to pre-empt the situation. The murderer knew he had read their dossiers. This made him the next target, of that he was convinced. Now to test his theory!

CHAPTER FIFTEEN

The explorer went to the bar where Brent had last been seen alive, and ordered a drink. He downed it in a few thirsty gulps, and immediately ordered another. This one he also drank quickly. He ordered a third and went to sit at a table near a potted sea plant. For a while he watched the Neptunians as they drank and socialized with their friends. A beautiful woman climbed on stage and began to gyrate sensuously to haunting music. Craig sipped some of his drink and, surreptitiously poured most of it into the potted plant. In this way he ordered more than a dozen drinks, but he was careful to sip only some of the contents and throw the rest away. He needed a clear head for his plan to work. However his outward appearance deteriorated for the benefit of the onlookers. He spoke to some of the patrons and slurred his words. At a table not far away he saw his guard watching him, a worried look on his face, but he didn't acknowledge the man at all.

A lovely Neptunian woman came up to him and sat down. She was breathtakingly beautiful, and her long dark hair hung sensuously down her back. Her dress was low cut in the front and cut high up on the thigh. Her voice was silky and she introduced herself as Ambrosia. Obligingly he bought her a drink and reflected wryly that even here on Neptune, prostitutes preyed on unwary customers. The evening was going to prove interesting – if he didn't get killed first.

More drinks arrived and he made a show of drinking them while most of them went into the potted plant next to him. Ambrosia questioned him about his work, saying that she loved Earthlings because of their generosity. Carter grinned like a silly schoolboy and whispered in her ear.

"I know that my friend was murdered!" he mumbled. "The police don't believe me! They think that it was an accident, but I know differently," he bragged.

He stood up and stumbled against her. Ambrosia giggled and put her arms around him. "Hey, be careful honey! You're quite drunk."

Carter smiled and stroked her hair. "I'm not that drunk honey! C'mon get me another drink huh," he smiled crookedly. "And get another one for you."

Her green eyes looked into his blue ones, and she gently lowered him back into his chair.

"I think you've had enough for tonight mister. My room's just down the passage. You need to sober up and I know just the remedy. I can do things to you in places you never dreamed possible. You interested?"

He leered at her through watery eyes. "Oh you are so beautiful! I've never been with a Neptunian woman before."

"Oh this will be an experience you will never forget, I promise you that!" she crooned. "Here let me help you," she offered, as he stumbled to his feet. She put her arm around him and led him away.

The security guard got up to see where they were going, and suddenly another woman grabbed him.

"Come on big boy, they are playing our song," she invited.

"Your friend is in good hands. Ambrosia is one of the best hostesses here."

She spun him around and when he looked again, Craig and Ambrosia had disappeared. Angrily he brushed the hostess off and went to look for Craig. Several Neptunians converged on him and pushed him out the door.

Meanwhile Ambrosia had half carried, half dragged the 'inebriated' explorer to her room. They fell together on the bed and he reached out to kiss her, but she pulled away. "Hey hold on a second; I have to get ready first!" she giggled.

"You look just fine as you are. C'mon, gimme a kiss!" he pleaded.

"This won't take a minute lover boy!" she teased.

He grinned drunkenly and lay back on the bed, putting his hands behind his head. "Don't take long now!"

"I won't," she promised and disappeared behind a door.

When the door had closed he got up and looked around. He quickly searched through her things but found nothing of importance. The door started to open and he jumped back onto the bed and assumed his former position. Craig closed his eyes and opened them when he judged her to be nearby.

"You took your time!" he grumbled impatiently. She wasn't standing there, but several very well-built Neptunian men were. Craig stared crossly at them.

"Hey, where did Ambrosia go? She promised me a good time," he slurred. "I'll complain to the management if you don't bring her back. Is this how you treat your guests?"

He began to get up, but the men pushed him down firmly.

"Don't move Mr Carter!" one replied commandingly. "If you try anything stupid, I'll kill you immediately. We have been waiting for you."

The explorer feigned stupidity. "I don't know what you mean. I came here to have a good time and now you want to rob me."

One of the Neptunians folded his arms across his chest and spoke to the reclining man. "You can drop the drunken act Mr Carter! We have been watching you ever since you arrived. You're just as sober as I am. Oh by the way, we took care of your minder, so don't expect any help from him."

Craig eased slowly into a sitting position, and glared at the man. "All right so you called my bluff! What do you want?"

The space explorer looked at the beings gathered around him and all were now pointing guns at him. He noticed some of the weapons were ones his team had brought from Earth, and the final piece of the puzzle clicked into place.

"Mr Carter you are far too inquisitive for your own good! You shouldn't have carried on snooping when that warehouse caught fire."

"You made it personal when you murdered one of my team!" he snapped. "Why?"

"Your colleague was very greedy. He saw something he shouldn't have and decided to try and blackmail us, so he had to die, just as you will."

The Neptunian placed his gun against Craig's cheek, and his hand rested on the trigger. Cautiously the explorer moved the weapon away from his face. 'Hey you want to watch where you're pointing that thing. It has a hare trigger which can cause plenty of damage, as well as alerting every cop in the neighbourhood, and they are here, you can trust me on that!"

The crook sneered at him. "You're lying! No one is within a hundred furlongs of here."

"Fine, so you are just going to kill me right here in a public place! The moment you fire that gun, the authorities will be swarming around here."

One of the beings looked at his friend in alarm. "He's right you know. We have to do it elsewhere. We don't want to call attention to ourselves right now."

The first man spoke. "I'm not going to kill him yet. First I want to find out just how much he knows."

He threw a pair of handcuffs onto Craig's lap.

"Handcuff yourself to the bed rail, Mr Carter," he demanded.

Craig was reluctant and the man ordered two Neptunians to come forward.

"Assist Mr Carter, boys. You can rough him up a bit if you like. I don't think the fish will mind snacking on damaged goods."

The beings smiled in anticipation, and advanced on their captive. The explorer held up his hands in a gesture of surrender. "All right, I'll do as you say!" he complained. "You should really do something about your temper."

He put the handcuff on one wrist and put the other section through the bed rail, snapping it closed.

The blow took Craig by surprise and his head smacked painfully against the bed rail. For a moment he saw stars, and shook his head.

"All right now let's talk. I want to know everything that you've found out, but whether you talk or not, you'll still die soon. If you want to prolong your life for a while anyway, tell us what you know."

"Why do you want my version of the story? You stole the dossiers from my room, so you know what I've been doing."

The man smiled. "You are very clever, Earthling! Yes I did that, but I still don't know what conclusion you have reached. As I said before, I don't mind whether you give the information voluntarily or I take it by force. Either way you will cooperate! It's up to you."

"In that case I prefer the first option," Carter replied. "What do you want to know?"

"Have you discovered who the guilty party is yet? I read through the dossiers you had on all the delegates obviously opposed to the weapons being brought here. Who is your chief suspect?"

"It's the Minister of Defence," Craig replied.

"That was very smart of you Mr Carter. How did you reach this conclusion?"

The door opened again and Ambrosia came in. She was dressed in jeans and a casual top. Craig pointed to her with his free hand.

"Well he can't really be blamed with someone like her taking an interest in him I suppose. My guess is that she made friends with him and he liked the attention that she showered on him. They became lovers. The minister is a married man, and the scandal isn't good for him. I'm willing to bet his wife doesn't know about the affair."

"Very good so far," the man replied approvingly. "You would make a good detective. Continue please!"

"Well Ambrosia was obviously obeying your orders. You're probably her boyfriend, or her brother."

"Boyfriend actually," he replied obligingly.

"Anyway, one night when the minister of defence and your girlfriend were together, he told her about the plans to upgrade the weapon system. You decided to get in on the act and steal the weapons for your own selfish purposes! My guess is that you wanted to cause as much delay as possible, so the weapons wouldn't be mounted on the ships. Did you plan to overthrow the kingdom, or just sell the weapons to the highest bidder?"

"I was offered a very good price for the weapons actually." The man replied. "I'm a businessman and it was just too good to refuse."

"Who's the buyer?" Craig asked curiously.

"None of your business!" the man snapped.

"You obviously paid someone to sabotage the warehouse and make it look like an accident. Your plans were foiled when the king simply found another warehouse and this time put guards on duty to protect the technicians and weapons, so the work continued regardless. What I want to know is why did Brent have to die?"

The man paced the floor and Ambrosia came up to him. He kissed her passionately before he answered.

"Your friend was having a late-night swim when my men set the timers to destroy the warehouse. He happened to see them do it. He could have gone to the authorities, but instead he followed one of my men home and told him what he had seen. He got greedy and threatened to blackmail us, unless we gave him some credits to keep quiet. My colleague set up a meeting at this club and Ambrosia did her stuff. She convinced him to come to her room, just as you did. In his case however we simply injected him with a strong sleeping drug. We took him to the cove where the police found him, but you know that already."

Craig kept quiet.

"Well it seems as though our plan is working Mr Carter. The weapons project has been put on hold for now."

"True, but it will continue in a few days, once all the evidence is presented," Craig replied.

"Who is going to be around to give evidence? In a short while you'll be dead, and I have no doubt that your boss will cancel the project. He won't risk losing anyone else. Then I'm going to get hold of every weapon not yet installed and sell them to my eager buyer. I'm still curious, because you haven't told us everything. How did you make the connection? The defence minister's credentials are impeccable. He had nothing shady to hide, except Ambrosia of course, and that didn't appear in the documents I obtained."

"In actual fact it did," Carter explained. "You were correct when you mentioned the minister hid his secret well. I must admit it puzzled me and I couldn't make the connection, that is, until I saw a photograph in the file. The minister of defence was arriving at a function with his wife, when the cameraman accidentally caught Ambrosia in the frame. The minister had turned to smile at her, and somehow this seemed out of character. She was supposedly just a face in the crowd, so why did he single her out especially? I acted purely on a hunch and copied her picture into the police data base. I was very surprised when a match was found. The lovely Ambrosia is really Trudy Mansefield, daughter of Robin Mansefield, an infamous arms dealer. Needless to say, I never printed that piece of incriminating evidence."

The Neptunian was amazed. "Well you certainly are clever aren't you? Armed with your new-found knowledge, you decided to play detective and solve the crime, so you came to the club."

"Yes," he admitted.

"Well that was a foolish thing to do! Knowing what you did, why risk your life to come here?"

Ambrosia stormed up to her boyfriend. "Instead of singing this idiot's praises you had better kill him right now! He knows everything and this will jeopardize the whole operation."

The man drew his weapon and pointed it at Craig. "She's right I'm afraid! This gun doesn't have a silencer on it, but the noise from the club will drown out the shot. Goodbye Mr Carter!"

The space explorer put up his hand and interrupted. "Don't be foolish! You've killed one person, but it can end right now. You're missing the whole point of the story."

The crook's finger began to tighten on the trigger and Ambrosia, or Trudy as she was really known, pushed the gun away.

"What do you mean by that remark?" she asked suspiciously.

"Just think for a moment Miss Mansefield, I came to the club, knowing who you were, yet I went with you willingly. You and your boyfriend knew I was suspicious, but you haven't questioned why I risked my life."

"You seem to be forgetting something Mr Carter. My people detained your police escort. Regrettably he performed his last function tonight! You're just trying to buy time."

"So you admit to having killed another being! Well you just keep on adding to your score don't you?"

"I look forward to you joining him in the near future."

"Sorry, I don't feel like dying today," Craig replied.

He jumped up and launched himself at the man holding the gun. It clattered out of his hand and slid out of harm's way. As Trudy reached for the fallen weapon, the door burst open and several policemen swarmed in. Subdued very quickly, the crooks were read their rights. Before they were led out the door, the man looked at him. "Mr Carter, how did you free yourself? I saw you handcuff yourself to the bed rail."

Craig held up a tiny piece of metal with a sharp point. "Meet my trusty lock pick! I never leave home without it! Oh, by the way, you can hire the best lawyer on the planet, but you'll all pay dearly for your crimes. This whole conversation was videoed! While Ambrosia over there went to get ready, I placed a tiny video camera above the mirror. The evidence is irrefutable. I took a risk, but it was worth it to put scum like you away."

The next day Craig was once again at the palace, with the king. The head of security was also present.

"Craig how can I thank you for what you've done? You went above and beyond the call of duty to help my people. Words cannot express my gratitude," the king replied gratefully.

"It was a pleasure Your Highness! I couldn't leave things unattended. I'm just sorry that Brent and that young policeman lost their lives. It was regrettable, but at least their murderers have been brought to justice."

"Yes, some good came out of the situation I suppose. What happens now?"

"Well Sire I came here to do a job and I must finish it. The rest of the weapons should be installed in your ships by the end of the week, and then I'll return home. Now if you'll excuse me, enough time has been wasted, and I must finish the job. We're already a week behind schedule."

Craig left and the two Neptunians discussed the reluctant hero. "Your Highness, Earth is very lucky to have a man like that in their midst. It is not his job to catch criminals, yet look what he did for us. That man is becoming quite a legend amongst the planets in space. Many of them have him to thank for their continued existence. In every case he put his own needs aside and risked his life for his friends. Truly we are fortunate to be considered friends of Earth. I will watch that young man's career with great interest."

"As will I my friend," the king agreed. "Commander Simms will be receiving an in depth report from me. He deserves to know what an amazing man Craig Carter is."

"I'm in total agreement Sire, and I'll be including my own report as well."

Craig kept his word, and by the end of the week, every weapon had been installed in the spaceships. He had trained some Neptunians in the use of the weaponry, and they in turn would train their fellow Neptunians. Now he was getting ready to leave the planet and return home. He said goodbye to the royal family and their household, and Lolita asked if she could swim to the surface to say her farewells. The king smiled indulgently at his daughter and gave his permission.

They reached the surface and Lolita climbed out of the water with her friend. She looked earnestly into his eyes.

"I'm going to miss you Craig," she sighed miserably. "When will I see you again?"

"I don't know, but you're always in my heart and mind and don't you ever forget it. We'll see one another soon I'm positive. Meanwhile you look after yourself. I wish I had been able to spend more time with you, but that didn't happen."

"Next time perhaps," she smiled.

"Yes, next time," he promised.

The princess stood on tiptoe and kissed him softly on his cheek. He hugged her wet body tightly and reluctantly let her go. Craig and the remainder of the technicians climbed aboard their ship. The last view he had of Neptune was that of Lolita waving goodbye. Soon afterwards the planet fell away as they set a course for Earth.

CHAPTER SIXTEEN

He breathed a sigh of relief when they landed at Mission Control once again. When he arrived home, he hugged his mother gratefully. "Oh mom sometimes I take you for granted and I never tell you how much I love you, but if it wasn't for you and dad, I wouldn't be the person I am today!"

His mother smiled at him. "I know how much you appreciate us, but thank you for that. I love you too."

Brent's funeral was held a few days later and Craig and Constance attended. Even though Carter had not caused the man's death, he felt awkward. They stayed for a short while only, then left the grieving family with their memories.

Constance took him to a restaurant where she ordered some beverages. She looked compassionately into her boyfriend's eyes and gently held his hand. "I don't know how you manage to get yourself into so much trouble. It follows you like a magnet!"

"I know," he sighed miserably. "Yet I don't go out visiting planets and looking for trouble. It just seems to find me."

"Craig you're the most unselfish person I know. You'd do anything to help your friends and I should know, because I'm in your debt as well. I seem to recall a similar incident not long ago when you came to my rescue."

"I was glad to help, you know that," he replied modestly.

"I know. Well I have to go on a mission for Commander Simms in a few days, so we may as well enjoy the time we have together. It'll be months before we see one another again."

"The joys of space travel!" he exclaimed ruefully.

"Yes, and neither of us would change it for anything, admit it," his girlfriend replied.

"You're quite right, I totally agree with you! What mission has Commander Simms got lined up for you though? Has he told you yet?" he asked Constance.

"Yes but it isn't anything exciting. I have to accompany another astronaut to Saturn. We must deliver some supplies, because one of the pilots suddenly became ill. There's no one else to help him fly the ship, so our boss asked me to step in. It'll make a change I suppose."

"I guess so," he agreed. "Well when you arrive, give my regards to Lara and the rest of the Saturnians."

"I'll do that. Right now though let's just concentrate on having a good time. The last couple of months have been pretty stressful for you."

Craig raised his glass and toasted his girlfriend. "Here's to us!"

She raised hers and they clinked glasses. "To us," she replied.

The next morning, Craig was summoned to see Commander Simms, He arrived and smiled at his boss's secretary and she smiled back. "You can go right in Craig. He's expecting you."

Carter knocked on the door and was asked to enter. His boss was reading something on his digital notepad and waved his employee to a chair. Dutifully he sat down and waited while Simms signed some documents and put the device in his 'out' tray. When the job had been done, he steepled his fingers and smiled at his astronaut. "Well Craig, I hope that you've been having a good rest. I know that you only got back from your last mission a week ago."

"Yes Sir. I used the time to catch up on some chores that desperately needed doing."

Simms got straight to the point. "How would you feel about going on another mission for me in two days' time?"

"Well Sir, you're the boss. What did you have in mind for me?"

"How would you like to go on a trip to Saturn?"

"Saturn? But isn't Constance going there soon?"

Commander Simms grinned at his employee. "Yes she is, but she needs someone to go with her."

"She does? But I thought that she was the replacement for someone else!" he exclaimed.

"She was, but now the pilot has had a family emergency, and I had to give him compassionate leave. His father died and he has to organize the funeral, so now I need someone else. Are you interested?"

Craig's face split into a wide grin. "Oh yes Sir! Thank you Sir!"

"You're most welcome I assure you! Should I tell Constance or would you like to do it?"

"I'll tell her Sir," replied his employee excitedly.

"Very well then; report back here on Thursday at 8 a.m. sharp."

"We will be here you can count on it. See you then, Sir."

Craig's boss smiled at his retreating back. When he was out of sight, Commander Simms's secretary joined him. "It's so refreshing to see how much in love those two young people are," she remarked wistfully. "That was very kind of you! Both you and I know there was someone else you could have asked to take the pilot's place."

Commander Simms put his hand to his lips. "Sssh, not so loud my dear; Craig may hear you! Those young people haven't had that much time together, and their holiday was a disaster. Besides, they have gone on the odd mission together. They complement one another beautifully. Anyway this isn't a dangerous mission at all. All they have to do is deliver supplies to the Saturnians. It should be a quiet and pleasant trip."

The two young people arrived well before time and went to see their boss in his office. He welcomed them and asked them to be seated.

"All right you two, I just wanted to tell you briefly what this mission is about. The Saturnians have requested a number of items which you will be taking to them. It's nothing top secret or dangerous, just food and medical supplies, plus some plants that they want to try and grow on Saturn as an experiment. I've given you one of the smaller cargo vessels because there isn't that much. The one I have requisitioned for you has only one hold. There are a couple of large crates, as well as a few smaller ones and these are still being loaded onto your ship. However the task has probably nearly been completed. If you want, you can get into the ship in the meantime and do your pre-flight checks. You should be underway in approximately half an hour or so."

Craig stood up and took Constance's hand. "Yes we should be getting ready. We'll talk to you later once we are airborne Sir."

"You do that. Goodbye and good luck. Enjoy the flight."

Both young people waved and their boss waved back.

They carried their suitcases into the ship and the techno mechanics greeted them. As they watched, a large crate was hoisted into the cargo hold and secured. Both astronauts climbed aboard and Craig sat in the pilot's chair while Constance sat down in the co-pilot's one. They flipped switches and checked dials, going through all the necessary checks. The computer confirmed their adjustments and made some of its own calculations. Finally, they were ready to leave, and Constance contacted Mission Control to tell them. Clearance was granted and they lifted off vertically. The roof of the building opened to let them out and soon they were once again in the blackness of space. When they were well on their way,

Craig put the ship on auto pilot and turned to his girlfriend.

"Well here we go again! I wonder what adventures are waiting this time?"

Constance laughed at him. "None I hope, silly! This is just a routine flight. We deliver the supplies and take anything that Saturn want us to deliver to Earth, and then we leave again. What could be simpler?"

"Nothing I suppose. Well my darling, how are we going to entertain ourselves in the few months that we will be alone together in space?" Craig asked mischievously.

"Oh I daresay we'll think of something!" she exclaimed secretively.

Carter held her in his arms and they kissed. She sighed and sat on his lap. "I think this is going to be a most enjoyable trip."

"It most definitely is," he agreed. Then he kissed her again.

A week passed uneventfully, and the couple watched the planets and stars go by. Suddenly the spacecraft lurched and they hung grimly onto their seats. They were buffeted about for a while and both of them strapped in firmly and tried to bring the ship back under control. The craft bobbed and weaved as though it had a mind of its own until Craig quickly put the force field on. Slowly the ship stopped bouncing and settled down. They watched in amazement as several huge rocks spun by them. Some hit the force field and bounced harmlessly off. Constance looked at the huge boulders in awe.

"Those rocks came out of nowhere! We had no advance warning! Why didn't the computer warn us, so we could take appropriate action?"

"I don't know but my guess would be it happened too suddenly. Somehow something must have exploded. I had better run a diagnostic check though, just in case there was some damage to the hull."

Carter checked the ship from end to end but the computer could find no serious damage. Both of them breathed a huge sigh of relief. Constance got up from her seat. "Craig, I think I should check on the cargo in the hold in case something was damaged."

"Good idea Constance," her boyfriend agreed.

Constance made her way down to the cargo bay, and unlocked the sealed entrance. She went inside and began checking up on the crates. Everything seemed to be intact at first glance, but she went inside to check anyway. All the crates and boxes were still securely tied down and she searched every crate for signs of damage but there appeared to be nothing wrong.

However, she noticed one of the crates had burst open and went to check it. Miss Gregg frowned when she looked inside for, apart from some soft padding material, the box was empty. She searched the hold thoroughly, but couldn't find anything that could have fallen out of the crate. The woman returned to the cockpit.

"Is everything okay Constance?"

"Everything seems to be, except for one crate. It was open but there was nothing inside. I searched the hold thoroughly, but found nothing that could have fallen out. It's really peculiar!"

Carter pursed his lips. "Well maybe it's not that strange. Perhaps the Saturnians wanted us to bring an empty one, so they could pack stuff in for us to take back to Earth."

"It's a possibility I suppose," Miss Gregg replied. "Well in that case then, everything's fine."

"I did a thorough check on the ship while you were down there and thankfully nothing has been compromised. We were lucky this time!"

"Glad to hear it. It's not as though we can call the nearest towing service."

"Not out here, that's for sure. Oh well, let's hope the rest of this trip is uneventful. We have two weeks left before we reach Saturn."

"Well right now I'm thirsty. Can I get you something to drink?"

"Sure, a nice cup of hot chocolate sounds like a plan."

"I'll make some for us. See you in a bit!"

Constance disappeared into the compact kitchenette and began rummaging amongst the shelves for the hot chocolate.

She finally found it right at the back and took it out. When she opened the can, it was half full.

"*That's funny,*" she thought. "*I'm sure this tin was at least three quarters full when last I checked.*" She shrugged her shoulders dismissively. "Craig probably had some earlier. It doesn't really matter I suppose."

She made the drinks and took them into the cockpit.

"Thanks honey. I really need this!"

They sat and watched the stars and planets whizzing by.

Much later, Constance took the empty cups to the waste disposal unit and threw them into the compacter. Then she went to use the facilities. While she was washing her hands, she heard the sound of footsteps passing by and she called out.

"Craig, what do you want to eat for supper tonight? I feel like warming up the spaghetti bolognaise. Will that be okay?"

There was no answer, and she finished up in the bathroom. When she opened the door, Constance heard footsteps going down the passage, towards their sleeping quarters, and she hurried towards the sound. "Honey did you hear me? What do you want for supper?"

Miss Gregg went into the bedroom, but it was empty. "Craig, are you here?"

She looked around curiously, but no one was there. "Craig?" she asked tentatively.

She began to leave the room, when suddenly someone came up behind her and a gun was jabbed into her ribs. She stood still.

"Look here miss, I don't want to hurt you. Please don't make me do that!"

The person was obviously nervous and Constance knew that this was an amateur, not a killer. However at such close range the stowaway couldn't miss her.

Slowly so as not to alarm the person, she raised her hands.

"Are you going to scream?" the voice asked.

She shook her head mutely, but the man continued holding the gun on her.

"Who are you?" she whispered. "What do you want?"

"Where's the other pilot?" he enquired.

"In the cockpit area."

The man prodded her with the gun. "Take me to him."

Constance put her hands down and went to the cockpit. The man followed a few paces behind.

When they reached the cockpit, Craig heard her footsteps and without turning around, he spoke. "Hey Constance, what's for supper? I don't know what it is about space travel, but I'm always hungrier when I'm in space."

"Uh Craig, we have a problem..." she began.

Something in the tone of her voice made him turn around. He gasped when he saw she wasn't alone. "What the hell...?" he began. "Who are you?"

The man put his hand on Constance's shoulder, and pointed the gun at Craig. "You just stay in that chair otherwise I'll shoot her," he stammered.

Carter placed his hands in his lap, and spoke calmly to the frightened man. "Hey that isn't necessary! I'm not going to do anything to jeopardize her safety. What do you want?"

The man gave Constance a hard shove. "You go and sit with your boyfriend," he commanded.

She did as she was told and sat down in the other chair. The man remained standing. "Who are you?" Miss Gregg asked curiously.

"I know who he is," Craig replied. "This is Conrad Burke! He escaped from prison a few days ago. It was all over the news! He was going to stand trial for murdering his secretary, and also for embezzling money from his company. The man invented a dangerous serum and tested it on human subjects. The police received an anonymous tip off and went to his apartment where they found some of the stolen money, as well as a few samples of the drug. He was caught trying to leave the country. Dr Burke is a well-known physiologist!"

Constance looked at their uninvited guest and nodded her head. "Yes I remember that now."

"I'm innocent!" the man protested. "I'm not a monster, and I never did all those things the press said I was responsible for."

"Sure, everyone is innocent until proven guilty," Craig remarked snidely.

"But why did you choose us? Of all the possible places you could have gone to ground, why did you stow away on this ship?" Constance enquired curiously.

"*Don't you understand, I never did any of those things!*" the man replied hysterically. "I was framed!"

"Do you know that this ship is going to Saturn," Craig remarked. "Why would you want to go there?"

"Look mister, I wanted to get as far away as possible, so I grabbed the first transport out of here and it just happened to be yours. I stowed away on board when you were preparing to leave."

"Wait a minute; the empty crate!" Constance exclaimed. "You were in that crate weren't you?"

"Yes I was," the physiologist confirmed.

Craig saw that the man's attention was on Constance, so he reached stealthily behind him and picked up a metal spanner. His aim was true and he hit the man on the side of his head, dazing him for a second, but that was long enough for the explorer. Within seconds he had thrown the gun to Constance, who caught it expertly and pointed it at their stowaway. Carter pinned the man's hands behind him and forced him to a chair, then he handcuffed him. Miss Gregg put the gun in a drawer and locked it, pocketing the key as she did so.

"Constance, get Commander Simms online and tell him that we have Dr Burke."

"All right, but we can't turn back now! We've come too far to do that. We'll have to take him to Saturn."

"Maybe that won't be necessary. Sometimes the troop carriers pass by here, and if I'm not mistaken, one should be in the vicinity within the next hour or so. They can take Dr Burke back to Earth with them."

Frightened tears began to roll down the man's face.

"Please I beg you, don't do that! I'm sorry I scared you, but I was desperate. I'm innocent I swear it! My partner is the one who should be arrested. He's responsible for all of the things I've been accused of. He planted the evidence in my apartment, and then phoned the police."

Craig looked compassionately at the man. "I'm sorry for what has happened to you, but you have to understand we aren't policemen. I don't know what was found in your apartment, nor can I take your word for it. Maybe you are innocent, but it isn't our problem. If we don't report your presence, we could be named as accessories to murder and we have our own problems to contend with."

The man began to shake uncontrollably. "I'll never live long enough to prove my innocence! Once I'm placed in jail I'll have an unfortunate accident, and then my partner will be free to do exactly as he wants. Please help me!" he pleaded earnestly.

Constance spoke to the man. "I don't think you are being honest with us. Your being on this ship was no accident was it? Why did you want to go to Saturn of all places? There are transport ships going to every known planet in the universe. Why didn't you choose another one to stow away in?"

"You don't understand! I have immense respect for the Saturnians and I admire what they are doing. I would give anything to consult with them. I'm a scientist and I can learn so much from them. I was going to ask for political asylum on Saturn."

The two young people looked at one another.

"What should we do with him?" Craig asked. "Even if he is innocent as he says, where can we put him? This is a cargo ship, not a prison transport and we have nowhere to confine him. There's only the hold but he got out of there before."

The stowaway appealed to them once more. "Look, if I was really a murderer you would both have been dead already! I've been here all the time, yet not once have I tried to harm either of you. If your girlfriend hadn't surprised me, I would still be in hiding, and you would never have known about me until we landed on Saturn."

Constance looked at her boyfriend. "He's right you know! As much as I hate to admit it, he has had every opportunity to do away with us and he hasn't. My instincts tell me that there's more to this story than we realize, but out here we have no way of proving anything. We have to continue to Saturn, and sort this out, once we have landed."

"What do we do with him in the meantime?" Craig asked. "We would have to take turns to guard him, and we still have at least ten days before we reach Saturn."

Miss Gregg smiled tentatively at the man. "I'm not over-joyed about the prospect of spending the rest of the journey with a stranger, but we have no choice. I'm sure our stowaway cannot fly this spaceship, so he needs us. Am I correct Dr Burke?" she enquired.

"Absolutely," he replied. "It would serve no purpose to harm you in any way. We all need one another."

"Doctor, if we agree to free you, there will be some conditions involved." Carter remarked.

"Name them!"

"Well I'm prepared to keep silent about your presence here on this ship, but once we reach Saturn, you'll have to apply for political asylum. Once I hand you over to the Saturnians I'll have no say on what happens to you. I'll have no choice but to tell Commander Simms about you stowing away on the ship. He will then contact the relevant authorities, and their decision will be final. If you can think of a way to prove your innocence, now is the time to do so. I don't need to remind you that we are out of the jurisdictional zone of Earth, but Saturn is one of our allies. They will send you back to Earth if they think it is in everyone's best interests."

"Very well I accept those conditions – I don't really have any choice. Now could you free me please?"

Craig looked at Constance, and she nodded. He went to the man and freed his hands.

Dr Burke rubbed his wrists and thanked them. He looked like a lost puppy and Constance felt sorry for him. Her instincts had served her well in the past and she believed the man was innocent as he had said. "Would you like something to drink?" she asked kindly.

"Thank you, I would," he replied gratefully.

She returned with a hot drink for the doctor and they all sat down.

"Dr Burke, you said you are innocent. We have plenty of time, so would you like to tell us why the police arrested you?" Craig asked curiously.

"I might as well, I suppose," he sighed. "As I mentioned before, my partner is the guilty one.

"We were both involved in trying to perfect a drug that could help the human immune system repair itself quicker. Imagine having a serious operation, and by using this drug, you could heal in half the time! Most people would welcome something like that. Both of us were doing experiments to improve the drug, and my partner wanted to rush through the procedure. We were making headway, but there was still plenty of work to be done before we could test it out on a human being. However, my partner kept on insisting we use someone as a guinea pig, just to see how much more work needed to be done. I refused because I didn't feel it was in anyone's best interests at that point. He protested and tried to make me change my mind, but I refused. Afterwards he never asked again.

"About a month later someone came to see him in the laboratory, but he was out, so I spoke to the person. The lady was very distraught and angry. Apparently, she had undergone an operation a few months earlier, and for some reason the scar refused to heal properly. My partner told her about the drug we had invented, but left out a number of salient points, namely the fact that it had not been used on a human being.

"The woman was a beautiful model and very conscious about her appearance, so she decided to try the drug. The scar did in fact heal much quicker, and within a few months it was hardly visible, so she said. The problem only appeared a few months later, when she fell pregnant. The baby was aborted at two months and when she asked why it had died, no one wanted to tell her. She managed to sneak into the mortuary by bribing one of the janitors, and found her baby. It was so badly deformed it hardly even looked human. It was cremated quietly because the woman didn't want to face a scandal.

"I had no reason to believe the drug had been responsible then of course, but I did have a few harsh words with my partner and he denied the incident, saying she was a former girlfriend of his anyway and she was just looking to make trouble for him, so the matter was hushed up. The baby could have been deformed for a number of reasons of course, so I gave him the benefit of the doubt.'

'Over the next couple of months, my partner gave the drug to several people without telling me. I found out purely by accident when I was passing his office one evening. He was speaking to a woman who was hysterical. She complained of tumours developing all over her body at an alarming rate. I didn't want him to know that I had heard anything, so I waited until the woman was leaving and I caught up with her as she approached the lift. We rode down to the next floor together and I asked her if I could examine her. A doctor friend of mine works downstairs and I had the spare key to his office. The woman agreed, and when I examined her, I was repulsed because the tumours were forming everywhere. In some cases, they were growing on top of ones already formed. She told me my partner had given her some new tablets to try because she had been told she had cancer. H assured her the wonder drug would kill the affected cells almost immediately.

"I took a biopsy of one of her lumps, and swore her to secrecy. Then I contacted my friend and asked him to analyse the tissue sample, because I didn't want anyone else to know about it. He came to my house two days later, ashen faced and in a state of shock. The analysis revealed the woman was now so riddled with cancer, death was imminent. She had about one month to live, if that. Instead of helping her, he had made things worse!

"I went to see the woman and gave her the test results. She was angry, but I knew I couldn't prove anything, even though I was one hundred percent positive what had caused the cancer to spread so rapidly. I knew I couldn't save her, but a plan began forming in my mind. I asked her if I could take photographs of her, because I wanted to get enough evidence to have my partner arrested. At first she was reluctant, but then she changed her mind.

"Promise me you'll stop him," she begged. "It's too late for me but that man is a monster. Help others and I won't have died in vain."

'I gave her my word and we parted company. A few days later she shot herself, and the records showed that her body had been cremated almost immediately. I began to do some snooping and discovered several people who had been injected with the drug. In each case I went to see the patients secretly, and all had developed some kind of deformity on their bodies. Wherever I could, I gathered evidence and hid it in a safe place."

"Where did you store this information?" Craig asked curiously.

"I stored the evidence on my computer. My partner will never find it, because it's in an encoded file my doctor friend created for me. I didn't want my partner to know I was aware of his secret, so I never told him what I found out. When I questioned him about the drug, he swore he had never tested it on anyone and I pretended to believe him.

"Finally, I reached the point of no return when I discovered that many of the patients he had treated with the drug, had died suddenly. I decided to go to the police the next morning and show them all the incriminating evidence.

"I had a lot of work to do that night though, and I asked my secretary to work late. When I was ready to leave, I offered her a lift and she declined, because her boyfriend was going to pick her up within the next half hour.

"The police came to see me early next morning when I was preparing for work. They informed me that my secretary had been murdered the previous evening, and asked when I had seen her last. I had to tell them she had worked overtime and that when I left her, she was fine, but I knew they didn't believe me. They had a search warrant and began looking through all my belongings. They found some notes about the 'experiments' I had allegedly performed on human beings, as well as a few graphic photos of the mutations. Conveniently there was a sample of the drug in my cupboard. The police arrested me, and I was told that my gun had been used to kill my secretary. Only my fingerprints were found on the murder weapon. The evidence against me was damning, and I knew then I hadn't been careful enough. Obviously my partner had found out what I had been doing and wanted to stop me telling the police, so decided to frame me instead. I went to jail and my partner got away with it.

"I spent a year in jail and during that time, I met up with someone who believed in me, as you have. He helped me escape and for obvious reasons I won't divulge that information. I knew I didn't have a strong enough case against my partner to secure a conviction, so decided to cut my losses and run away. Saturn seemed like a good idea because I'm a scientist and I would love to consult with them about various things. I didn't think I would be discovered though. I just hoped I could slip off this ship quietly and throw myself at their mercy."

"Why didn't you approach us earlier?" Craig asked. "You can't solve your problems by running away from them. Heaven only knows what your partner has been up to since your incarceration! I have some good friends on the police force, who could have helped clear your name."

The scientist shook his head. "I don't think so! If I had stayed on Earth, I would've died like the rest of the mutating humans, because my partner is unscrupulous, and I'm a loose end. That's why I'm afraid to go back. He knows I'm aware of his ghastly experiments and he'll do anything he can to shut me up forever. Anyway the moment I show my face, I'll be arrested again, so what will going back to Earth really achieve?"

Constance turned her cup thoughtfully around and around in her hands. "I see your dilemma, but think about all the people who are looking for help on Earth. If your partner is giving them dangerous drugs, a lot more people are going to die."

"Maybe, but if I know my partner he's probably keeping a low profile now. Imagine if some people complain about the new medication. The authorities will know I'm innocent and he won't like that at all."

"You could be right doctor," Craig replied. "However, he sounds like a greedy man, and I think he'll continue to use the drug, because there are many desperate people in the world. Maybe he'll just be a lot more careful now. Anyway, we can speculate all we like, but that won't solve anything. When we reach Saturn, I'll have a word with Lara and her colleagues. Don't lose hope just yet!"

The man smiled gratefully at the two space explorers. "I'll try to remain optimistic. Thank you both for believing in me. It means a lot to me and I'm really sorry I pointed a gun at you."

"Well at least no one got hurt," Constance replied.

The couple found Dr Burke very interesting to talk to and they were never short of anything to discuss with him.

CHAPTER SEVENTEEN

The group landed on Saturn ten days later and Karnd was there to welcome them personally. He shook hands with Craig and hugged Constance. He looked curiously at the third occupant.

"No one said anything about another guest," he replied. "Who's your friend?"

"Karnd, this is Dr Conrad Burke, and we didn't know we would be bringing a guest either. I'll explain later, okay," Carter promised.

The Saturnian took them to their hotel and got them settled in. The room opposite was given to the scientist. When they had settled in, the group was taken to visit Jorrel, Lara and the rest of the scientists. They talked pleasantly for a while and then Karnd came to take the scientist on a tour of the facilities.

When he had gone, Lara spoke up. "What's going on? We weren't told that you were bringing anyone with you – not that we mind, you understand," she replied hastily, "but you always tell us how many to expect. Why were you so secretive?"

"Because we didn't know we had another passenger," Craig explained. "He stowed away on the ship. We only found him about ten days ago. Lara, he's a fugitive who escaped from jail and hitched a ride with us."

"He's a criminal!" Lara exclaimed in amazement. "How did he manage to hide away?"

"He came aboard in a large crate," Constance interjected. "Anyway he's innocent! He was framed for the crimes he was supposed to have committed. I believe him."

Lara looked curiously at her friend as though she had lost her mind and looked to Craig for confirmation. He nodded in agreement.

"She's right – he is innocent. It's a long and involved story Lara but I cannot keep this from Commander Simms. I have to tell him about the stowaway. Dr Conrad Burke is a scientist who invented a drug that speeds up healing, but something wasn't quite right with the formula, and it speeded up some harmful things as well. Dr Burke wanted to continue improving the formula, but his partner had other ideas and used the untested drug on human beings. They suffered terrible mutations. When Dr Burke tried to put a stop to the experiments, his partner had him framed for the mutations, plus a number of other crimes. He was in jail for a year when someone helped him escape, and he stowed away on our ship. The good doctor wanted to come here specifically, because you are all scientists and he was looking forward to working with you."

Lara paced backwards and forwards worriedly. "What are we supposed to do with him now?"

Carter shrugged his shoulders helplessly. "I don't know. He's going to ask for asylum here and obviously the decision rests with you whether you would like to have him here, or return him to Earth. You should meet with him to discuss the matter."

"The council most certainly will meet with him. Did you tell him their decision will be final?"

"Yes I did," Craig replied. "He is prepared to accept whatever the council decides. Now if you don't mind I'll go and tell Commander Simms the news."

"By all means do so. We'll talk later."

Craig went to his hotel room where he contacted his boss and soon the commander's face appeared on the mobile device's screen.

"Ah excellent Craig; I see that you made it to Saturn safely. You can stay there a few days and then return to Earth."

"Yes Sir, but I have a problem and I don't know what to do about it. Remember Dr Conrad Burke?"

"Yes; he managed to escape from jail and, the authorities haven't been able to find him, despite a nationwide search. Why are you asking?"

"Well Sir, the police need look no further. He's here on Saturn."

"*Saturn! How did he get there?*" Commander Simm's eyes widened in surprise, as realization dawned. "*Oh no, don't tell me! He stowed away on your ship didn't he?*"

"Yes Sir he did," his employee confirmed.

Commander Simms narrowed his eyes suspiciously. "Why didn't you tell me? We have spoken a number of times in space, yet you never mentioned him. He's a wanted felon!"

"I know that Sir but he's innocent! We only discovered him halfway through the journey here. If he really was a murderer, we would have been dead by now. Constance and I felt it was pointless telling you while we were still travelling to Saturn. He told us his partner framed him. The doctor is going to ask for political asylum here. What do you want us to do?"

Commander Simms rubbed his jaw pensively. "I don't know what to say! Obviously since he's on Saturn, I'll have to respect their decision. If they don't want him there, he will have to come back to Earth."

"Yes, sir but he's afraid to go back. He says his partner will kill him if he does. If he's forced to return to Earth, we cannot bring him back. We have no facilities to keep him locked up on our ship, and anyway he escaped from the hold where he was obviously hiding out, so that isn't an option. He came with us willingly enough, but he won't be that accommodating if he hears that he has to return to Earth against his will."

"All right Craig, let me know when the council have their meeting and what their decision is. It's no use speculating, until we know what the council have decided to do."

"Yes Sir. I'll contact you when I have some more news."

The young man disconnected and went back to Constance. They discussed the incident until they were joined by Dr Burke. He had nothing but praise for the Saturnians and spoke excitedly about their planet.

"Oh I'm going to love working with Lara and the rest of the scientists! They are so far ahead of us, it is phenomenal. Maybe with their help I can find out why my project failed."

"Didn't you leave all your notes on Earth? Surely your partner knows how to make the serum?" Carter asked curiously.

Doctor Burke smirked. "No, I have never made any hard copies of my formula. I did make a large amount initially, but once that's finished he won't be able to duplicate it." He tapped the front of his head. "My formula is stored up here where no one can get at it."

"I don't understand!" Constance replied. "If you are the only one who knows the complete formula, why were you so afraid your partner would kill you? Surely he wants that too badly to eliminate you?"

"You would think so Miss Gregg, but you don't know him at all. He doesn't care about the serum anyway, because he knows it doesn't work. I'm a threat to him because I know the truth about his escapades, that's why he would kill me. All he's interested in now is how much money he can make out of the poor victims. Unfortunately, until all the serum has been used up, there will be many more mutations."

"That maniac has to be stopped!" Craig complained.

"I agree with you but I cannot stop him, and without any proof, he has free reign to do exactly as he pleases."

Further conversation was interrupted by the arrival of Jorrel.

"Craig the council has been convened. It was short notice, but the nature of the situation has made it a priority. Lara has requested you and Constance be present at the hearing."

"I don't understand why. We aren't asking for political asylum," the young man stated.

"Nevertheless your presence has been requested," Jorrel replied stubbornly. "These proceedings are very important."

"Then we must comply," Craig replied simply. "When will the session begin?"

"You have one hour to prepare. Dr Burke must accompany me now. There are a few things we need to explain to him. I'll see you later."

Conrad Burke looked nervously at the Saturnian. "Why can't I stay with them?"

Constance put her hand on his arm. "Doctor this is normal procedure. May I remind you that you are the one who asked for asylum? If you cannot respect their rules, then maybe you should return to Earth. This is Saturn and their requirements are different to ours."

He nodded nervously and then followed the Saturnian. When they were out of earshot Constance questioned her boyfriend. "Why do you suppose they want us to be present at the hearing?"

"My guess is that they want us to serve as character witnesses. If they decide they want Dr Burke to stay here, his credentials must be impeccable."

"Oh I understand what you mean!" Miss Gregg replied. "Oh well we can only relate what happened out in space I suppose."

The young couple arrived at the community hall fifteen minutes early and were shown to their seats. Exactly on time, Lara, Jorrel and Karnd escorted the doctor in. He sat down in the front row before the rest of the council members were shown in. It reminded Craig of a courthouse, but seemed a little less threatening. Once the council members had taken their places, the audience sat down.

The chairman of the council stood up and his wings fluttered gently. He introduced the members and explained the reason for the meeting. Afterwards Dr Burke was called to state his case and explain why he wanted to stay on Saturn. He was questioned at length, and his whole life history was discussed. After a few hours, the Doctor was finally told to return to his seat.

The convener then addressed Craig and Constance.

"Who discovered the stowaway?" he asked them, and Constance put up her hand.

"I did Mr Chairman," she replied.

"Come forward please," he instructed her.

She obeyed and bowed politely to all the members of the council.

"Miss Gregg, how did the discovery come about?" another asked.

"It was quite by chance actually. I had gone to the galley to get a drink for Craig and me and I heard footsteps. Thinking that it was Craig, I called out to him, but received no answer. I heard footsteps heading towards the main cabin and went to investigate. It was there that Dr Burke surprised me."

"What transpired then?" the Saturnian asked.

"Well he pointed a gun at me," she replied hesitantly. "Then he asked me to take him to Mr Carter."

"Was his manner threatening in any way?" asked the council member.

"Well as I said, he had a gun, but he didn't seem at all sure how to use it," she replied.

"Am I to assume that you did not think he was a killer?"

"No sir, I did not. He just looked sad and desperate. I felt under the circumstance though that I should do as he said, so I took him to the cockpit area."

"When he saw Mr Carter, what did he say?"

"He warned Craig he would shoot me if he tried to do anything foolish, so Craig backed down. Then he told me to join Mr Carter in the other chair and I did so. We recognized him as an escaped prisoner, but he denied the charges and pleaded his innocence. He told us he had stowed away on board our transport, because he wished to seek asylum on Saturn. Mr Carter then tricked and overpowered him. He handcuffed Dr Burke to one of the chairs. The doctor then explained why he had stowed away on the ship and told us the story that you have just heard."

"Did you believe him?" the Saturnian asked.

"Yes I did. I have met with many trained killers, but this man was an amateur. If he had been a killer, we would never have reached Saturn alive, because we only discovered him when we were halfway through our journey."

The council member paced up and down thoughtfully. "Miss Gregg do you believe this man to be an unstable individual?"

"No Sir," she replied emphatically. "He was just frightened."

"Aren't you angry because he pointed a gun at you?"

"I was at first I suppose, but when he told us his story, I understood why he threatened us. I would probably have done the same thing, had I felt uneasy in any way."

"What happened after you had heard his explanation?"

"Craig freed him and we completed the journey peacefully. He never tried to harm us at all."

"I see; well thank you Miss Gregg. Please take your seat."

She obeyed and Craig was called up. He gave his version of the story and it was similar to the one that Constance had related. Afterwards as it was late, the meeting ended and they were informed it would re-convene after eight the next morning. Dr Burke was taken elsewhere that evening and the couple was curious, but they never asked the Saturnians why. He was allowed to join them for breakfast and he looked tired and apprehensive, but otherwise he was fine, he assured them.

The council re-convened and some of the questions were re-phrased. All three of them testified once again. Finally the head of the council stood up and spoke to everyone present.

"We put Dr Burke in an isolation unit and monitored his behaviour last night. It is the verdict of this council that the man is not dangerous, but only nervous, as both Mr Carter and Miss Gregg had said." He turned to Conrad Burke. "Approach please."

Conrad Burke approached hesitantly and bowed politely. The leader continued. "Doctor we are sorry you find yourself in these unfortunate circumstances, but we are satisfied you meant well when you invented the serum. You were manipulated by an unscrupulous man who didn't care about human life, only the wealth that this so called wonder drug could bring him. However that is now Earth's problem and not ours. I am sure Mr Carter and Miss Gregg will report to their superior when they return to Earth. I will also furnish Commander Simms with a report of this gathering. It is the decision of this council that you may remain here on Saturn if you wish to do so."

Craig and Constance smiled broadly and Dr Burke's face lit up in delight.

The Saturnian raised his hand for silence and continued. "There is one further condition. If you do not allow us to proceed with the next phase, this decision will be revoked and you will return to Earth. We are prepared to trust you, but now you must trust us. We wish to perform a mind probe on you, to ascertain the honorability of your intentions towards Saturn."

The doctor looked helplessly at Craig and Constance and leaned over to them.

"What is a mind probe?" he asked nervously. "I don't like the sound of that."

Craig raised his hand. "May I speak?" he asked politely.

"Continue."

"Mr Chairman, Dr Burke is not familiar with the mind probe device. May I suggest a recess of fifteen minutes while I explain this to him?"

The winged being shrugged his shoulders dismissively. "Very well, we will adjourn for fifteen minutes."

The council members went out in single file and everyone stood respectfully to attention. Then the rest of the audience followed.

Craig and Constance walked some distance away and Dr Burke went with them. They sat down on a bench. Dr Burke looked very anxious indeed.

"You have nothing to fear from the mind probe doctor," Craig assured him. "It is a helmet that is put on your head and electrodes are connected to it. You will be given a sedative to calm you down. It is very relaxing and you might even fall asleep for a while. Then the machine is switched on and it feeds images onto a large monitor, which records them. What it means, in simple terms, is that it reads your mind. If you have lied about anything, it will surface and could be used against you. If you have answered every question honestly then you have nothing to worry about. It is non-invasive and doesn't hurt at all."

"But I don't understand! If they believed me, why do I have to be subjected to this mind probe?"

"You have to look at it from their point of view," Craig reasoned. "The Saturnians are a delicate race and they do not reproduce very easily. Even with all their technology, they cannot increase their lifespan, or their population any quicker than at present. If you were a very good liar and convinced them of your honourable intentions, yet later they found this to be incorrect, you could destroy them. They are just being cautious."

"Have you ever been subjected to this mind probe thing?" he asked the explorer.

"No, there has never been any reason for this, but if they ever asked me to submit to one, I would do it without hesitation. If you are really serious about staying here on Saturn, and we both know they are interested in having you here, then you must agree to this willingly."

"But if I allow them to probe my mind, won't they know everything about me? What about the calculations for the formula?"

"Yes they will learn everything you have stored in your brain, but aren't you going to ask for their help in perfecting the drug anyway?"

"Yes of course I am," he replied.

"Then you have nothing to worry about. You heard what he said. Unless you want to go back to Earth, you have no choice. It's up to you."

"I guess that I'll have to do it then," Dr Burke sighed.

Constance looked at her watch and stood up. "Well time is up so we had better be getting back."

They all went to the hall and took their places. The most senior member stood up and addressed the group. "Have you made your decision yet Dr Burke?"

"Yes I have. I have nothing to hide so I will co-operate with you in every way. Mr Carter has explained what will happen and I am happy with his explanation."

"Good then it will be done tomorrow morning."

Everyone left the building and went their separate ways.

The next morning Dr Burke went to have his mind probe done and the two young people went off to be alone for a while. That afternoon Lara spoke to them. "The mind probe was very satisfactory. Dr Burke is a very ingenious man and we look forward to consulting with him. The council has told him he can stay as long as he likes. You can contact Commander Simms now if you wish. I'm sure he wants you both to return speedily."

"I'll contact him in a little while Lara. Right now I need to speak with Dr Burke. There are a couple of loose ends that need to be tied up first."

Carter looked for Dr Burke and found him without much trouble. The man was beaming from ear to ear. "Did you hear the news? The Saturnians have given me permission to stay as long as I want to!"

"I'm very glad for your sake. Congratulations; I know you'll enjoy it here. The Saturnians are very accommodating."

"Yes they are! I must apologize once again for threatening you with a gun. Despite my actions you and your girlfriend believed in me. Thank you!"

"Don't mention it!" he replied kindly. "Just always do what is best for mankind and everything will be fine."

"I will, I promise!" he exclaimed cheerfully.

"There now remains only one problem doctor. As long as you stay here on Saturn everything will be fine, but when you return to Earth it will be a different matter entirely. Remember you're still wanted for murder. I know you are innocent and you know it, but the police won't be so accommodating. You still need to clear your name and your partner needs to pay for what he has done to his fellow humans. I'm sure you don't want to wait until all the serum has been used up before doing something about it. Your partner could kill a great many more humans before the supply is exhausted."

"What can I do about it?" he asked helplessly. "I won't go back to Earth, not for a long time."

"You mentioned you had hidden the evidence in your computer. I know a few experts who could find that file, with your permission of course! Are you prepared to hand over your secret codes to me and I'll pass them on to the right people. Then we can destroy your partner's reputation once and for all. In that way, you'll receive a pardon and he will go to jail. The rest of the formula will have to be destroyed, but you can make more here I suppose. Then you can work on it, with the Saturnian's help of course."

"Can you really do that for me?" he asked incredulously.

"Not me!" Craig laughed. "My policemen friends will deal with this. I am a space explorer, not a computer hacker. What do you say? It's your decision."

The man shook Carter's hand excitedly. "How can I ever thank you for what you are going to do?"

"Just do the best you can for the human race and others, that's all I ask." Craig replied kindly.

"I'll have those codes for you within the hour," Conrad Burke promised.

He kept his word and produced the information, down to the last detail, and gave step by step instructions as to how this should be done. Craig then asked if he could be left alone and he was shown into a private office where he contacted Commander Simms and brought him up to date on all the news. He sent him the detailed instructions and Commander Simms promised to follow it up.

The next day Craig and Constance prepared to return to earth once more. Their cargo hold was again filled to the brim with provisions that had to be given to Earth. Lara, Karnd and Jorrel went to say their goodbyes and Doctor Burke accompanied them. He shook Craig's hand vigorously and hugged Constance.

"Goodbye my friends, I'll never forget you! I'm very fortunate to have met you."

"We'll meet again I can guarantee that. I wish you every success for the future," Carter replied sincerely.

The couple went to their ship and waved goodbye, and soon they were in the blackness of space. Saturn faded from their screen and Constance sighed. "Well so ends another adventure! I never thought that a simple trip to Saturn could have been so eventful!"

"Well in this case all's well that ends well. Now we can relax all the way home."

"That sounds like a good plan! Who knows what will be waiting for us when we return," Constance replied pensively.

"As long as it's a few quiet days to rest and relax I'm not fussy. This journey has been quite an experience." Craig replied.

"It most certainly has," his girlfriend agreed. "However it wasn't in vain because now Dr Burke can resume his research with intelligent beings who can help him. If the Saturnians can't fix his formula then no one can."

The couple looked out of their observation window and for a while they were silent as they watched the stars twinkling in the distance. Later on they were enjoying a snack when Miss Gregg put down her plate and looked at her boyfriend. "Craig, do you think Dr Burke's name will be cleared now? Will the authorities manage to get the files from his computer?"

"I don't see why not! He gave me precise instructions as to how this could be done and I repeated them just as he gave them to me. Anyway, we'll see when we get back to Earth. It's out of our hands now."

CHAPTER EIGHTEEN

Back on Earth, the matter was indeed being given priority. Commander Simms had great respect for his employee's opinions, and had wasted no time in informing the head of his security detail about the incident. That, coupled with a letter from the Saturnians confirming Craig and Constance's story, had led to an investigation being launched. Very few people were involved in the case, and only those with the highest security clearance were told of the facts.

One such person was Helen Spencer, one of the police's rising stars, who had made a name for herself with her above average intelligence, which left most of her classmates at the police academy in the shade. Her specialty was computer hacking and there wasn't a code she couldn't break sooner or later. Her skills had proved invaluable over the years, and she had broken many secret codes in the few years that she had worked in this division.

Helen Spencer had pitch black hair cut in a fashionable pixie style. Her eyes were a startling green and when she looked at anyone, it was as though she was looking directly into their very souls. Her figure was trim and athletic and she was slightly built. Many of her male colleagues had learnt, to their embarrassment that she packed a punch which could floor most men twice her size. One of her many talents was also that of disguise. She often played tricks on her fellow policemen, and none of them had ever recognized her. Miss Spencer was given the task of infiltrating Dr Wallace Jessup's rooms and ordered to find the secret hidden in Dr Burke's computer. Dr Jessup was Conrad Burke's unscrupulous partner, and his previous secretary had quit, because she was tired of being insulted by the man whose manner was condescending to say the least.

It was a very different Helen Spencer who arrived for the interview with Dr Jessup.

Her black hair was pinned into a bun, and scraped away from her face. She had changed the color of her eyes by using plain brown contact lenses. Helen wore a pair of horn rimmed glasses. Her clothing was smart and expensive but she wore baggy items, giving the impression that she was a little overweight. Her shoes were smart, but plain and sensible. When Helen spoke, she never looked him straight in the eyes and she spoke softly. Now she sat on the chair opposite him while he read her work history, most of which was untrue.

The doctor looked her up and down and smiled. "Miss Spencer you certainly are very qualified for this position. I was just wondering though, do you have a boyfriend."

She blinked owlishly at him "Sir?"

"I was just wondering, because I'm a workaholic who has a very successful business. I have many patients who consult me on a regular basis and as part of this job, you will be asked to work late on some occasions. There is plenty to do here, and if you have a boyfriend then I'm afraid I'll have to look for someone else. I need you to commit to me one hundred percent, am I clear?"

Helen smiled at him. "Oh no doctor I don't have a boyfriend! I live alone and have plenty of free time. It won't be a problem I assure you."

"I'm glad to hear it my dear. Ever since my partner was arrested for using an untested formula on his patients, I have been left with his workload as well."

Miss Spencer made the appropriate sympathetic noises.

He shrugged dismissively. "Having said that, I do have a number of other candidates to interview, but quite frankly I don't have time for this! You seem like a competent young woman. If I gave you the job, when could you start?"

"Would tomorrow morning be convenient doctor?" she asked timidly.

The Doctor smiled genially. "That would be wonderful Miss Spencer." He stood up and they shook hands. "I'll see you tomorrow morning then!"

"Yes doctor, thank you!"

Miss Spencer left the building and went home to her flat.

There she made a phone call to her superior.

"I'm in!" she remarked triumphantly. "He gave me the job."

"Of course he did!" her superior responded. "Even if he had interviewed more secretaries, we would have persuaded them to come up with various excuses not to join him. When do you start?"

"Tomorrow morning."

"Excellent!"

The next day Dr Jessup showed her to her desk and asked her to order whatever she needed. He then took her on a tour of the laboratory and everything was neat and tidy. Wallace Jessup showed her the various samples of drugs and explained briefly what some of them were used for, but he didn't elaborate and she didn't ask.

One of Helen's talents was her ability to type quickly and efficiently and the day passed in a whirlwind of activity. Dr Jessup kept her very busy, and she could see why the secretarial position had to be filled so urgently. That night she went home on time but she had the feeling that it wouldn't happen very often. Whenever she had a moment, she would pass by Dr Burke's office and see his computer on his desk, but she never got a chance to look at the data, because his partner never left her alone in the office. Every time patients wanted to see him, he asked that they come to his consulting rooms.

None of the patients however, exhibited signs of any mutations that she could see and she wondered if he went elsewhere to treat them. A safe stood in her boss's office, but she was never asked to fetch anything out of it, and she had no opportunity to try and open it because the doctor was always around. She had risked a look through the files of some patients, but found nothing out of the ordinary in the cabinets or on the computer that she had access to.

One evening however, the doctor put on his coat and got ready to leave for the day. He was in a hurry, and waited impatiently for her to pack away her things.

"But Doctor Jessop, I still have some work to do. I don't mind staying a bit late tonight. I'm sure I can ask the security guard to lock up the office," she protested mildly.

The man shook his head impatiently. "It can wait until tomorrow Helen! Come along now!"

Looking longingly at the computer in Dr Burke's office, she reluctantly followed her boss out.

She returned home to her flat and decided to take matters into her own hands, because it was taking too long to get the evidence, and she was growing impatient. The undercover policewoman showered quickly and put on a pair of black jeans and a dark top. She tied her hair into a ponytail and took out the brown contact lenses. Doctor Jessop was a very cautious man and she never had keys to anything. Smilingly she attached a lock pick set to her belt and headed back to the office. The one thing she did have was a laminated card that she used to enter the building. Helen knew the guards would see she had entered the premises after hours, but that couldn't be helped. She wanted to find the evidence so that Dr Burke's name could be cleared.

Miss Spencer went inside and slid along the walls to avoid the security cameras. She had noticed there was a blind spot on every single closed-circuit television, and she used this to her advantage. When she arrived at her office however, she placed a picture of the room over the screen which made it look as though the room was empty. She did this with the camera in both Dr Jessop and Dr Burke's offices as well. The policewoman didn't switch on any of the lights, except the one on Dr Burke's desk. Helen powered up the computer and flexed her fingers.

"*Let's see what secrets you can divulge,*" she thought.

The computer screen lit up and she consulted the much worn piece of paper in her hands. It asked for a password and she typed in what Dr Burke had told Craig on Saturn.

Miss Spencer had to go through a number of steps and each asked for another password. She had been given strict instructions on the order in which the passwords had to be typed in, and she knew one wrong move would deny her access to the hidden files. Worse still, she could activate a booby trap and the computer would subsequently destroy the evidence. It was a good fail safe mechanism in Dr Burke's hands, but should it be activated, he would have no proof of his innocence.

Her palms began to sweat and she rubbed them on her jeans. She bit her lip and continued with the sequence. It took her an hour to bypass all the booby traps and finally the file was revealed. She called it up and began looking through them. Miss Spencer's stomach lurched, and she thought she would be sick as the grisly evidence of Dr Jessop's greed became evident. Despite the horrible mutations, Dr Burke had written concise notes on what had happened. The patients he had managed to see secretly also wrote their feelings down, accompanied by full length naked pictures of their grotesque bodies.

Helen wanted to throw up and she had a sour taste in her mouth. She was filled with loathing for the man she had been working for, and wondered how a doctor could go to such terrible lengths to experiment on unsuspecting human beings who looked to him for help. In almost every case the word "deceased" appeared in their files. Not many people were left alive to testify about what they had gone through. There were many files – too many to read and she had an idea. She emailed the file to her home PC. She pressed the "send" key and straightened suddenly when she heard footsteps coming down the hall.

Helen wished fervently she had brought her weapon with her, but she knew it was a bad idea, because it would have triggered the door alarms. The policewoman quickly switched off the light and the computer screen, leaving the central processing unit on. She hid under the desk, just as the door opened and a figure came inside. Miss Spencer peeped out and saw Dr Jessop arrive. He switched on the reception light and walked straight through to his office without putting on the light in his partner's office. He passed so close to the desk that she could have touched him, but fortunately he never saw her.

The doctor walked to his safe and opened it. She saw him take out a small electronic tablet, which he put in his pocket. Then he bent down again and took something else out of the safe. He held it up to the light and the green liquid in the vial glowed eerily. Dr Jessop smiled in a way that made her flesh creep, and suddenly she felt the urge to get up and put as much distance between them as she could. He locked the safe and switched off the light. Helen sat immobile under the table for quite a while after he had left, and then climbed out from under the table. She switched on the screen and saw the data had transferred to her computer. Helen smiled and deleted the sent email. The policewoman then reversed all the codes and returned to the main menu before switching off the computer.

Afterwards she took out a small torch and moved to the safe. Helen selected a number of lock picks and after a few attempts the safe door opened. Her eyes widened in disbelief when she saw several tubes of the green liquid inside. She took one vial and wrapped it carefully in some tissue paper. A data device was in the safe and she took it out and switched it on. It was protected by a pin but it only took Helen a few minutes to crack the code. She was amazed when she saw the number of credit transfers listed on the device. The policewoman quickly took out her mobile device and copied a few pages off the data reader. She emailed the list to her home computer and replaced the device in the safe, locking it once again.

Helen managed to get out of the building without incident and by the time she got home it was very late, but there was still a lot to do. Before she had left though, she had used a special card reading device on the outside doors, deleting the time frame that she had been in the office. She couldn't delete it entirely, but the computer at the main desk now showed she had entered the premises and left ten minutes later. She made a phone call and left a message with the answering service. Afterwards she opened her emails and retrieved the files she had sent to herself. While she drank some coffee, she transferred the damning evidence Conrad Burke had hidden so carefully in his files onto a small memory stick. She yawned and just wanted to go to sleep, but the files she had read unsettled her, and she remained awake.

The next morning as the sun rose in the sky, she got into her helicar and went to the laboratory, where she dropped off the vial of liquid, issuing strict instructions that the analysis of the item was to take top priority. She took the memory stick to her superior in the police department and left it with him. Afterwards she went to work as usual.

Helen Spencer was seated at her desk when Dr Jessop walked in. He greeted her sourly and stormed into his office, where he slammed the door so hard that everything in the office rattled. She saw him pick up the mobile phone he had placed on his desk. Half an hour later he came out of the office and beckoned her inside.

Helen wanted to run away, but instead she stood up and went into his office. He pointed to a chair and she sat down. Dr Jessop came straight to the point. "Why did you come back here last night?" he demanded.

"I...I'm sorry if I did something wrong! I never meant any harm!" she explained. "I left in such a rush last night I forgot my cellphone in the ladies' toilet downstairs. I only came back to fetch it and then went home."

"Didn't I tell you not to come back if I wasn't here? Surely you could have fetched your phone this morning when you came to work."

"I needed it and anyway I have just recently bought a new one. I was afraid someone would steal it! My mother isn't well and I have to have it with me, in case she calls. I'm sorry, it will never happen again, I swear. I was only in the building for about ten minutes! I didn't even come upstairs to my office."

The doctor paced the floor and glared at his secretary.

"Who are you really Miss? I was in earlier this morning, and I found a vial of liquid missing from my safe. What have you done with it?"

Helen stared at him in mock horror. "I don't have the key to your safe! Why would I care what you keep in there? I just do my job, that's all! Maybe you took it out and forgot about it."

Jessop towered over her and placed his hands on the armrests.

"I know exactly what I keep in my safe, and one vial is missing. Your access card shows that you were here last night, so it had to be you. Where is it?" he snapped.

"I don't know!" she exclaimed. "I never took it!"

Dr Jessop went to his desk and sat down in his chair. He

opened a drawer and pulled out a gun which he levelled at his secretary.

"You know I was suspicious of you from the very beginning! Your credentials were just too good, too perfect to be true! Now how about telling me the truth?"

"I am telling the truth! I don't know anything about this!"

The gun remained steady in his hand. "Come now Miss Spencer, if that's your real name; tell me the truth! Did you steal one of my vials?"

"No I didn't!"

"Okay then, answer this question. Is your name really Helen Spencer?"

"Yes it is."

"Who are you?" he asked again.

"I'm just a secretary, that's all," she insisted.

The doctor stood up and waved her out of the chair.

"Lock that door and come with me," he ordered.

Helen did as she was told, then he pushed her into his office and handed her a key.

"Now open the safe!"

She did so and he instructed her to remove a vial of the green liquid, which she then handed to him. He waved her back to the chair and took out a syringe. Then he uncorked the bottle and sucked up some of the liquid.

"Do you know what this is?" he asked her idly.

"N...no," she stammered.

He placed the syringe down and closed the bottle. Helen watched him carefully, but the vial was too far away for her to reach, because the desk was large. She weighed up the possibility of jumping him, but decided against it. He could kill her before she got close enough to cause any damage. Wallace Jessop stroked the vial lovingly and spoke wistfully.

"This is the future! This liquid has such possibilities, but it has a few kinks that need ironing out. Look we can play this guessing game all day if you like, but you know more than you are letting on. Now, unless you tell me the truth, I'm going to inject you with this syringe. In such a small quantity it won't kill you, but you'll be unconscious within a few seconds. Afterwards I'll keep on filling the syringe and injecting the liquid into your unconscious body, until it's all finished, causing you to have a massive heart attack. You'll be dead within minutes."

Helen Spencer knew that had reached the point of no return, and she decided to tell him the truth. "All right I'm an undercover policewoman. My name is really Helen Spencer though."

The doctor grinned maniacally. "Ah, finally we are getting somewhere! You *do* know what this liquid is I assume?"

"Yes I do. It's a formula invented by your ex-partner Dr Conrad Burke. His calculations were incorrect though, and he developed a dangerous drug. You were so blinded by greed, that you had him arrested and framed for murder when he found out you had used the liquid, despite his pleas not to. When people began developing terrible abnormalities, you hid the results by killing the victims. People flocked to you to get this new wonder drug and paid a fortune for a useless formula. You have earned a fortune off other people's misery. Why did you do it? As a doctor it's your code to save lives, not destroy them."

"You're missing the point my dear! In order to perfect the formula, I have to sacrifice a few people. How else can I learn to fix the problem?"

"Doctor Jessop, you cannot fix the problem until you have the formula, and my guess is that you haven't got it. Dr Burke invented it and only he knows how to make more of the serum."

The doctor shook his head emphatically. "It's written down somewhere. I just have to find it. Then I can perfect it. I have tried looking on Conrad's computer but he has nothing on record."

Miss Spencer smiled, despite the circumstances. "You're mistaken doctor! Conrad Burke never wrote that formula down anywhere! I have it on good authority that he kept all the information stored in his head. You had him framed for murder and various other things, and you put away the only man who could really perfect the formula. Now he has escaped and you are no nearer the solution than you were in the beginning."

The doctor waved away her comments. "I'll find him sooner or later. Then I'll get the formula from him and manufacture the potion myself."

"I doubt that! If you want to find him, he's on Saturn and he doesn't plan to return anytime soon. You made a fugitive out of him, because of your greed!"

The doctor raised his eyebrows. "Another reliable source told you this?"

"Yes indeed. He's far away from Earth right now. So tell me doctor, what do you plan on doing when you finish all the remaining vials of liquid?"

Wallace Jessop smiled evilly. "If I can't get hold of Conrad, I'll just continue using people, and making an exorbitant and obscene amount of money. Then I'll retire comfortably and never have to worry about a thing anymore."

Helen glared at him and put her hands on the table, intending to stand up, but the gun remained steady in his hands.

"Of course, before I can do anything about this, you'll have to die, you know that. It's a pity, but I can't have you telling tales about me."

Miss Spencer sat down in the chair once again and put her hands on her lap.

"Why did you kill one of your secretaries? What did she do to deserve that?"

Dr Jessop felt confident that he had the situation well in hand, so he smiled wickedly at his new secretary.

"The problem with her was that she just couldn't keep her mouth shut! One of the patients I had used as a test subject, complained to her and showed her the results. Marjorie was horrified, but she didn't go to the police. Instead she told me what the woman had confided to her. I think maybe she planned to blackmail me, although she never told me that outright. I gave her an immediate salary increase and in that way I paid for her silence. Unfortunately, she got greedier, and one day when she left the office, I found an unfinished letter on her computer. She had planned to expose me to the newspapers.'

'When I questioned her the next day, she told me she had been in touch with a reporter, who had offered to pay her a very large sum of money for the exclusive exposure of yours truly. I killed her and made it look as though Dr Burke had done the deed and it worked! She was dead and he was in prison. I thought I was cleared, but obviously the authorities weren't convinced, otherwise why would they have sent you to investigate? Anyway it doesn't matter now because you are going to have to die as well. I think in your case though I'm going to have to be a lot more creative."

He moved around the desk and Helen pushed the chair away to make more room for her legs. He laughed at her attempt to escape and approached confidently. She waited until he was almost on top of her before kneeing him in the crotch. He swore angrily and the gunshot went wide, slamming into a picture on the wall. Before he could raise it again, she punched him in both ears and he dropped the weapon. In that instant she got to her feet and they began to fight. The policewoman was amazed by the strength in his arms, but his anger was uncontainable and it gave him strength.

Dr Jessop flung her against the desk, and the vial toppled over and rolled a few centimetres, before stopping against his pen holder. He made a grab for his gun and she kicked it out of reach. The man grabbed a heavy glass ornament and smashed it against her face, but fortunately she realized his intention and moved her head a fraction, causing it to smash down on her shoulder instead. The pain was intense but she ignored it, and they fought for a while longer. She tripped him, making him stumble against his desk, where he reached out for the vial. His fingers touched it but he overbalanced, and succeeded only in pushing it off the desk instead. Both of them heard the tinkle of the glass as it shattered.

Helen Spencer put all her strength into the next punch, and it caught the doctor solidly on his jaw. He somersaulted over the desk and fell down on the other side, pushing his chair into a filing cabinet. Helen got ready to kick him again, but he had lost interest in her. Instead he was looking in dismay at his bleeding hand, from which some glass still protruded. His face was ashen.

"*Oh heavens, no; this can't be happening!*"

Miss Spencer stared mesmerized at the green liquid on his hand. It had mixed with his blood and filled the large cut on his palm. Shakily he removed the glass from his hand and stared in morbid fascination at the blood welling up. He held his hand pleadingly up to the woman he had just tried to kill.

"*Help me please!*" he begged.

Helen took a few steps back and watched him in disgust.

"*Please, you have to inject me with another vial! I don't want to mutate! I would sooner die!*"

Callously the policewoman moved further away and smiled triumphantly. She retrieved the still intact syringe from the table and placed it in a plastic bag, which she sealed.

"I believe that justice truly has been done!" she remarked. "You have caused several innocent people to suffer, and who knows how many more are still out there! I can think of no better sentence than the one you have just received. You put them and Doctor Burke through hell. Well, welcome to hell Doctor Jessop! Let's see how you like it! By the time your case is tried, you'll probably wish you had never been born! Who knows though; perhaps your ex-partner will discover the cure for this condition and maybe, just maybe you'll be helped. Personally I hope that day doesn't come in your lifetime!"

Helen Spencer took out her mobile device and spoke into it. Soon afterwards the security guards arrived and she showed them her badge.

"Did you video this as I specified?" she asked.

"Yes maam we did," a guard confirmed.

"Was the conversation clear enough?" she asked again.

"We heard and saw everything!"

"Excellent! Well this video, coupled with the evidence I found on Dr Burke's computer should be enough to convict this piece of slime."

She went over to the doctor who was still sitting on the floor, and knelt down a safe distance away.

"Yes, Dr Burke had compiled evidence against you but he was caught and arrested before he could clear his name. I'm really a computer expert and thanks to the co-operation of your ex-partner, I retrieved his file. You've been a very bad boy!"

As Helen got up to leave the room, Doctor Wallace Jessop began to cry.

CHAPTER NINETEEN

Craig and Constance returned to Earth soon afterwards. After their usual debriefing session, they went home and unpacked their belongings. The next day they met Commander Simms for lunch at an exclusive restaurant. While they were having their drinks, Helen Spencer joined them.

Craig hugged her and she sat down in the seat opposite him. He introduced her to his girlfriend.

"Constance this is Helen Spencer, undercover policewoman *extraordinaire* as the French say."

"You know one another?" she asked incredulously.

"Know him!" Helen remarked. "He was the one who recommended me for the undercover assignment."

"Well congratulations are in order then! I believe that Dr Jessop got his just desserts!" Constance replied.

"He most certainly did! I got his whole confession on video. The doctor thought I was so frightened of him and because he planned to kill me, he wasn't shy about sharing information. He'll spend the rest of his life behind bars," Helen replied triumphantly.

"I knew you could do it!" Craig exclaimed happily. "Personally I'm very happy with the result!"

"It was a wonderful effort on your part my dear," Commander Simms stated. "At least that will now put a stop to the mutations. Unfortunately some people will be scarred forever, but thanks to the data on Doctor Burke's computer, the police should be able to track down those who are still alive. The doctors and scientists will do whatever they can to help the unfortunate ones."

"What happened to the rest of the serum?" Constance asked curiously.

"It's been destroyed! Now no one else will suffer. Dr Burke thought he had created something good, but who knows, perhaps with the Saturnian's help, it will serve its intended purpose." Simms remarked.

"I have some more good news," Helen interjected. "Dr Conrad Burke's name has officially been cleared and I personally deleted his record. If he ever decides to return to Earth one day, he'll have nothing to worry about."

"That's good news indeed," Craig agreed. "Commander, have you told him yet?"

His boss smiled. "No, I thought that you or Constance would like to do it. You had a chance to get to know the man a lot better and it would be fitting if you told him. Besides it was your information, Craig that got the ball rolling."

"We'll tell him later!" Craig promised. "Right now I plan to enjoy a sumptuous meal at your expense Commander Simms. It's not often that my boss pays for something, so I plan to enjoy every moment."

Everyone laughed and toasted one another's successes.

Later that same day, Craig and Constance contacted Saturn. Karnd answered and his face broke out in a radiant smile.

"It's good to hear from you my friends! You made it safely back to Earth I assume."

"We did indeed. Could you link us with Dr Burke please? He must be very anxious by now."

"He certainly is! Wait just a moment!"

They were transferred to the laboratory where Lara greeted them. She then called the doctor over. Craig and Constance were amazed by the change in his appearance. He still looked tired, but the worry lines around his eyes had diminished and he looked a lot more relaxed. He smiled at the two space explorers.

"Doctor we have good news for you. Your name has been cleared and all the remaining serum has been destroyed. The police managed to find the information, thanks to your precise instructions, and they'll waste no time in tracking down the unfortunate patients who were treated by your partner." Craig assured him.

"Thank you so much! I feel a lot better now, knowing that everything is in order. I love it here on Saturn, but Earth is, and always will be my home. I'm glad that I can return there whenever I want to. How can I ever thank you both?"

"There is no need to thank us. Just work on that formula, because it will help many people when it has been perfected."

"I plan to do that Miss Gregg," he promised. "Maybe I'll see you around sometime?"

"It's always a possibility!" Constance replied. "Good luck to you on your future endeavours."

"I wish the same for both of you. Goodbye dear friends."

The screen went blank and Craig put his arm around his girlfriend's shoulders and squeezed her affectionately.

"Another happy ending for a satisfied customer," he grinned.

"Yes," she agreed. "Now we can put that matter to rest and move on. So, where do we go from here?"

"Well for now, I'm going to go home and just do nothing. My mom can spoil me all she likes and I won't complain. I'm looking forward to that! What are your immediate plans?" he enquired.

"I plan to do pretty much the same as you! I'll just vegetate on the couch and rest up until the next mission. I'll have to visit with my grandmother as well. She gets cranky when I don't stop by for a while."

"I don't really blame her. It must get pretty boring in that old age home," Craig remarked.

"Well I'm heading home. See you tomorrow, okay."

"Sure, I'll see you then." Craig replied.

They kissed and parted company.

Constance arrived home and thankfully placed her small hold all in her bedroom. Like Craig's family, they too lived in a small townhouse. She went looking for her mother and found her watering her flowers. They hugged and spoke about the mission she had just returned from, but Constance deliberately didn't tell her about their unexpected guest. Some things she decided should remain a secret, because she knew her mother would worry about her.

Later that same day she went to visit her grandmother. The old lady usually sat quietly on a bench in the grounds, or else could be found listening to a book in her bedroom. This time however, she was waiting at the entrance for her granddaughter and was twisting her hands anxiously. She held out her hands to her granddaughter and embraced her tightly. "Oh my dear, thank the stars you're okay! I've been so worried about you!"

"Why would you do that Gran? It was a simple mission, just like every other one I've been on."

Her grandmother fixed her with a withering stare. "Don't lie to me child!" she chided her.

Several people were watching them curiously and Beth took her granddaughter by the hand and headed for her bedroom. Once inside she closed the door and rounded on Constance.

"I love you very much and I know that you're lying to me! I'm glad that Dr Burke's name has been cleared, but not the way he went about it."

Constance stared at her grandmother in amazement. "How did you find out? I know that various things are shown on the news, yet you seem to be aware of events deliberately kept out of the media. Why is that?"

"It's just a talent of mine," Beth hedged. "Well are you going to tell me what happened or do you expect me to guess?"

Miss Gregg sighed and sat down on the bed alongside her grandmother. She told her briefly and concisely what transpired on the journey to Saturn and Beth nodded sagely.

Constance left out a few details of the trip but her grandmother didn't comment until the tale had reached its climax. Afterwards she held her granddaughter's hands tightly.

"Oh my dear child, I wish fervently that you had never decided to explore space. I worry so about you. I was content to live as a housewife, taking care of your grandfather while he lived. Your mother also showed no desire to do anything quite so dramatic, although she has, and still does work for a living. What made you want to explore space in the first place?"

Constance smiled at her grandmother. "I guess it was just the rebel in me. I mean, dad is a General in the army and he commands respect wherever he goes. This may sound really silly to you Gran, but I like the way that he is admired for what he believes in. I think somehow I disappointed him when I was born. He wanted a son to follow in his footsteps. Instead he got me. I guess I wanted some of that awe and respect for myself."

Beth stared at her granddaughter in surprise. "Did you decide to explore space because you wanted to please your father, or was it to please yourself?"

Constance looked into the enquiring eyes. "You know the answer to that question Gran. At first I did it because I wanted Dad to love me more. He just seemed so...well, indifferent if you know what I mean. Then when I began training as an astronaut, I realized just how much I loved it. I'm good at what I do and I love exploring space. Yes, there have been bad moments on some missions, but mostly they have been uneventful. It's what I trained for and I love my job."

"I understand," her grandmother replied softly. "I hope you realize just how much your father loves you. He may have wanted a boy, but he soon came to terms with having a girl. You didn't have to prove anything to him you know! Anyway I'll still worry about you when you go on a mission if that's okay with you."

Constance's eyes were misty. "It's just fine with me Gran. I need someone to think of me when I go out into space. It isn't always glamorous, but someone has to do it. I've come to realize that I don't need constant praise to make me grow. Sometimes the bad times are necessary, so that I can become a better person through the trials and tribulations."

Her grandmother stroked her arm tenderly. "Then I'm satisfied, because you have the right attitude. I love you dearest!"

Constance hugged her back. "And you know how much I love you Gran!"

Beth smiled radiantly behind her granddaughter's back. "Yes I most certainly do!" she confirmed.

They visited for a while longer before Constance reluctantly took leave of her grandmother and returned home. Her father had returned, and she hugged both her parents impulsively in turn.

"I love you both so much!" she gushed. "I'm lucky to have you in my life."

She skipped out of the house and went to look up at the stars. Inside the house her parents looked at one another in surprise.

"What do you suppose that was all about?" Mark Gregg enquired curiously.

Alexis grinned. "I don't know why but that child returns from her missions feeling tired and drained. Then she visits my mother and everything is okay again."

"Well they have a very close relationship dearest," her husband replied.

Alexis smiled secretively. "They most certainly do! Then again they have a lot in common!"

"More than Constance could ever imagine!" her husband sighed.

Alexis put her hand on her husband's arm, silencing any further talk.

"I think I'll make us something to drink," she responded.

Outside on their small patio, Constance sat in their swinging couch and her father joined her. "It's a beautiful evening!" he sighed, looking at the bright stars. "It's not often we can see them so clearly."

"No I guess not. Usually clouds seem to cover them up."

"What's it like, out there in space?" Mark asked curiously.

"Quiet and peaceful!" she replied wistfully. "It gives you a lot of time to think about things in general."

"How are you feeling honey?" her father asked kindly. "I heard that your trip to Saturn wasn't as smooth as expected."

Constance waved away his obvious worry.

"We did get quite a surprise dad, but everything worked out fine. Dr Burke was just a worried man, and we soon dealt with the situation!"

"My sources tell me that his partner, Dr Jessop, got what he deserved."

"He did, but neither Craig nor I had anything to do with that! Craig just made a few phone calls and the police did the rest."

"I know sweetheart. The chief of police is one of my closest friends. He couldn't resist telling me the story," her father grinned. "It does help to have friends in high places, you know!"

Miss Gregg smiled at her father. "Dad, how do you really feel about me exploring space? I only tell mom the good things and not the bad. She's always worried when I go out on missions."

"That's what parents do my child. They worry about their children, because that's the way things are. Answer one question for me before I answer yours, okay?"

Constance shrugged her shoulders. "What do you want to know?"

"Why are you exploring space? Is it because you want to please your mother and me, or is it because you love doing it?"

"Granny asked me the same question today! I'll tell you what I told her. I'm doing this for me, not for anyone else. I love my job, even though sometimes it does have its perils."

Mark Gregg smiled proudly at his daughter. "You must always follow what your heart tells you to do. You've obviously done that, so always hold your head up high, and know that you are doing something that benefits mankind in the end. It's a long process, but the universe will be a better place for humans one day, when we have explored every planet and swapped technology with other beings. Knowing this, how can I not be proud of you and your achievements! You have my blessing and you always will. I'm very proud of you Constance."

"Thank you Dad; it means a lot to me!" Constance replied.

Alexis arrived with their drinks and they watched the stars together for a while. After her parents went inside Constance stared into the heavens and gave thanks for her job and her parents' support. She felt a great weight had lifted from her heart.

Craig meanwhile was alone at home. His parents had been there when he arrived but had left soon afterwards. He sighed and stretched, making his aching muscles creak. "Oh boy do I need to go to the gym! The problem with being out in space is that one cannot exercise properly, and I need to work off some steam."

It was dark outside and he didn't feel like exercising, but he promised himself he would go to the gym the next morning. That night he lay in bed and looked at the familiar surroundings. He smiled in the darkness. "It's wonderful to be home again. This place is my refuge when things get tough. I'm lucky we still have some ground to call our own. These days everyone lives in high rise buildings and it won't be long before every available space is used up."

He closed his eyes and slept peacefully.

The next morning Craig woke bright and early and looked in on his parents. They were fast asleep, and he went for a run around the neighbourhood. He returned home to find his parents awake. After breakfast his mom and dad left to go shopping, and he dressed casually in a track suit. He headed outside towards his car.

Suddenly Carter paused and looked towards the bottom of their garden. The wall was in deep shadow, but he thought he saw something move.

He shook his head. "I'm being ridiculous! There's nothing there! I must be going crazy! I guess I'm still tired from the last space journey."

Craig put his hand on the door of his car and felt a strong breeze tousle his hair. Suddenly, inexplicably he tensed and whirled around, his eyes going automatically to the bottom of the yard. Something silver materialized and he was filled with a sense of danger and foreboding.

"*No, it can't be!*" he whispered in disbelief.

Someone or something tapped him on his shoulder and he knew instinctively that trouble was brewing. He spun around once more, and ducked as something flashed past his face. He knew why he had been so edgy. "*Tyrus!*" he gasped. "*But how is this possible?*"

Carter ran around his car, putting it between himself and the alien. He stared at the three hostile red eyes that glared back at him. "*Hello Carter,*" Tyrus replied telepathically. "*It's so good to see you again. I have missed you.*"

"What are you doing here?" he snapped. "More importantly, how did you find this place?"

"With a little help from a friend," he replied secretively.

"You can't stay here! This is a residential area and you'll cause panic amongst the neighbours."

"Oh, I don't plan to stay very long. I propose we go somewhere a little less crowded and...ah...catch up as it were."

"You must be kidding! I'll never go anywhere with you!" Craig replied stubbornly.

Tyrus looked around thoughtfully. "Nice little place you have here. I believe this house belongs to your parents."

"They aren't here right now. Anyway how do you know this?"

"Idle chatter!" he snapped. "I could cause an awful lot of damage here! I want you to come with me immediately, or I'll start annoying the neighbours."

He sensed Craig's unwillingness to comply, but he knew the man had not taken his gun with him. Tyrus stretched out a hand and a bolt of pure energy flew from his fingers. His quarry dodged the blast and it missed.

Several people had been alerted by the awesome sight of the

strange and menacing creature. Someone screamed, and Craig realized it would turn ugly very soon if he didn't do something quickly.

"I'm not going to ask you again Carter! I haven't got time for this nonsense!"

The creature pointed a finger at the house, and immediately an orange flame appeared in the lounge. Craig stared helplessly at the house as it began to burn, and he ran towards it, intent on dousing the flames, before they could cause any serious damage. Distracted by the sight of his house burning, Carter turned his back on the alien creature, which swiftly wrapped its arms around him. He struggled to free himself.

"*No, I must put out that blaze!*" he cried desperately.

Tyrus looked down the road. "No time for that now. See the fire brigade has already been alerted. Time to go I think!"

Craig blinked and suddenly he was in another place. He recognized it as one of the few parks that still remained. His mind processed the information subconsciously, they were alone in the park. His feet touched the ground and angrily he pulled away from Tyrus. "*How dare you come to my house and desecrate it!*" he replied angrily. "*Go away and leave me alone!*"

"No, not now when I finally have you. Besides, someone is dying to meet you. You have questions to ask and the answers will be provided by this person."

The young man followed the pointing hand, and a shadow detached itself from a tree and walked into the light.

"*Petrovsky; I should have guessed!*"

Colonel Ivan Petrovsky smiled lazily. "Hello comrade; it's a pleasure, as always!" he made a mock bow, and the explorer's hands bunched into fists of rage.

"So, this was your plan, I assume!"

"It was indeed," he confessed.

Do you have any idea what you are dealing with?" he snapped irritably. "Tyrus cannot be trusted! You're a fool to make any kind of alliance with him."

Petrovsky smiled. "We both want the same thing, namely your capture and eventual demise, once we have what we want. It seemed like a good idea to team up."

Craig shook his head in exasperation. "What do you really know about Tyrus, Petrovsky, apart from the fact that you both dislike me?"

"Well for one thing, he gets the job done. I gave him your coordinates and here we are! I think this will be the beginning of a good friendship."

"Any friendship with Tyrus is strictly one sided," Craig warned. "Tyrus isn't a trained pet, available for your exclusive use. Do you know for instance that he is an electrical being? A bolt from one of his hands could kill or maim you instantly."

"I believe so," Petrovsky replied. "What's your point?"

"Tyrus does things only because it suits him to do so. I should know, because he has no concept of right or wrong. Right now, he's cooperating with you, because he'll get something out of the deal. The moment he no longer needs to dance to your tune, he'll betray you."

"You would say that of course. I see where this conversation is headed. You want me to distrust my new friend and pit us against one another. Well it won't work!" The Russian smiled at his enemy. "You're at a disadvantage right now, and will say anything to avoid the inevitable. Why not give up gracefully and let us do what we must?"

"Let me guess! You want information from me. Tyrus I suppose, just wants to kill me. He does seem to have a one track mind! He's not very bright, but definitely tenacious!"

Tyrus growled menacingly and extended a finger. "Let me just kill this annoying worm! That way we can save a great deal of irritation."

"Not now!" Petrovsky snapped. "I need him. Afterwards you can do what you like with him, I don't particularly care."

"Oh by the way, did you know that Tyrus is telepathic?" Craig continued conversationally. "He is probably reading your mind right now, so be careful of what you're thinking!"

Petrovsky looked startled and Craig continued. "He didn't share that little detail with you I assume!"

The Russian stared at the silver creature thoughtfully. "No, he didn't, but it doesn't matter."

"Maybe not to you, but did you really discuss what you planned to do with me once you had me?"

"Obviously! He was to capture you, and then I was going to take you away and question you at length about some top-secret projects. Afterwards I was going to give you to him, whereby he could do whatever he wanted to alleviate his anger."

"That is not what we discussed," Tyrus replied coolly. "I get him first and pass the remains on to you."

"Really, well you can think again!" the Colonel replied evenly. "He belongs to me first and then you can have him."

"Children; children!" Craig chided gently. "See what I mean Petrovsky? You have no idea what you're dealing with!"

Petrovsky drew his weapon and pointed it at Craig. "We'll come to an amicable agreement I assure you! Either way it doesn't look good for you."

"Why choose Tyrus of all beings?" Craig asked. "You have so many connections, yet you went off-world and partnered with someone so unreliable. Believe me I know him a lot better than you and you are wasting your time."

"We'll see about that," Ivan replied.

Craig was furious. "I don't care what you think you can or cannot do to me, but you had no right to endanger my parents! Your fight is with me and not them," Carter snapped.

"So says someone who had my father dishonoured," Petrovsky replied snidely.

"I did nothing of the sort and you know that! Your father betrayed people and he deserved what he got. Mine have never harmed anyone in their lives. Luckily they had gone out before Tyrus tried to burn their house down!"

Petrovsky was amazed. "He did that? Well I'm learning new things every day."

Carter glared at both of them in turn. "Tyrus, you had no right to involve my parents in our feud. What I do out in space has nothing to do with my parents, and they aren't responsible for my actions, so don't punish them because you hate me!" As for you Petrovsky, the same thing applies. I'm out in space all the time so anytime you want me, you can try and capture me out there. Don't bring our differences of opinion to my doorstep! Leave my parents out of this, understand!"

Petrovsky grinned. "Ah, but it's so tempting! You are at such a disadvantage down here, because you won't cause trouble amongst your kin."

Craig had the urge to punch Petrovsky viciously and Tyrus watched in amazement as he felt their hatred for one another.

"You two really hate one another!" Tyrus remarked drily. "If you could read his thoughts Petrovsky, you would be most surprised."

"No he wouldn't," Craig replied. "The feeling is mutual."

"You know Petrovsky, you really shouldn't mess around with this man," Tyrus warned. "He's very cunning. Why not let me kill him now and save you the trouble?"

"That offer is very tempting but alas I must refuse! I'll take him back to Russia where he will most certainly wish he had never been born. He has knowledge in his head that my country would find very useful."

"Not to mention the prestige it would bring you to deliver such a prize, not so?" Tyrus remarked slyly.

Ivan Petrovsky was speechless for a moment and then he smiled. "Remarkable! You read my mind didn't you?"

"I did," Tyrus confessed.

"That must be a handy talent to possess. Imagine knowing in advance what people will do, or what they think about you. It must be quite fascinating."

"Depends who you are with at the time I suppose," the alien agreed.

"It's not much fun in the social circle he frequents," Craig taunted. "His own kind are quite boring. Personally I wouldn't put them on the tourism map for future generations."

Tyrus unleashed some of his power, and Craig grunted in pain. He rubbed his tingling arm and the colonel smiled at his discomfort.

"He needs help controlling his temper as well," Carter stated.

Tyrus extended his arm once again and Petrovsky caught it in a firm grip.

"Save the torture for later Tyrus. Right now I want him in one piece."

"All right, we'll do it your way for now, but time is moving on and soon this place will be full of people. Unless you want an audience, I think that we should leave soon."

"We still have time on our side," Petrovsky replied. "Look my car isn't far from here. I can take him to Russia now and I'll contact you when we're finished with him."

The silver creature fixed its three red eyes on Petrovsky. "I want him first! I'll soften him up for you and when the time comes, he will be only too willing to share information with your country."

The Colonel planted his feet firmly apart. "Tyrus we have been over this already! This was my plan, so he comes with me first."

"No, your people will kill him before I even get a chance to have my revenge."

Both of Craig's enemies were so busy arguing they forgot about their victim, who slowly took a few steps backwards. His back came into contact with a tree and he slipped quietly behind it. He wanted to run away as fast as he could, but he knew that the rustling of the leaves would alert his enemies, so he walked stealthily until he was a fair distance away. Only then did he break into a run. Craig knew where he was, but it was too far to walk back home, and he knew it would be only a few moments before he was pursued. With Tyrus's ability to teleport, Carter didn't stand a chance if the alien knew which way he had gone. His first instinct was to head for the main road and get a ride with someone, but he knew that was the first place they would look, so he continued to run through the trees, putting as much distance as he could between them.

In the distance he heard Ivan Petrovsky's shout of rage when he realized his prize had fled. The Colonel shouted an unintelligible order to Tyrus, but Craig was sure they would have split up. He dashed through the trees and headed for the darkest part of the bushes where he dug a small depression with his hands and hid, hoping desperately not to be seen.

After all they would pursue a running target and not expect it to hide nearby.

Tyrus did in fact appear and Craig hugged the ground tightly, trying to blend into it. The creature looked everywhere but was tall so he mostly looked in the branches of the trees. Petrovsky approached and Craig held his breath.

"Any sign of him?" he asked Tyrus.

"None whatsoever; if he had come this way I would've found him by now. That man is sneaky! You should have let me kill him when I had the chance. Now this place is getting busy and I cannot stay here without attracting attention! You ruined a perfectly good plan!"

"*I did?*" Petrovsky asked angrily. "*Why did you let him out of your sight?*"

"*Why didn't you notice he had escaped?*" Tyrus growled. "We will never find him now."

"I suppose not but I'll get him next time. He can't hide from me forever."

Both of them walked away but Craig stayed put in his makeshift hiding place. An hour later, cramps forced him to his feet and he made for the road.

Carter took out his mobile device and contacted Commander Simms. Briefly he told his boss what had happened and asked him to organize somewhere safe for his parents to stay, because he feared that Petrovsky or Tyrus would return to the house, if it still stood, and kidnap one or both of them. Commander Simms assured him it would be done immediately. He also arranged for his employee to sleep in the single men's quarters at Mission Control for a few days.

He was taken secretly to his parents and hugged them tightly. "I'm so sorry about what happened to the house. It's my fault!"

His father sighed. "No it wasn't! That damn Petrovsky is to blame for what happened. If he hadn't given Tyrus the address, everything would have been fine. His urge to capture you made him desperate."

"If you had been in the house, you could have died!" Craig said.

"Well we weren't and the insurance will cover it. Fortunately only the lounge caught alight. The rest of the house is just fine," his mother assured him. "We can move back into our place in a few weeks."

Craig left his parents and passed by his house. He looked at the charred room, and the police cordon around it gave him no comfort at all. He knew he would never feel safe in that house again.

That night he informed his parents he wouldn't be staying with them when the house had been repaired. He was given a room in the single men's quarters until he could find a place of his own.

He stood on the enclosed balcony that led off from his room and looked into the sky.

"Exploring space is my life and I cannot imagine doing anything else, yet I've been in danger so many times, both up there and even down here on Earth. I wonder sometimes if I've made the right decision. All I ever wanted was to be up there among the stars, yet that desire has cost me a great deal."

Craig's mind wandered to the missions he had been on over the years and he began to smile again. He remembered all the good things that had come out of space exploration and when he thought about them, they did outweigh the bad.

"I'll continue exploring space. It's my destiny!" he decided. "As long as even one human being is in danger, I want to be able to make a difference to mankind. Technology is advancing at an incredible rate and I want to see it through to the end. Who knows what tomorrow could bring? Each new day brings a promise of a better future for all!"

Craig Carter, space explorer looked up at the twinkling stars and smiled. "Here's to tomorrow, and all the tomorrows that will follow!"

www.ingramcontent.com/pod-product-compliance
Lightning Source LLC
Chambersburg PA
CBHW050357030726
47503CB00006B/1897

* 9 7 8 1 9 1 2 4 1 6 4 5 5 *